Black Magic

Look for these titles by

Russell James

Now Available:

Dark Inspiration

Sacrifice

Black Magic

Russell James

Samhain Publishing, Ltd.
11821 Mason Montgomery Rd., 4B
Cincinnati, OH 45249
www.samhainpublishing.com

Black Magic

Print ISBN: 978-1-61921-345-6
Digital ISBN: 978-1-61921-300-5

Editing by Don D'Auria
Cover by Scott Carpenter

First Samhain Publishing, Ltd. electronic publication: May 2013
First Samhain Publishing, Ltd. print publication: May 2013

Dedication

For Mom,

Thanks for all the creative genetic material.

If only I had used it for good instead of evil.

Chapter One

A single fried egg stared at Lyle Miller from the center of the white plastic plate. It was sunny side up, a perfect match for his ebullient mood. He was about to banish his ennui and embark upon a new Grand Adventure. He picked up a bottle of hot sauce from the diner counter and painted a ring around the egg yolk.

He noticed that Gloria, the waitress, watched him from the end of the counter. Lyle wasn't the usual Sunrise Diner customer, who was generally of the south Florida cracker variety. Lyle combed his thick, black hair near straight back, razor part on the right. High cheekbones gave his face great definition and his eyes sparkled sapphire blue. Despite the stifling summer heat, he wore a black, long-sleeve silk shirt. No doubt he looked a cut above Gloria's usual ten-percent tipper.

Lyle touched the yolk with the tine of his fork. It shuddered, as if in protest at its coming fate. He gave the egg the slightest pressure and pricked the sac. Others attacked a fried egg, slashing the liquid yolk in half and mixing it with the hard fried white. But Lyle preferred to savor that moment of victory. Bright yellow yolk oozed from the egg's wounded side. Lyle smiled at the almost imperceptible drop in the yolk's crown and the slow trickle from the base that telegraphed the inevitable end.

With his fork, he led the streaming yellow liquid in a counterclockwise journey around the egg and through the red hot sauce. By the third trip, the yolk sac was flat and Lyle had a masterpiece, threads of swirled red, orange and yellow that covered the white of the egg. It reminded him of his new Grand Adventure.

Gloria sauntered up with a carafe of steaming coffee at the ready.

She was well past thirty with platinum hair and the kind of skin damage only tropical sun can inflict at that age. She tucked her gum into the corner of her mouth with her tongue and fired up a big homespun smile.

"Warm you up?" she said with a dip of her carafe to his coffee mug.

Lyle looked up from his plate. He guessed her life story. High school cute. A failed marriage or two. A variety of addictions and a slide down into a career at the Sunrise Diner off Alligator Alley. Nursed a stubborn denial that she was as past her prime as week-old fish. Nobody anyone would miss. He flashed her a shining salesman's grin.

"Has anyone ever turned down that offer?" he answered.

She refilled his cup. "So what brings you out into swampy south Florida today?"

Lyle caught the arrival of an old man in a green John Deere baseball hat. He shuffled in and took a seat in a booth. Collateral damage.

"I'm a magician," Lyle answered. "A master of illusion and prestidigitation."

"Like that Criss Angel?"

Lyle kept from cringing. "Exactly. Allow me."

He pulled a deck of cards from his shirt pocket, though it had appeared empty. All fifty-two cards expanded into a fan in his right hand. Gloria's eyes locked on the large dark blue sapphire ring on Lyle's third finger.

"Pick a card," he said.

She passed her hand back and forth across the deck, hesitating as if the fate of the world rested on her selection. Lyle swallowed his impatience. She pulled out a card. He placed the rest of the deck against his forehead and closed his eyes in mock concentration.

"Seven of diamonds."

"Oh my gawd!" she shrieked. "How'd you do that?"

Lyle winked away the world's stupidest question. He extended his hand and she returned his card. He tucked it into the deck and cut it in half, face down. He held his hand over it and the top card levitated into his palm. He flipped over the queen of hearts and handed it to her with a flourish.

"For you," he said. "The queen of hearts, as you are destined to break so many."

Gloria managed a star-struck smile and stared at the card. Lyle rose and left ten dollars on the counter for his uneaten three-dollar breakfast. By the time Gloria looked up from the face of the playing card queen, Lyle's black convertible was pulling away in a cloud of white dust.

She tucked the card into the breast pocket of her white working blouse, behind her hand-lettered name tag. She walked the coffee pot over to the old man in the booth.

"A little java, Sid?" she asked the Sunrise regular.

She started to pour and she felt the card in her pocket get hot. A look of shock crossed Sid's face. His mouth opened in a silent scream and his eyes bulged. He went red as a beet, looking like some horrific Christmas decoration in his green hat. Sid clutched his chest and fell against the table so hard his coffee mug jumped with a clank.

"Sid!" Gloria screamed. She dropped the coffee pot. It shattered on the floor into a muddy sunburst. She bent to help Sid.

The card in her shirt went white hot.

She jerked upright. Fiery fingers dug into her chest and wrapped her heart like bands of flaming steel. She hitched one last, incomplete breath and collapsed to the floor.

Ten miles away, Lyle's black convertible took a right on CR 12 and headed north. It passed a sign that said: *CITRUS GLADE 35 MILES.*

Chapter Two

The WAMM-TV morning news had a weathergirl, all feminist wrath for the title set aside. The WAMM evening news featured staid meteorologist Chuck Randall, a weather*man*. The a.m. show had a former high school cheerleader named Whitney.

This morning she wore a tight red top with a plunging neckline that should never have seen the light of day before noon. She had mastered standing in profile to better display the pair of assets that landed her the job. Few complained when they obscured the projected temperature for Ft. Lauderdale that day. Her long blonde hair swirled as she made each overly dramatic sweep of the weather map with one hand.

"A cold front stalled out waaay up here in Tallahassee, the capital," she said, as if her report was part of a geography test. "So we'll be under the influence of high pressure all week."

The screen behind her flipped to a radar map. It appeared to startle her as she saw the change in her off-stage monitor. She scooted to the other side of the screen and pasted her smile back on.

"The barometer," she said, "is up three-tenths this morning." She pronounced it *barrow-meter* to confirm to any sentient viewer that she had no idea what she was talking about.

"Our radar is clear right now but expect scattered storms to pop up later this afternoon as the temperature climbs. The high today will be ninety-two degrees with super high humidity. You won't need a sweater today."

It was August in south Florida. Half the population spent the day in a swimsuit.

"For Miami, winds are switching to come from the southwest." She pointed to Miami with her left hand, and made a clockwise windmill with her right. She looked like a football ref calling a penalty.

One of the cameramen groaned.

"Calm surf and bright sun. A great day for the beach!"

She bounced a bit, like she was still leading a cheer.

The whole report could have been recorded yesterday, or the day before. South Florida summer days were all the same. Claustrophobically humid at sunrise, blisteringly hot by mid-morning, and afternoons peppered with sporadic downpours. The only reason viewers tuned in was to make sure they weren't in the path of a hurricane. Or to watch Whitney jiggle.

"Back to you, Bud," she said and pointed at him with both hands, even though the director had told her not to a dozen times.

Bud came back on screen with a look of resignation on his face.

"Thanks, Whitney."

The rumor was that he really missed doing the evening newscast.

Chapter Three

A few miles south of town, surrounded by a sagging chain-link fence and centered in a weed-infested slab of buckling asphalt, rose the rusting hulk of the Apex Sugar Mill.

Apex had selected Citrus Glade for one reason, and it wasn't the quality of the potential employees. Citrus Glade was in the middle of nowhere, halfway between Naples and Miami, but it was the only high point for miles. CR 12, running north and south through town, was the only road in and out, and it had to bridge canals to make the transit each way. The low ground was perfect for sugar cane and a centralized mill on this slight elevation was the perfect processing center.

Opened in 1941, the mill had sent packets of K-ration sugar to American soldiers fighting around the globe. The end of the war and of civilian rationing sparked a sugar boom. Adjacent to the cane field that grew on reclaimed Everglades land, the plant churned out tons of refined sugar around the clock as Americans rediscovered baking cakes and Kool-Aid. A ban on Cuban sugar in 1960 only pushed demand higher. The swelling population of Citrus Glade sold their farms to large growers and snagged high-paying punch-clock jobs.

All good things, though, must come to an end. By the turn of the twenty-first century environmental pressures and dropping prices hit Apex hard. Sugar cane borers and whiptail disease devastated the local sugar fields. An independent operation could not turn a profit. Production sagged and a downward spiral of layoffs began. By 2000, Apex had cut its losses and closed the doors.

Like the sunken Titanic, the remains of the mill were a reminder of past glory. The weathered three-story brick shell towered over the flat

Florida landscape, a dun and red tombstone for the dead industry. The sides were mostly large glass windows segregated into dozens of panes, most of which had been shattered by vandals and the elements. A lightning strike had toppled the smokestack years ago and it lay like a crushed brick snake across the parking lot. A rust-red water tower stood near the building, a reminder of the prodigious pumping from the Florida Aquifer the plant used to require.

Amidst all these ruins of 1940s technology stood an intrusion from the current era. A massive steel tower with satellite dishes at its peak rose from a new concrete pad. The fence around the base had warning signs with government logos.

With the mill closed, the panicked town council needed a new employer of choice. They bet their futures on the National Security Agency. The spy agency's latest brainchild was a communications receiver, a reception station for intercepts from across the globe. South Florida's least appealing feature, an endless expanse of pancake-flat ground, became Citrus Glade's selling point. Line of sight was unlimited.

With the promise of a government employer, the town volunteered the abandoned Apex site. Sure, the Federal Government paid no property taxes, but they would clean up the eyesore at the edge of town and dole out jobs to idled Apex employees.

But the best laid plans...

The town council didn't read the fine print. The huge vacant parking lot on the Apex site meant that the NSA didn't need to bulldoze the decaying factory. They also may have confused the agency with NASA. The council members had Project Apollo-type images of hundreds of communications workers bustling around spinning magnetic tape reels. But the current reality ended up being an unmanned receiver that sent all its data elsewhere through fiber optic cables. The only local jobs generated were the three guys from Poulsen Construction who poured the tower's concrete slab. The jobs lost were the five city councilmen, whose positions were abolished.

But the tower's location, the town's water supply and the mill's history all converged to create the perfect setting to attract one new business. Two days after Lyle Miller arrived, workers gave the façade of the former Everyday Shoes store on Main Street a fresh coat of glossy black paint. The next morning, hand-painted letters appeared in the window that spelled *MAGIC SHOP.*

Chapter Four

"How's she doing today?"

Andy Patterson had learned years ago to start every visit to his mother at the Elysian Fields Retirement Home that way. It was best to be prepared for the mood of the day.

"Today's a good day," Nurse Coldwell said. She had a face uncomfortably similar to a bulldog and the no-nonsense demeanor to match it. In her nursing whites she looked like a stout chunk of marble behind the reception counter. "She didn't need to be reminded you were coming today."

Andy breathed a sigh of relief. It was always a crap shoot when he arrived. Today he rolled a seven.

Andy still wore the tan uniform of the Citrus Glade Department of Public Works. On his thirtieth birthday this year, he'd shaved his surviving hair down to stubble, a look that brought back a few uncomfortable memories of his recent military service. But the look accentuated his round cheeks; people said it made him look younger. He could live with that.

He walked down the light yellow corridor towards his mother's room. Each door he passed reminded him how lucky he was. Some of the occupants were on IV drips and lay immobile on beds that looked uncomfortably close to hospital gurneys. A few empty O_2 canisters lined the hallway, their contents sacrificed to maintain the lives of others. Within one room, a man in urine-soaked pajama bottoms stared at a TV without comprehension. An orderly cleaned the floor while a nurse tried to help the man up to get changed. Compared to most of these patients, his mother was healthy as a newborn.

The sharp impact of a wheelchair footrest against his shin refocused Andy's attention.

"Watch where you are going, jackass," the old man in the chair growled. It was Shane Hudson, the eighty-year-old scourge of the Elysian hallways. His face had all the features of a shriveled raisin and his legs had atrophied to little more than candlesticks. But his silver hair was still styled in the pompadour of his prime and his eyes burned with a tiger's ferocity.

The angled chair pinned Andy against the wall. The old bastard had nailed him on purpose. Andy shook his head.

"Sorry, Mr. Hudson. I need to keep my head in the game."

"Goddamn right," Shane said. He fingered the black oak cane he had across his lap. Years ago he could still walk with its help. Now it was just a link to his past. Or an attitude adjuster for a less-than-attentive member of the staff. He spun his chair back a few inches to let Andy pass.

Andy's mother's room was a welcome relief from the stark clinical décor of many of the others. The shades were open and bright Florida sunshine streamed in to illuminate a collection of her artwork. Framed watercolors filled the walls. Still-life studies of orchids, landscapes of the Everglades, children flying kites on a sugar-white beach. An unfinished work of butterflies among cattails stood on an easel in the corner.

Dolly Patterson beamed as soon as she saw her son. Andy smiled back in happy recognition. That was her adoring smile he remembered blazing from the bleachers at his baseball games, from the crowd at high school graduation and from the gate at Miami International when he returned from his time in the Army. Even in the shared public space of the retirement community, that smile was a "welcome home". The comfort it gave him made its frequent absence taste so much more bitter.

Dolly only stood five foot three now. Seventy years had shaved a few inches from her height and now Andy had to look down into her eyes. Her hair was the same shade of auburn she always favored and had a sensible style that stopped just short of her shoulders. A paint-dappled white apron covered her pink sun dress.

"Andy!" She pulled the apron off over her head. "Is it the afternoon already?"

Andy held his breath, afraid she was on the edge of a backward slide into confusion. "Sure is."

"This day has flown by," she said. "We spent the morning out in the gardens and you should see the flowers we have going this year. After lunch I went to a ceramics class, you know, to try something new, and well, let's just say I know why they call it 'throwing pots'. I had clay in my hair! That inspired me to a bit of painting. I had no idea so much time had gone by."

Andy exhaled. This was Mom. The real Mom who had more creative energy than the world had time and more enthusiasm than human beings a third her age could muster.

"I had the pleasure of Mr. Hudson's company on the way in," he said.

"Nasty old coot," Dolly said. "Mean when he ran the mill, meaner when they closed it, meanest when his legs deserted him, soon followed by most friends he ever had. You should steer clear of him."

"If it was a question of steering," Andy said, "I think he was at fault."

Dolly hung up her apron.

"Are your ready to go out for an early dinner or can you not bear to miss an Elysian meal?" Andy said.

"I've been dying for fresh snapper," she said.

They left the building and Andy had her wait under the front canopy as he retrieved his car. As he pulled back up, his stomach knotted. His mother's breezy smile was gone, replaced by a tight grimace. Her eyes darted around the parking lot.

"Oh, please, no," Andy whispered. "She was doing so great."

Andy pulled the car up in front of her. She took a fearful step back. She clutched her purse in a panicked, defensive way that made Andy realize how old she really was. He sighed and got out of the car.

"Mom?"

"What are we doing out here, Andy?" she said. "Where are we going?"

He could try to explain it to her, try to make her remember, but that road had been rocky each time he took it and was always a dead end. When she got confused, she got scared, and only the familiar things in her room made her feel safe.

"We're going inside, Mom. We're going to sit for a while before you have dinner."

"Good," she said with a look of relief. She scooted back in through the door, like a tortoise back into its protective burrow.

He pulled his car back into the same parking spot. He killed the engine and sat in silence. A good day had gone bad. But at least part of it had been a good day. He popped open the car door. Odds were, by the time he got in there she'd have forgotten he was ever there in the first place. But he'd give it a try anyway.

She was his mother.

Chapter Five

Felix Arroyo yanked the pull cord on the pole saw. It sputtered to life and settled into a lumpy growl. He released the safety and the cutting chain at the end of the nine-foot pole spun up to speed. He swung the blade far up over his head and aimed it at the shattered branch at the top of the orange tree. The chain churned through the branch and it crashed to the ground. Felix flicked off the saw and tossed it into the back of his pickup. If only a broken branch were his sole problem.

He tipped his battered straw cowboy hat back and wiped the sweat from his dark brow with a rag. He stood in the shade between two rows of navel orange trees in his orchard. His wife, Carlina, came up behind him and slid her arm around his waist.

"Look at you, scowling at the trees," she scolded. "Like the tiny fruit is their fault."

Felix plucked a sickly green sphere from the orange tree's branch. At this point in the year it should have been quadruple the size and bright orange.

"We left the violence and corruption of Mexico to grow our own fruit," Felix said. "Now frost and rain and citrus chancre conspire against us."

"We've had tough years before," Carlina said. She was short and plump as an olive. Even in these dark times she exuded her trademark glass-half-full outlook. "We lived on less in Juarez."

"In Juarez it was just the two of us," Felix said. He pointed a thumb at the peeling white clapboard farmhouse where their two children, Angela and Ricardo, were. "Now it is four."

"And God will provide," Carlina said. "This fruit will bounce back in no time. The Lord can work miracles."

That's what it will take, Felix thought. And he was certain that with the world such as it was, God did not waste miracles on things so small.

"I'm sure He will," Felix lied.

He gave his wife a hug and they went back to the farmhouse.

The house was just far enough away from CR 12 that the dust passing trucks kicked up settled before it reached the front porch. The house stood on short, concrete-block pillars to let the air flow under the floors and draw off some of the Florida swelter. Two ancient oaks shaded the homestead's sides. The realtor who sold Felix the property had assumed the new owner would bulldoze the old place and put up something new. But, while a house without air conditioning that still boasted a stained claw-footed bathtub wouldn't cut it with most people, it was a mansion to a dirt-poor kid from Juarez and his new wife from a Mexico City barrio.

The two entered through the back door into the kitchen. The omnipresent smell of cayenne pepper and hot chilies filled the air, though the stove sat cold and empty. A ceiling fan fought a slow, lazy battle against the home's retained heat.

"Where's Ricardo?" Felix asked. It was Saturday and the thirteen-year-old should have been out with him in the orchard.

"He was in his room," Carlina said. "And it's 'Ricky' now, remember?"

Felix shook his head. "So Ricardo, my father's name, isn't good enough?"

"Felix," Carlina cooed. She stroked his shoulder. "He thinks 'Ricky' sounds tougher."

"He thinks it sounds less Mexican."

"You rebelled at his age," Carlina said, "and in worse ways."

Felix went down the hall and pushed his son's door open. Posters of bands he had never heard of covered the walls. Strange shapes flickered back and forth as the screen saver played on his son's desktop computer. The boy lay on his bed, eyes closed, earbuds from his smartphone shoved in his ears. Felix was sure the new phones made you stupider, not smarter. Ricky's shaggy black hair swayed back and forth as his head bobbed to the beat of some unheard tune. He wore a solid black T-shirt and baggy jeans with square holes ripped into the knees.

Felix banged on the door without acknowledgement. He walked in and gave the bedpost a kick. Ricky opened one eye and looked at his father. He extracted one earbud. A raspy version of a rap song eked out.

"Yeah, Dad?"

Felix made a gun with his fingers, pointed at the phone and dropped his thumb. Ricky sighed and hit pause.

"We need to clear brush in the orchard," he said. "Tomorrow after church."

Church services were a reference point only for Ricky. He hadn't joined his parents at services since the spring, after he'd started hanging out with the Outsiders, as they called themselves. Ricky rolled his eyes.

"Yeah, sure. Mañana." He reset his earbud and tuned out the world.

Felix stifled his frustration and walked out. Somehow his values of hard work, God and family had not penetrated his son. As recently as last year, they had worked together in the grove, harvested oranges with smiles and laughter. But now...

Carlina waited for him in the hallway.

"It's a phase," she said. "He'll grow out of it. His hormones will calm down and reason will return."

"He needs to be quick about it," Felix said. "If I'd spoken to my father that way when I was thirteen..."

"You'd have never made it to fourteen," Carlina said in a sing-song monotone.

Felix gave her an irked look. She took his hand.

"But you aren't your father. Give him time."

Felix shook his head and then kissed her cheek.

"I'll give him until tomorrow, how's that?"

"A start," she said.

They walked back out into the grove, hand in hand.

Chapter Six

Mañana was *mañana* as far as Ricky was concerned. He'd worry about working the grove when he needed to worry about it. He had other things to do *hoy*.

As soon as his father left his room, he checked the message that had arrived on his phone. Two words from Zach. "Scorpion blasting." Excellent.

Ricky slipped out the front door and hopped on his bike. Halfway down the driveway, his little sister Angela darted out in front of him, hand raised like a traffic cop. Ricky hit the brakes and skidded sideways in the sand.

"Damn, Ange," he snapped. "You trying to get run over?"

Angela's big brown eyes went wide and her mouth opened into a silent, mortified O.

"D-word!" she said. She was five and had accumulated a list of words the Sunday school had banned. "Very bad. Where are you going?"

"Zach's, if it is any of your business, and it isn't."

She threw her long black hair over her shoulders and raised her chin in defiance.

"Then you have to pay the toll."

Ricky knew the going rate in their running game. He pulled out a pack of gum and put one stick in her outstretched palm.

"And one for the cursing," she said.

"Now you are just a robber," he said. He put another stick in her hand.

Angela stepped aside and unwrapped the gum. Ricky rolled by her and ruffled her hair.

"Next time you'll get run over," he said.

"Mommy will be mad," she mumbled through a mouthful of gum.

He pedaled out to the highway, away from the decrepit old embarrassment of a house his parents condemned him to inhabit, away from the stupid trees that his father treated better than his children. He rode along the narrow shoulder for a few miles until he got to Poulsen Acres.

When TV was still broadcast exclusively over the air in black and white, Poulsen Acres had been the place to live, a grid of small concrete-block starter homes with vertical-slat windows that closed with a crank and a carport for your Ford Edsel. Poulsen Construction stopped building tiny homes about the same time Ford canned the Edsel, both items eclipsed by models that kept up with the times. The unfinished neighborhood had degenerated into an assembly of shabby rentals. Zach Vreeland's house was no exception. The carport was so swaybacked no one dared park a car underneath it anymore.

The front door was open with just a punctured screen door to fend off the mosquitoes. Ricky walked in without knocking. Parents were never home before evening at the Vreeland house. Zach Vreeland sprawled on the bumpy living room couch, feet braced against the lip of a coffee table. He wore the unofficial uniform of the group, jeans with missing knees and a dark Tshirt. His advertised a band called Metal Maidens today. His cheeks were covered with acne, the red, lumpy painful kind you couldn't pop to make go away. He kept his shaggy brown hair long to cover it. A seventh-grade academic retention made him a year older than the rest of the Outsiders.

Zach's fingers danced over the game controller in his hands. His eyes were glued to the widescreen HD TV that hung on the wall. The Vreelands might eat mac and cheese for dinner, but they had a killer TV. Animated soldiers ran across the screen and blasted enormous alien scorpions with laser rifles. The TV volume was maxed and each blast of the soldier's weapons filled the room like overhead thunder.

Barry Leopold sat next to Zach. The pudgy kid wore the kind of owlish glasses that might have looked cool on Harry Potter, but only served to amplify the boy's eyes into a permanent look of wonder. His mother cut his dark hair as if an inverted salad bowl had been the guide. The holes in his jeans knees were cut so recently that they had yet to sprout white cotton fuzz around the edges. Barry mashed the controller in his hands, desperate to save his soldier, who was taking serious hits from the scorpions' stingers.

"Dudes," Ricky said as he stood behind the couch.

On screen, a scorpion impaled Barry's alter-ego soldier and then slapped him down against the ground a half dozen times. The soldier flashed red and dropped its weapon.

"Son of a bitch!" Barry said. It was funny to hear him curse, as out of place as the sound of screaming guitars coming out of a 1930s cabinet radio. The effort to sound cool made him seem even less so. "Now look what you did, Ricky. You broke my concentration and I'm dead."

"Yeah, that's it," Ricky said. "You were kicking that thing's ass until just this second, and I screwed it all up."

"You're dead, loser," Zach said to Barry. He hit the pause button and the action froze on the screen. "Switch out."

"But Ricky—"

Zach picked a BB pistol up off the coffee table, pointed it at Barry's meaty shoulder with only the vaguest attempt at aiming. He pulled the trigger. The gun popped.

"Hey, what the hell?" Barry said. He pulled up his sleeve and exposed a tiny red welt.

"Low pressure, woosie," Zach said with derision. "You got the padding to take it."

Barry dropped the controller in defeat and left the couch. Paco Mason took Barry's place.

Paco was a wiry little kid with a nose like a ski slope. The frayed white denim around the holes in his jeans stood up like brush bristles and swayed with each stuttering step. Perpetually ADHD, all his movements had a jitter to them. His eyes lit up as he took the controller.

"This is the ultimate, dude," he said. "Let's waste some aliens."

The game restarted and Paco's fingers flailed across the controller. His soldier looked like a marionette controlled by a meth head. Volume of fire overcame its random nature and he racked up points.

The four of them had banded together as the Outsiders over the last few months. They all had issues that kept them out of the mainstream. Zach had been at the bottom of the pecking order since he'd been held back. Now kids his age looked at him as if he was retarded and the younger kids in his class thought he was a freak since he was so much further into puberty. Ricky was poor and his Mexican parents farmed. Paco was jittery as hell, and always in trouble for something, usually involving fire.

But Barry had it the worst. Short, fat and spectacled, he might as well have had a big red bully bull's-eye tattooed on his forehead. Asthma kept him out of PE and sidelined in the schoolyard. Watching one of Barry's panicked grasps for his inhaler was practically an invitation to punch him. His horribly overprotective mother was a constant source of humiliation. If he hadn't fallen in with the Outsiders, even *they* would have wailed on him after school.

Barry sat to one side and massaged his left shoulder. He could not hide the anxiety on his face. Ricky sat next to him. Barry moved his hand from his shoulder and straightened up in his chair. Something exploded on the TV screen and the boys on the couch cheered.

"Don't sweat Zach," Ricky said. "He was raised by wolves."

"It didn't hurt," Barry said, his voice an octave too low.

"You know you need to shoot the green diamond on their heads," Ricky offered.

"Huh?"

"The aliens. Nail that green diamond and they go down in one shot instead of having to slice them to pieces."

Barry's eyes widened to fill his glasses. "For real?"

"For real. Try it next time. Take my turn."

"Okay," Barry said with a grateful look in his eyes.

Ricky propped his feet up on the table. Zach shot the stinger off an alien. All was right with the world.

Chapter Seven

Downtown Citrus Glade was dead as road kill the next morning and not just because it was Sunday.

Back when Apex Sugar had the mill going, it was a different story. The six blocks that centered on Main and Tangelo bustled with activity. Hundreds of workers lived in Citrus Glade. The town provided all they needed, including movie theaters, car dealerships and a thriving downtown square. Fourth of July parades were good for two dozen floats.

But that Citrus Glade was gone. Like an aging actress with a fizzled career, the town tried to keep up appearances. But just as thicker makeup cannot cover the ravages of time, fresh paint on the town's central water tower and a politician's stirring speeches could not mask the town's internal economic rot. The tax base evaporated like summer rain on blacktop. Services dwindled. Stores closed. Many moved.

Downtown now was a shell of its former self. All the two-story brick buildings were there, the sidewalks and streetlamps ready to guide customers from shop to shop. But empty storefronts dominated the square. The movie theater marquee had shed all its neon finery and the "Roxy" lettering underneath it had long peeled away. Glade Hardware made a valiant stand at one corner, Gentry's Drug at another. Harper's Video rented DVDs and repaired electronics and thus had cornered the market on obsolete business models. A few small businesses populated the rest of downtown, scrapbooking and antique shops that only broke even with free rent.

That morning, Zach Vreeland pedaled his bike down the empty

street, past the parking meters the few visitors roundly ignored. His knees poked through the big square holes in his jeans with each pump of the pedals. The ninth grader had about outgrown the BMX bike, but a new one wasn't one of his parents' priorities

He'd mastered his new *Scorpion Assault* video game to the point of boredom. He'd texted the rest of the Outsiders that he'd be here. Now he just awaited a four-person flash mob.

He hopped the curb and did a lazy slalom down the uneven sidewalk. He jerked the bike to a halt in front of what used to be Everyday Shoes. The empty shop sported a repainted black facade with a glossy shine. The old tiles in the recessed doorway glowed like they had when first laid in the 1950s. A *CLOSED* sign hung in the door. Sunlight shimmered on the polished display window. Black Gothic letters with gold trim crossed the glass in a wide arc. They spelled:

MAGIC SHOP

Underneath in smaller print it said:

ILLUSIONS AND PRESTIDIGITATION

Zach's reflection in the glass disappeared as he pulled his long brown hair from his pimply face and leaned in for a closer view. A new wall behind the window blocked the view to the rest of the store. Two old posters flanked the middle. The one on the right had the word *Houdini* across the top and a painting of the great magician hanging upside down in a straight jacket inside a water-filled box. The poster on the left was a drawing of a man at a table in a bejeweled turban, left hand around a crystal ball like it was an old friend at a dinner party. He stared straight out from the sheet with a mesmerizing gaze. Lettering at the top read *The Amazing Alexander of the East* and *Futures Foretold.*

Only one item sat in the display area. Three joined silver hoops hung on a black post. They gleamed against a black velvet background.

Zach thought that was weird. He remembered, when he was a kid and Dad had money to burn, he had a birthday party. Some guy in a clown suit came to perform. Honestly, the guy in the white face paint and big shoes gave him a case of the creeps. His balloon animals all looked like twisted-together hot dogs. But the clown had a set of magic rings. As the birthday boy, Zach got to touch them to prove that they were solid. Then in front of everyone, the clown juggled the silver rings. They flashed in the sun like some Hollywood special effect. Then fast as lightning, he linked and unlinked the rings. At the time Zach thought it was magic.

On the other side of the door, a hand snaked into view and flipped the door sign over to *OPEN.*

It's ten-twelve a.m., he thought. *Who the hell opens a store at ten-twelve? On a Sunday?*

Nothing else was happening out here. He leaned his bike against the front of the store and walked in. A bell tinkled to announce his entrance.

The shop was empty. The walls were painted black. A layered curtain of beads covered the doorway between the shop and a rear storage room.

Lyle Miller sat on a vacant display counter. A huge brass cash register took up the other end. Lyle wore a solid red silk button-down shirt. He gave Zach a grin that made Zach think of a spider in a web, though he didn't know why since spiders don't smile.

"C'mon in," Lyle said. "Lyle Miller's the name."

Zach gave him a quick snap of his head in return. "Zach."

"Welcome to the shop," Lyle said.

"Dude," Zach said with a quick glance around, "you got nothing to sell."

Lyle slid off the counter and stepped to the front display window.

"It's called 'just-in-time inventory' in the business world," Lyle said. "I only carry what I need to sell."

He reached in through a door in the back of the window display and pulled out the three rings. He looped one through his arm and it slid down to his elbow. He held the other two, one in each hand.

"*Bakshokah shuey,*" Lyle said. He swung the two rings together. When they touched each other they rang instead of clinked, like someone had struck a musical triangle. He handed them to Zach. Zach tugged at them and they remained united.

"So what's the trick?"

"No trick," Lyle said. He took the rings from Zach, scooped them side by side, and peeled them apart. "It's magic."

"Bull. There's always a trick." He took the rings from Lyle and examined each one. Flawless, continuous metal. He slammed them together and they would not join.

"It doesn't work because you don't believe," Lyle said. "And you won't believe because it doesn't work. A nasty cycle. Elements attuned to magic can do amazing things. But without belief, you cannot channel the power to make the magic happen."

Lyle reached into his pocket and pulled out a polished gold coin the size of a quarter. The edges were uneven and engravings worn, as if the coin had passed through millions of hands over hundreds of years. He tossed it to Zach.

"Put that in your pocket," he said. "And then try again."

Zach had enough of this weird dude doing party tricks in his empty store. He tossed back the coin and turned to return the rings to the display.

"I can see how you would be afraid," Lyle said. He bounced the coin in his hand. "The power of magic intimidates the weak."

Zach spun back to face Lyle.

"I ain't afraid of nothing."

Lyle delivered a victorious smirk and tossed the coin back to Zach. Zach slipped it in his pocket.

"Now," Lyle said. "Focus."

Zach felt like an idiot. He held one ring in each hand. He closed his eyes. Nothing.

"The phrase," Lyle said. "*Bakshokah shuey.* Say it."

This was so lame. "*Bakshokah shuey.*" Zach sighed.

The coin in his pocket warmed. His arms tingled, like they bristled with static electricity. He swung the rings together. When they hit they emitted a high musical note. But Zach didn't feel them hit. He opened his eyes. His heart skipped a beat. The rings were joined.

"Awesome," he whispered.

He let one of the linked rings drop. He flipped the other off his wrist and into his palm.

"*Bakshokah shuey,*" he said with conviction. This time he felt the tingle right away, like the magic had found its path of least resistance and now sought it out on its own. Something in the back of his brain purred like a kitten. The two rings pulled toward each other as if magnetized. He let them swing together. Ping! A chain of three.

Zach's jaw went slack.

"Feel that power?" Lyle said.

Zach nodded as if drugged. The exhilaration of channeling the magic was beyond description.

"There's more where that came from," Lyle said.

"Bring it on, dude."

"In good time," Lyle said. "You have some friends who might also enjoy learning some magic?"

"Hell, yeah," Zach said.

"Have them come by," Lyle said. "One at a time."

Zach was afraid of the answer to his next question.

"What do these rings cost?"

"How much do you have?"

Zach paused at the odd answer. He pulled his cash from his pocket.

"Eight bucks," he said.

"Lucky for you they cost four," Lyle said.

Lyle held out a hand. His fingernails had a shine to them, like they were coated in clear polish. Zach shrugged and peeled off four dollar bills. Lyle crushed the bills in his grip.

He pushed the keys of the old register. Each one responded with a deep mechanical click, like the sound of a jail cell locking. The register's bell rang and the drawer slid open. Lyle placed Zach's money in the empty tray. The drawer closed and swallowed the payment.

"Remember, no returns," he said.

Zach didn't know why he'd want to.

"Come back Tuesday afternoon," Lyle said, "and learn the craft."

The jingling bell ushered Zach back out the door. He looped the rings over his handlebars and took the coin from his pocket.

On one side was a man's face in profile. Strange symbols circled the coin's edge. On the back were a crescent moon and a five-pointed star within a circle. The coin felt warm, and not in a particularly comforting way.

He picked up his phone and texted the Outsiders.

dudes u need 2 go 2 town now coolest place just opened.

Zach pedaled off and Lyle watched him weave his way down Main Street. The boy was young, very young. But he'd used younger. And the downside of a little less developed *whapna,* or inner being, was more than balanced by this one's upside of missing moral balance. The power would flow through him with no resistance. If the rest of his friends were as disaffected as he, as ripe for the picking, the Grand Adventure in Citrus Glade would be one for the ages.

But unlike some of his past Grand Adventures, such as Tangshen, Bhola and Huascarán to name a few, he'd need some inadvertent assistance here as well, some people with a natural inclination to evil that he could cultivate and enhance. He felt the presence of some fine candidates. He'd start that search tomorrow.

Chapter Eight

Zach Vreeland sat in his room with the three magic rings. He'd just learned that without the coin in his pocket, the rings were solid steel. He could bang them together as hard as he wanted to and nothing happened.

He put the coin in his pocket, closed his eyes and tried again.

"*Bakshokah shuey.*"

The coin heated up like a stovetop element. That wonderful rush of energy hit his hands and he felt like he could throw lightning bolts. He studied the rings as they passed through each other. He could not see the transition event. No noise, no pressure. He had learned in science class that everything was made up of atoms with lots of space in between. It was as if the molecules of one ring went out of phase and steered around the ones in the other.

"*Bakshokah shuey.*"

The coin cut back to half power. He pulled the rings apart, and this time they nearly hung together halfway through. He gave them an extra jerk and they came apart.

"What the hell?" He tried the trick again. This time when he said the incantation, nothing happened at all. No rush of power, no warming coin. He made a second useless attempt. He felt like an idiot.

He threw the rings against the wall. The trick was a trick. He'd been taken in by that guy in the magic shop. Barry texted that he was on his way down there now. He'd head into town as well and get his damn money back.

Once Zach got there, he couldn't wait for Barry. He had a defective product and Lyle was going to answer for it. He barged into the Magic Shop, rings in hand. Lyle came out of the back room in a clacking swirl of the black beaded curtain.

"Dude," Zach said, "these things don't work."

Lyle's mouth tightened. He stared down Zach and his eyes seemed alive with a blue fire behind them. Zach's bravado withered and his resolute advance through the store slowed to a stop. Something ice cold took residence in Zach's chest. Lyle stepped up next to Zach and stared down at him like a god from Mount Olympus.

"Perhaps you want to rephrase that," Lyle said.

"I...I couldn't get the rings...the rings to join."

"And when are you supposed to come back?"

The air around him felt thick and...dark. "T-T-Tuesday."

"Then come back then," Lyle said. "Walk in with an attitude like that again and you'll walk out a changed boy, and not for the better."

Zach felt like he'd just stepped to the edge of a cliff. He wheeled around and restrained himself from running for the door.

He stepped outside into the bright, liberating sunlight. He shuddered, rounded the corner of the building and leaned against the brick wall. The sunbaked stone felt good.

Barry appeared at the corner of the square. From head on, the round kid on the bike looked like an oversized lollipop. He gave Zach a nod of his head. Zach straightened up and slapped on a measure of cool. It was Barry's turn with Lyle. And he could have the old man to himself.

Barry saw Zach in front of the Magic Shop and sighed with relief. He'd answered Zach's text and hoped Zach would still be there. He wasn't going to admit it, but there was something just a bit sinister about the place. He was much happier entering the store with backup.

He pedaled up and his bike screeched to a halt.

"Go on in, dude," Zach said.

Barry gave the Magic Shop a sideways look.

"You already know the dude," Barry said. "Come in with me."

"He said to send in my friends alone," Zach said. "Just go in, you woosie."

"Woosie" was Barry's hot-button word. Seven years of being the picked-on fat kid had rolled to a stop when he joined Zach's merry band. He'd been the woosie when he was out there alone, but those days were sure as hell over.

Barry set his double chin and marched to the store. He stopped to look in the front window. Between posters of an inverted Houdini and a fortune teller in a turban, there was only one item in the window. A black silk top hat.

Barry wiped his sweating palms on his shorts. He glanced at Zach, who gave him an exasperated look. Zach made a W with his fingers. Barry plunged through the door. A bell at the top rang. As the door closed behind him, the *OPEN* sign flipped over to *CLOSED* on its own and something clicked, like the door deadbolt being thrown. The sound echoed in the dark empty store.

Lyle Miller leaned against the vacant main display case. The huge brass cash register next to him had a bit of a glow to it.

"Barry, I'm Lyle. I've been waiting for you to drop by."

No adult had ever decided to be on a first name basis with Barry before. He instantly felt older.

"I see you have your eye on the magic hat," he said.

Barry repressed a smart-ass comment about there being little else to have his eye on in the shop.

Lyle walked to the front display and pulled out the silk hat. He balanced it on one finger and spun it like a top. Then, a flick of the wrist, and he caught it in his hand with a flourish. He stepped to the other side of the display counter. He upended the hat so Barry could see the bottom.

"It's quite an amazing hat," Lyle said. "You see it is completely empty. You see it was sitting unattended on the front display before I just extracted it. Nothing could be hidden within."

Lyle put the hat on the counter, open end up. He pulled a white handkerchief from his shirt pocket, though the pocket had hung flat against Lyle's chest and had clearly been empty. He flipped the handkerchief open and spread it across the open end of the hat. He placed his hands over the hat, palms down.

"Now I say the magic words," Lyle said. "*Bakshokah apnoah.*"

He whipped back the handkerchief. Barry held his breath.

Lyle reached in and extracted a bright yellow parakeet with pale blue eyes.

"Whoa, dude," Barry exhaled.

The bird chirped twice and perched on Lyle's finger. He gave it a flip and the bird fluttered off through the beaded doorway.

"How'd you do it?" Barry asked.

"Magic, Barry. Magic."

"Can you pull anything out of the hat?"

"Anything that breathes, as long as it fits. One can't pull out money. One can't pull out a tiger. Other than that, it's up to the owner. Give it a try?" Lyle slid the hat across the countertop.

Fresh sweat broke out on Barry's palms. He grabbed the hat by the brim and looked inside. Empty. He ventured a finger inside and ran it along the sides and bottom. The red silk inner lining glided across his fingertips.

"Don't worry," Lyle said. "Nothing's going to bite you in there. Not yet." He slid a gold coin across the counter. "Put this in your pocket to focus the energy."

Barry put the coin in his pocket. When he touched the hat again, it hummed, like an A/C adapter after it's plugged into a socket. He jerked his hands back.

Lyle laughed. "Not everyone can handle the power."

Barry furrowed his brow. He could handle any power the guy

wanted to dish out. Zach had done it. He gripped the hat again and pulled it closer.

"Now what shall we conjure?" Lyle said. "Let's start small. A cricket. Cover the hat."

Barry laid Lyle's handkerchief across the hat.

"Now close your eyes and make a mental picture of the cricket. Both hands over the hat and say *bakshokah apnoah.*"

Barry shut his eyes and saw a cricket in his mind. Small, black, shiny, long black legs tucked up in inverted V-shapes. He extended his hands. "*Bak-sho-kah-ap-no-ah.*"

The coin in his pocket warmed. His hands tingled. He froze in fear. He opened his eyes and stared at Lyle.

"Well?" Lyle said. He pointed at the hat.

Barry slipped the handkerchief off the hat. He reached inside. Something hopped in his palm and his heart skipped a beat. He pulled out his hand and there sat a glossy black cricket. Barry smiled in wonder. The cricket hopped onto the counter and chirped.

"Well done!" Lyle said. "You're a natural."

Barry tilted the empty hat toward him. "I so want this hat," Barry said.

"I'd give it to you," Lyle said. "But it doesn't work that way. The owner must have skin in the game. How much money do you have?"

After hearing what Zach had found in the Magic Shop, Barry had emptied his shoebox bank in preparation. He dumped a handful of cash on the counter. Twelve dollar bills, two quarters and four pennies. He gave Lyle a hopeful look.

"It's $6.27," Lyle said. "Tax included. Your lucky day." He counted out his cut. "All sales are final, of course."

Barry nodded like a bobble-head toy and Lyle rang up the sale on the old cash register. The bell sounded like the bell at a boxing ring, the one that announced the round was over. Or just begun. Lyle pressed at the top hat and it collapsed flat. He slid it toward Barry with one finger.

"Come back on Tuesday afternoon," he said. "Learn your new craft."

"You bet!"

Barry left the shop thrilled. For a kid whose parents never let him have pets, what could be cooler than an avenue to create as many as you wanted. Zach waited for him next door.

"Whatcha got?" Zach asked.

"Most radical thing you've ever seen," Barry said.

Back in the shop, Lyle polished the top of the display case with his handkerchief and then tossed it into the air. It vanished in a puff of white smoke.

The parakeet flew back into the room fast as a streak of yellow lightning. It alighted on the top of the register. Its pale blue eyes now glowed bright cobalt. It cocked its head at the cricket on the counter.

The cricket chirped. The parakeet launched itself like a golden rocket. It hit the glass counter top with a thwack and speared the cricket with its beak. It tossed the insect in the air and devoured it whole. Its eyes blazed brighter.

Lyle scooped up the parakeet in one hand. He stroked its head with the other.

"Excellent kill," he cooed.

He grabbed the bird's head and snapped its neck. The light in its eyes died like a burned-out campfire. He tossed the carcass in a trash can.

"But it is too early to tip our hand with you flying around. In time, all will be revealed."

Chapter Nine

The two boys returned to Zach's house, a safe place to experiment with both of his parents gone. Barry saw this as a step up. Anytime the Outsiders gathered, he was usually fourth to the party, the one invited as an afterthought. Today he was Zach's guest of honor, his Number One.

Zach gave Barry the details on his silver rings, save that he could no longer make them work. Barry proudly popped the top hat into the open position for a demonstration.

"Watch this."

He placed the hat on the kitchen table. The brim hummed as he touched it. The coin in his pocket warmed. He unfolded a paper napkin and laid it across the top. He wondered what to pull from the hat. Nothing too dangerous. A lizard, one of the small green-gray ones always racing across his back patio, snapping up ants and mosquitos. His hands hovered over the hat. He closed his eyes and made a mental picture.

"*Bakshokah apnoah,*" he said.

He pulled away the napkin and reached in. A small green lizard climbed up his arm.

"No shit," Zach gasped. He pulled the hat in front of him. "What can I wish for?"

Barry reached for the hat. "My trick. I bought it."

Zach raised a clenched hand in Barry's face. "My fist. You want to buy that? Now what can I wish for?"

"Any animal that will fit in the hat."

"Cool. I'll do a monkey!" He pulled the napkin over the hat and put his hands out the way Barry did. "*Bakshokah ano*...what's your magic words?"

"*Bakshokah apnoah.*" Barry sighed.

"*Bakshokah apnoah.*"

Zach yanked off the napkin. He reached into the hat with a devilish grin. His smile dissolved as he ran his hand around the inside of the empty hat. He looked inside. He tossed the napkin back on top.

"*Bakshokah shuey,*" Zach said, giving his own phrase a try. He pulled the napkin away. Still nothing

"What the hell? What did you do?"

"Maybe..." Barry said. He picked up Zach's rings from the table. He closed his eyes and concentrated. The coin in his pocket stayed cool. He muttered his magic phrase and yanked the rings in opposite directions. They clanked together, still linked.

"We can't do each other's tricks," Barry said. "Just the one we own. Maybe that's why Lyle said we had to buy them."

Zach took his rings back. He closed his eyes and an overly concerned look crossed his face. He pulled on the rings with theatrical effort.

"Now mine doesn't work," Zach said. "No hot coin. Like the juice got turned off."

Barry touched the brim of the hat. It did not hum. "Same here."

"Son of a bitch," Zach said. His face got that dark look that reminded Barry of vampires in movies. The dark face always brought trouble. "We both got ripped off."

"We go back Tuesday afternoon," Barry reassured him. "We'll get a recharge."

Zach banged the joined rings against the table. "We'd better."

Chapter Ten

While two of the Outsiders struggled with the dissipation of their powers, a third stood before Lyle Miller. Paco Mason still harbored doubts about what Zach had told him of the Magic Shop.

"So you're some kind of magician?" he asked.

Lyle gave him a wry, condescending smile. "My boy, I'm the best kind of magician. A real one."

He walked Paco over to the front window display. He reached inside and pulled out the only item there, the one that had immediately captured Paco's imagination. A black magician's wand.

The wand was a solid dowel about six inches long. One tip was white. Lyle held it in his hand, white tip out.

"Now think of the white tip as the end of the barrel," he warned. "Point that thing away from you."

He returned to the counter with Paco in tow. Two paper cups sat at one end. The rest of the display case, and store for that matter, was empty.

"It's a wand like Harry Potter has?" Paco said.

"Please," Lyle said. "Wands that can do anything. That's all make-believe. A real wand has one true task."

He held the wand with the grace of a great painter with his finest brush, a delicate touch to direct great power.

"Now all the finest magicians master this skill one way or another," Lyle said. "A woman enters a box, a coin hidden under a scarf, a sheet draped over an item, the setup is immaterial. One way or another, they all disappear."

Lyle touched the wand's white tip to the lip of one of the cups.

"*Bakshokah korami,*" Lyle said.

There was a tiny flash. A puff of white smoke appeared and dissipated in a split second. The cup was gone.

A look of awe appeared on Paco's face. It was the same look he had when he watched a campfire burn, the same look he had when he saw fireball explosions on TV, the same look he had at the moment of ignition when a magnifying glass focused the sun's rays on the back of an ant.

"Where did it go?"

"It didn't go anywhere," Lyle said. "It just ceased. Spontaneous endothermic combustion. Always leaves the crowd wanting more. Usually because they now have less. Want to try?"

Paco could not speak. He just held out his hand. Lyle gave him the wand. He positioned Paco's fingers to hold it like a chopstick.

"There, hold it with reverence. It's not a plastic fork."

Lyle held up a hand and waved his fingers. A gold coin the size of a quarter appeared. He put it in Paco's other hand.

"Now focus and feel the power," he said. "It will surge to the wand at your command of *Bakshokah korami.*"

"*Bakshokah korami.*"

The coin in Paco's left hand heated up. A tingle ran up that arm, across his shoulders and down the other. The wand between his fingers began to thrum. His pulse pounded harder.

He tapped the remaining cup. The wand jolted like the kick of a shotgun. The cup flashed and vanished.

"Awesome!" Paco shouted.

"You are a natural," Lyle said. "The wand and you are one."

Paco stared, enchanted by the stick in his hand. No more matches. No more firecrackers.

"How much for it?" he asked.

"How much do you have?"

Paco pulled a twenty and two fives from his pocket. It was as much as he thought he could take from his mother's wallet without the loss being noticed. Lyle took the twenty. He pumped two keys and a *$10* and a *$5* tab popped up on opposite sides of the register's glass window, like two eyes awakened. The drawer consumed Paco's money. The two eyes dropped back into satiated sleep. Lyle returned a five to Paco's cash hoard.

"That's fifteen with five change," he said. "Remember, the white tip points out. Come back Tuesday afternoon to master your new craft."

The wand still had Paco mesmerized. He nodded and went out through the front door. He blinked in the sudden sunlight. The street was empty, but it was still best to hide his new acquisition. He slipped the wand into his pocket and mounted his bicycle for the trip home.

During the ride, his mind raced from idea to idea, the way it always did. The ADHD gift did him no good at school, where they gave him drugs to douse it. But he liked it out in the world, where it made him feel free and powerful, like he was jumping from stone to stone in a fast running stream. He faked taking the pills that slowed him down for just that reason. Yeah, it made school easier, but who cared about that when your mind no longer ran like the wind.

He thought of what he wanted to make disappear. There were a few kids from school who made the short list, as did the school itself. He wondered how big something had to be before he couldn't make it vanish in a flash and a puff of smoke.

By the time he returned to his house, he knew what weekly nemesis was first on his list to make vanish. He made a beeline for the kitchen and pulled open the refrigerator door. His target sat alone on the second shelf, wrapped in a clear plastic bag.

Broccoli. The dark green vegetable pointed its mutated heads at him like a pack of accusatory radiation victims.

Paco hated broccoli like vampires hated garlic. Tonight it was going to be him or the green stalk, and this time the stalk was going to lose. He touched the wand to the vegetable.

"*Bakshokah korami.*"

The coin in his pocket warmed and his hands tingled. The wand twitched in his fingers. A tiny flash sparked in the refrigerator and the broccoli disappeared in a little cloud of white smoke.

"Excellent!" he shouted and slammed the refrigerator door shut.

Next item on the list: Ritalin. He was done getting that crap shoved down his throat. He went to his mother's bathroom and pulled open the medicine cabinet. There were more bottles here than he expected. He shuffled through them until he found the prescription with his name on it and pulled that one out. He set it on top of the toilet tank.

"Adios, buzz killer," he said. He touched the wand to the cap, white tip to white top. "*Bakshokah korami.*"

The pocketed coin barely warmed. His shoulder registered a quick twinge, but no power reached his hand. The wand did not respond. It was like when his mother tried to start the car with a dying battery. Paco gritted his teeth.

"*Bakshokah korami,*" he said more firmly.

This time nothing happened at all. No juice.

"Son of a bitch," he said. Just when he was getting started. Lyle had better refill his magic gas tank on Tuesday. This little wand was going to be way too much fun.

Chapter Eleven

Ricky Arroyo stood outside the Magic Shop and stared at the *OPEN* sign. The early evening sun had dipped lower in the sky and cast the shop front in shadows. Lately, he'd been the last to jump at whatever the Outsiders were into. Barry had always been the Pluto of the Outsiders' solar system, but recently the little fat kid had tightened his orbit and been first to follow Zach's lead. Ricky had sensed himself drifting a bit outside the inner circle. Now he was the last of the four to make a purchase at the Magic Shop.

He'd stopped by their houses on the way here and seen what the other kids had purchased. Magic rings, a wand that made things disappear, the hat that could deliver live animals. All cool tricks, and though none of the others could actually make them work, he believed them when they said that the things just needed a jump start of some kind. He just wasn't sure if he was ready to mess with that kind of power.

One item sat in the window display, a deck of playing cards arranged in a fan. The box at the center of the fan had *Magic Deck* across the face.

Card tricks. That might just be okay. Nothing got destroyed. Nothing got created. No laws of physics were broken. Cool, but kind of safe. And if his mother rifled through his room, as she often did, how much suspicion could a deck of cards arouse?

The bell on the shop door rang a tattling proclamation of his entry. Lyle Miller stood at the rear of the empty store. His black shirt had long flared sleeves and a V-shaped corset lacing at the open neck, very theatrical looking. Ricky exhaled, relieved to see someone more entertainer than warlock.

"Ricky," Lyle said as he approached at a trot. "Last but not least. I'm Lyle."

He extended his hand. At first touch, he felt...sharp. It was the way frozen metal and a hot stove element both have the same initial dangerous feel. The sensation faded. Lyle's grip engulfed Ricky's smaller hand then released it.

"All magic must be tailored to the magician," Lyle said. "The illusion must speak to him."

He walked to the front of the store and scooped the deck of cards from the front window. Ricky followed him back to the vacant display case. Lyle took position on the far side and set out the deck.

"These speak to you," he said with a soothing, easy patter. "The familiarity of the cards is the card's draw. Fifty-two cardboard rectangles are so simple, the audience expects nothing."

He hovered a palm over the cards and swept right. The deck spread out along the counter, but Ricky swore Lyle's hand hadn't touched them. With nothing but fingertips, Lyle flipped the entire deck back to front and back again. He swept the cards back together and held the deck in both hands. He pulled his hands apart and the red-backed cards fluttered from left to right like a flight of robins. He closed his hands together and spread the deck into a tight fan. Ricky stared, dumbfounded.

"Now the dexterity tricks are just the warm up," Lyle said. "The people want the magic, the demonstration of the inexplicable. Pick a card. Don't let me see it."

Ricky pulled one card free with a hesitant finger and thumb and tilted it up. Six of spades.

"Now back inside," Lyle said.

Ricky slipped the card back into the deck. Lyle cut and rearranged the deck with one hand. Then he shuffled the deck and fanned it again. "*Bakshokah serat.* Pick again."

Ricky pulled a card from the deck. Six of spades.

How could that be...?

Lyle closed the deck, flipped it over and fanned it again face up. The cards were all the six of spades. He took Ricky's card and reinserted it.

"*Bakshokah serat.*" He flipped the deck, shuffled it and fanned it out again face up. Fifty-two different cards.

"Killer trick," Ricky said.

Lyle slid the deck across to Ricky. The blue sapphire ring on Lyle's finger flickered with different shades. "Your turn. Show me some moves."

Ricky picked up the deck. He felt foolish. He could barely shuffle cards without having them end up all over the floor.

"Focus," Lyle said. "Magic is all around you. You must focus it to move through you."

Ricky stared at the cards. He waved his hand across the deck. Nothing moved. He stared harder and tried again. Nothing.

Lyle slid a gold coin across the counter. The careworn face on it stared at Ricky. "Here, put this in your pocket, say '*bakshokah serat*' and try again."

Ricky picked up the coin and got the same fleeting feeling he had when he first touched Lyle's hand. He put the coin in his pocket.

"*Bakshokah serat,*" he said. The coin warmed his pocket. He touched the deck. The cards hummed with a rhythmic pulse, like they had a heartbeat. He raised his hand over the deck and swept it right. He could feel his hand pull the cards, as if they were attached to his fingertips by spider webs. He moved his hand back and the cards restacked.

"Whoa."

"Now the magic," Lyle said.

Ricky picked up the cards and swore they fanned themselves in his hand. Lyle picked one from the pack, flashed the king of diamonds to Ricky and replaced it. Ricky's hands tingled like they were plugged into a wall socket. He shuffled the deck like a Vegas pro and fanned it again. Lyle pulled out a card and turned it face up. King of diamonds.

"Easy as pie," Lyle said. "Nothing to be concerned about with a simple deck of cards, right?"

Of course not, Ricky thought. It's not like he conjured up something from thin air, or made something disappear into it. This was cool. The hard part was coming.

"What do they cost?" he asked. The others told him what they had paid. It hadn't been much, considering what they had bought, but they had more money than Ricky did. He doubted he would have enough.

"What have you got?" Lyle asked.

Ricky pulled out two bills and an assortment of change that totaled $3.50. "I can work off whatever it costs extra," he offered, red-faced.

Lyle broke into a crocodilian grin.

"No need. You have more than enough. It's your lucky day."

He counted out $1.75 and pressed three keys on the big register. The cash drawer rolled open with a solemn ding of the bell. Lyle deposited the money and when he pushed the drawer back in, it returned with a soft guttural sigh.

"Now come back with your friends on Tuesday. Great mysteries will be revealed."

"We'll be here!" Ricky said. He shoved the remaining cash in one pocket. He stuffed the cards into the other. He hit the door in a euphoric sprint.

Lyle watched him go with great satisfaction. Four would be a good number. Manageable, yet still able to spread the power across town. At first he thought the boys' ages would be a problem, but now he saw it as an advantage. The irresistible lure of the magic combined with limited life experiences meant things would spin out of control quite quickly.

And that was just what the Grand Adventure needed.

Chapter Twelve

"What's that?" Angela said.

Startled, Ricky jerked and magic cards sprayed from his hands all across his desktop. The desk in his room faced away from the door his little sister stood in. He shot an annoyed glance over his shoulder as he reassembled the deck.

"Pest! Stop sneaking up on people."

"I'm not sneaking," Angela said. "My shoes are just quiet."

Since her fifth birthday she had started shadowing Ricky more often, wondering what her big brother was up to. Rather than flatter him, her curiosity had gotten on Ricky's nerves. He wanted to kick himself for forgetting to close his bedroom door. She wandered in and stood by his desk.

"Playing cards?" she said.

"Yeah, that's it."

"I can play too," Angela said. Her little bangs bounced as she shook her head up and down in affirmation. "I know how." Last week she had learned to apply her counting skills to playing Go Fish. A lamer game had never been created.

This deck wasn't going to stoop to Go Fish-ing. But while Ricky had been able to practice some of his tricks, he hadn't been able to test some without a participant to pull a card and be amazed. Angela might have a purpose after all.

"These cards are for a different game," Ricky said. "A magic game. You can play if you will keep it a secret."

"A secret?" Angela looked wary.

"Sure," Ricky said. "The magic will be a surprise for Mom and Dad later. You will just be first."

"I'll be first," Angela said. She straightened up like a soldier about to be decorated with a medal.

Ricky turned to face her and spread the cards into a tight fan. "Pick one."

Angela ran her hand back and forth along the edge of the deck. She stopped and pulled out a card. She showed Ricky the four of diamonds. "How about this one?"

"No." Ricky said. He shoved the card back in the deck. "Pick one and *don't* show it to me."

"You didn't say that," Angela said. She pulled out a second card, slapped it to her chest, folded up one corner and peered down at it. She looked back at Ricky in satisfaction.

"Now back in the deck," Ricky said.

She slipped it back in. Ricky cut the deck one-handed and then shuffled the cards with the fluidity of running water.

"*Bakshokah serat,*" he said. He felt the coin in his pocket get warm, but nowhere near as warm as it had before. He fanned the deck again. "Pick again, Angela."

Angela selected a card from a new place on the deck. She looked at it with confusion and flipped it around to Ricky. "King of Clovers," she called the ruler of Clubs. "I had the six of diamonds before."

Ricky turned the deck over. Fifty-one different cards. Damn.

Angela put the card on his desk and patted his shoulder. "I won't tell Mom and Dad until you are good. Promise." She gave an "oh, well" shrug and left the room.

Ricky slapped the deck down on his desk. He'd hoped it would be different for him, but it seemed that the magic drained out of his purchase just like everyone else's had. Whatever stream of wonder he'd tapped into earlier had run dry.

Tuesday, he thought. Tuesday it would all come back. For all of them.

Moments earlier, a third pulse of energy, weaker than the two that had preceded it, had come to life beneath the Arroyo house. It wrapped itself around the old copper piping like a boa constrictor and then corkscrewed down to the main water line, following the path of its brethren. The pulse shot across town along the pipes, pinging from junction to junction like a disk in a pachinko machine, bouncing left and right but holding one overall course. It finally found the rarely used line from town to the abandoned Apex sugar plant.

The pulse hit the plant's long-dead pumps and then angled down. It plummeted several hundred feet until the pipe opened up into a vast underground limestone cavern, drained by decades of the plant's thirst for processing water. The energy flew in the darkness like a shooting star. It hit one wall, ricocheted across the cavern and bounced off another, leaving an afterglow trail.

A half dozen other pulses rebounded from wall to wall, flashes in the inky void, the first fruits of Lyle Miller's new Grand Adventure.

Chapter Thirteen

Setup: How many DPW employees does it take to change a light bulb?

Punch line: One, because there's only one to do it.

The "Department" in Citrus Glade's Department of Public Works was a bit of a stretch. Monday through Friday, Andy was it. Andy reported to the mayor. Back when the mill was humming and the streets were alive, Andy, and the rest of the crew, would have reported to the Chief of DPW. But the city payroll had dwindled with the tax base. The town council found they could ax the position of chief, but if they axed Andy, no one cut the grass. And someone had to cut the grass. And scrape up the road kill. And man the dump twice a week.

Andy balanced on the top rung of a stepladder Monday morning at the corner of Tangelo and Main. He removed the dead bulb from the quaint iron post streetlight. After nightfall, downtown was as popular as a haunted house, so there was an element of absurdity to Andy's morning task. But it was on the list anyway.

The clomp of high heels on concrete sounded below him. Mayor Flora Diaz had put the bulb replacement on Andy's list and he knew she'd want to check on progress. She approached the corner wearing a sharp white linen suit, skirt professionally to the knee, and a pair of beige pumps. With shorter black hair and tasteful makeup, she looked the part of a small-town mayor. Andy always thought that looking the role of Citrus Glade's mayor was more than half the battle. The job had shrunk to near figurehead status.

"Madame Mayor," Andy said with teasing reverence.

"Super, super, super!" she said with the enthusiasm of a child at

Christmas. "I saw the light out last night and it just isn't right for the town to have dead lights on Main Street."

Her positive attitude hadn't changed since they'd both been at Citrus Glade High a lifetime ago. Andy admired her sunny disposition about the town and its future. There were days it made the difference in his outlook on his work. Add in that he felt he worked *with* the mayor, rather than *for* her, and the DPW looked pretty good.

"It will be shining brightly this evening," Andy said. "Ready to light our new business across the street."

He pointed his thumb at the renovated Magic Shop. Flora rolled her big brown eyes.

"Now don't you start," she said. "I've already had Reverend Wright call me twice about how Satan himself had moved onto Main Street. We're going over together tomorrow morning to chat with the owner and put the Reverend's fears to rest. I hope."

"The store isn't open much," Andy said. "Or maybe at all. I've never seen the *CLOSED* sign flipped over, now that I think of it."

"I'm sure he's planning a big grand opening," Flora said. "I'm just happy to have some new business downtown."

Andy had to stifle a laugh every time she used the word *downtown* as if there was an "uptown" to Citrus Glade.

"Be safe up there," she said and departed to City Hall.

Andy gave the Magic Shop a bit more thought. There was something creepy about it. The bland name, the black paint, the empty storefront window. Since the flurry of activity to re-invigorate the exterior, the place seemed dead. Andy made plenty of passes through the town square all day and was now positive it had never been open, nor had he seen the owner.

As if on cue, Lyle Miller stepped out of the front door with a jingle of the little bell on top. He had on a black long-sleeve shirt reminiscent of pirate garb, the kind of shirt a magician would wear on stage. He looked over at Andy and their eyes locked. Lyle smiled and waved, but both gestures were cold, calculated. Even from across the street, Andy could make out a ring with a large blue stone on one of Lyle's fingers.

Lyle disappeared around the shop corner and into the alley. He emerged a minute later at the wheel of a jet black Cadillac Eldorado, convertible top retracted. He drove off down Main.

A chill shivered up Andy's spine. He twitched at the top of the ladder and grabbed the lamppost for support. That guy gave him a serious case of the creeps.

He shook it off. A mysterious shop and black clothes. All the type of hype a magician would spin to create an aura. The guy will be making balloon animals at birthday parties next week and selling Magic 8 Balls in his shop.

He climbed down and tossed the ladder in the back of the town pickup truck. Bigger fish to fry today, as they say. Today was Dump Day, after all.

Chapter Fourteen

The Elysian Retirement Home day room stank Monday morning.

At least it did to Dolly. It wasn't rotten like a bad banana or an open can of rancid tuna. It smelled clean. Too clean. A fake floral smell with an antiseptic aftertaste. As if it had worked hard to cover a host of scents no one wanted to acknowledge; the reek of soiled bed linens, the shuddering stink of vomit, and above all the musty smell of death. Before she had to live here, Dolly tended her own fragrant flower gardens where blooms sent out the bouquet of new life each morning. The day room's smell was just the opposite, a cover for life slowly winding down.

Nurse Coldwell bustled around the room from corner to corner like one of those robot vacuum cleaners. She gave each resident a cursory inspection and flagged attendants to assist those in need.

Dolly felt good this morning, which made her feel awful about her son's last visit to see her. She wished amnesia rode tandem with the bouts of dementia when they galloped up and trampled her brain, but it did not. She remembered every confused, embarrassing moment from her son's visit. Andy was a saint for never bringing those times up, pretending he was the one stricken with amnesia.

Her friend Walking Bear was up early this morning. His dry, gray hair was swept back in a ponytail. The sun backlit his profile and his prominent nose. Pronounced bags under his eyes gave him a very somber air, not that his brown, weathered face ever broke into a smile.

He had his usual chair. He positioned it to face the big picture window overlooking the center's patchy grass backyard and the small pond beyond. Hummingbird feeders hung from the roof's overhang and the brightly colored birds hovered around them for quick sips of sugar water. His gaze never wavered from the birds.

Walking Bear claimed he was an Anamassee, an obscure tribe without casinos whose dwindling membership still lived in south Florida. The name on his room chart was *Walter Connell*, but he only answered to Walking Bear. Dolly didn't know his history before he came to the home years ago, and he didn't volunteer it

Dolly took a seat beside him. "Good morning!" she sang.

Walking Bear gave a curt nod and kept his eyes on the birds. Dolly had learned not to take offense.

"What do the birds tell you this morning?" she asked. Walking Bear claimed that even through the glass the animals, few that there were, relayed news of the natural world to him.

"It is all in balance this morning," he said. "Light and dark, sun and moon."

"Sounds perfect," she said. Walking Bear gave the most poetic weather reports. They didn't make sense, but Dolly loved them, the way one loves a song with nonsense lyrics for its melody. She patted his hand and headed across the room.

Shane Hudson held morning court at one of the card tables. Chester Tobias and Denny Dean sat opposite him. Chester had the bulky, sagging physique of a formerly burly man. What remained of his hair was a crown of short silver fringe, though he tried to compensate with a bushy moustache. Denny was a scarecrow of a man with rheumy blue eyes and a non-existent chin. When Shane had been head honcho at Apex Sugar, Chester and Denny had been his right and left hands, hands that weren't afraid to get dirty, to slap down a worker who had forgotten his place in the pecking order.

Shane cut off his lecture to the two as Dolly passed. His black cane lay across the arms of his wheelchair. He gave it a few taps. She ignored his summons and took a seat in the far corner. The day was too lovely to spend a moment of it with the likes of him.

Shane screwed his face up in frustration as she walked away.

"Noticed how stuck up that Patterson bitch has become?" Shane said.

"You said it, boss," Chester said. "She could use a moment of education."

Dolly knew she had been on Shane's hit list since her environmental crusade to save the Everglades began. As far as Shane was concerned, her quest to save the environment had cost him the Apex plant, no matter what the Apex annual reports said about profits and losses and global competition. Not being Shane's pal wasn't much of a loss.

Nurse Coldwell led a slight woman into the day room. The twenty-something blonde had frizzy hair that went down to her shoulder blades. She wore a long denim skirt and a white blouse that was either homespun or trying hard to look it. She opened a brown leather rollup on the table top at the front of the room.

"All right, everyone," Nurse Coldwell said. "This is Janine, the woman I told you would be visiting us today. Let's give her our attention."

The nurse had a look of relief as she left the room in Janine's hands. The few residents who were coherent turned their bored expressions Janine's way. Walking Bear continued his study of the local fauna.

"Well, I'm Janine," she said in a sing-song voice better targeted to preschoolers. Her eyes bulged just a bit in their sockets, which made her look surprised at everything she said. "I'm from the Eastern Institute in Marathon. We've volunteered to come in and help you all focus your personal energy."

Janine pulled out a large, clear crystal from a pouch in her roll. The oblong stone was a few inches long, uncut and unpolished. She held it up and as she rotated it, the surface sparked on and off like Christmas lights.

"Crystals are nature's wonder," she said. "They channel and direct any energy they come into contact with."

Of all the stupid ideas... Dolly thought. She rested her chin in her hand and contemplated an upright nap.

"Now we all have energy that emanates from us," Janine said. She made a big sunburst gesture with her hands. "But it all escapes in every direction. Crystals can reflect the energy back so we can recycle it."

Dolly wondered if today was Caesar salad day. Management had changed the menu twice this month.

Janine grabbed a handful of crystals from her roll and began to flit around the room like some New Age pixie as she spoke. "So what we will be doing is placing crystals in strategic locations around the day room, where the most people are throughout the day." She slipped crystals on the edges of bookshelves and in windowsill corners. "These will collect and return all our radiant energies. Those with excess will share, and in return will get the energies of others from a different wavelength."

Janine passed before Walking Bear. He gave her a quick, sympathetic look and then refocused on the rabbit at the edge of the woods. She deposited the last of the crystals and returned to the front of the room.

"So we want to leave the crystals undisturbed," she said. "And all of you should feel the effects of these amazing stones in no time. You'll feel peppier, sleep better and be at peace with all."

She paused as if applause was supposed to follow. She looked crestfallen in the silence and folded up her leather roll. Nurse Coldwell stepped over to salvage her pride.

"Thank you, Janine," she said. "I'm sure we'll all see wonderful results."

She took the bewildered girl by the elbow and walked her back to the main entrance.

Dolly wished it were that easy. She wished there was a simple cure, an easy way for her to be the person she used to be *all* the time, not just during the good times like right now. She missed her house, though Andy took her home to it every week for a meal or a DVD movie. She missed her freedom, though she was free to come and go at the home as she wished when she wasn't in some fugue state. She missed her friends, though they all came by regularly enough. Life just wasn't the same, because even her best moments were spoiled worrying about the dark moments that might ambush her any second. If a few hunks of rock could cure that...

Well, if Janine's visit was supposed to bring hope and enlightenment, it had instead become quite depressing. Dolly knew just the way to shake that off. She headed back to her room to finish the still life of daisies on the easel. She passed by Walking Bear on the way. She pointed to a crystal in the corner of the window.

"What do you say about these?" she asked him.

Walking Bear did not look at her. "Another crazy white woman."

Walking Bear didn't look even remotely Native American himself, and Dolly smiled at the irony.

Chapter Fifteen

It was a big day for visitors at Elysian Fields. Crystal Janine in the morning and an afternoon of entertainment.

Lyle Miller entered fronting a smile worthy of a TV pitchman. The owners had snapped up his offer of a free magic show for the residents, something they could boast about on next year's brochure. "Acclaimed entertainers do personal shows" or some such crap. They thought they were using him to their own ends. Lyle allowed them their delusion.

Nurse Coldwell showed him to the day room where the staff had set up a long folding table draped with a white table cloth. He'd been specific about black and gritted his teeth as he ran his finger along the edge.

"You are scheduled for one-thirty," she said without looking at him. "It will be after lunch so a few residents may get sleepy."

"I will endeavor to keep them awake and entertained," Lyle said.

"The owners should take care of this," she fumed. "I'm a certified RN and I've spent half my day like some cruise ship activities director."

Lyle put his hand on hers. She shot him a warning glare for violating her personal space. But as she looked into his sparkling eyes, the scowl on her face turned softer.

"I'm sure that my little diversion will cheer up both the residents and the staff," Lyle said, "and make your job easier today."

Nurse Coldwell blushed just a bit and turned away in unaccustomed embarrassment. Lyle knew that little flirtatious foray would keep her at arm's length for the day. The little bulldog probably hadn't been hit on since high school, even by women.

Lyle had fifteen minutes until show time. Several residents already sat in the day room, but the drool-to-patient ratio said they weren't paying attention and wouldn't start when the show commenced. They weren't the ones he sensed here, the ones with the mighty *whapnas*.

He laid out a deck of cards, a red rubber ball and black plastic wand with as much magical power as a block of concrete. Table magic. The cheapest, oldest, stupidest stagecraft in the world. The whole idea of doing it made him ill. But today the ends justified the foul-tasting means.

Residents doddered in alone and in pairs. The staff wheeled in a half dozen like valets parking cars, dropping one off and returning with another. At the stroke of one-thirty, the room was full. Apparently, with little else to occupy the day, the group could be timely.

He studied each resident, assessed them through his body language translator, honed by thousands of years of existence. He listened to their interactions. Somewhere in here there was a threat to his plan, a *whapna* with all the wrong attributes. He would need a counterweight to check it and one of those was here as well.

So far, the residents were old, worn out. Physically, that was immaterial, but mentally his chosen one would need to be up to the task ahead and have the right disposition. But each resident he eyed showed little promise. They fidgeted in their sweaters and slippers, grandparents and great-grandparents, devoid of the fire he needed to feel. Had he misread the *whapnas* in this building?

One man caught his attention, a hulking specimen by the window, the only one looking outside instead of inside, silver hair pulled back in a ponytail. The outsider, perhaps. A good start. Lyle felt for the man's *whapna*. It was strong, integrated in a way he had rarely seen in a millennium. But the man had no fire, no flames waited to be kindled and released.

A woman walked in; she had short blonde hair and wore blue pastel pants. Lyle touched her *whapna* and almost spit in response. She had a fire that burned brighter than the others in the room, but it was all the wrong color. Fascinating how her age was no factor in the power of her *whapna*. This was the threat he'd felt from across town.

Just one like this could ruin his plan. He'd been down that road before.

Two minutes to show time and Lyle began to contemplate having to use the staff for his ends, a far less effective option. He straightened out his pitiful tricks on the table.

A thump and a muffled curse came from the back of the room. A woman in a pink fuzzy robe hobbled backward. A wheelchair made its way through the crowd, plowing residents aside like they were tilled earth. A haughty smile crossed the withered face of Shane Hudson as he rolled into a front row location. His black eyes burned bright. The woman sitting next to him cast him a look of scorn.

"I thought you said this magic show was stupid," the woman said.

"Shut your pie hole, sister," Shane said. He gave his cane a threatening twist. "Even for stupid I get front row seating."

Lyle touched Shane's *whapna*. He might be physically damaged, but mentally he was clear as pure alcohol, with the same volatility. And his *whapna* was perfect, fierce and dark, receptive to the energy that would soon pass beneath the building. The good could leak out anywhere, but the bad needed a bit of focal direction. This would be his counterweight.

Nurse Coldwell approached Lyle to introduce him to the room. But with his target acquired, he had no time to waste on such pleasantries.

"Ladies and gentlemen!" His voice thundered and the room went silent. "My name is Lyle Miller, recently arrived in your lovely town. I will astound you today with some feats of magic."

Lyle began his show. He did simple tricks where he did not even use true magic. Sleight of hand to make some coins disappear and return, then the old ball and cup routine, a few card tricks. He then tapped into some true power. He handed out some paper and had a few residents write down a three-digit number. He mystically "read" each one without seeing them, to the oohs of the coherent in the crowd. Even Nurse Coldwell at the back of the room looked impressed. Only Shane looked on with derision.

Lyle wound up with a special trick. He made a fist with his right hand and pulled a red scarf from within it. Then he draped the scarf over his fist and tapped the plastic wand to it with a whispered incantation. He whipped the scarf away and a white pigeon flapped from its perch on his fingers. Gasps went up from the crowd, but none louder than the one from Nurse Coldwell, no doubt concerned about the sanitation hazard the bird might create. Lyle had promised no animals. Oh well.

He flicked his right hand and the pigeon flew to the other. He draped the bird with the scarf. A wand tap and the bird vanished. A smattering of applause floated around the room. He was done with this demonstration.

He raised a hand in the air and a quarter-sized gold coin appeared at his fingertips. The careworn edges hinted at its journey from antiquity to the twenty-first century. He bent and extended his hand to Shane so that the coin glimmered before the old man's eyes.

"Last illusion," Lyle said to the room. Then he looked straight at Shane. "It's yours for the taking."

Shane wrapped his hand around the coin and snatched it away. Lyle showed his empty hand to the audience with a theatrical flourish. Shane smiled in triumph. Then his face fell. He opened his hand and the coin was gone. Laughter rippled through the room. He went red with anger.

"I felt it," Shane said. "I had it. Where did it go?"

"It's magic," Lyle said. He gave Shane a smiling fraternal clap to the base of his neck. When he pulled his hand away, his fingers gripped two stolen silver hairs.

Lyle thanked the residents and swept his props into his bag. He was out the front door before the first resident left the room.

Lyle had what he needed. An unknowing accomplice and the means to have him ready to take his role in the sorcerer's Grand Adventure.

Having a room full of residents get a good laugh at Shane's expense wasn't sweet enough to chase away the taste Lyle left in

Dolly's mouth. He made the skin at the nape of her neck do a slow crawl. She shuddered. His cheesy tricks and empty banter played like a cheap perfume over rotting fruit. She could still smell the decay beneath. And Lyle wasn't just smarmy, like Vicente at the used car lot. Lyle felt...wrong...black. She sought a second opinion from the man always in touch with the planet's vibe.

"So," she said to Walking Bear, "how'd you like the magician?"

"Anyone who gives a jab at Shane is worth having visit."

"How did he...feel to you?"

Walking Bear mulled his response.

"I have some experience with clothing. I know a cut-rate suit when I see one."

Dolly laughed. She let the creepy magician spark a bit too much of her imagination that afternoon.

"But I am much better with animals," he added.

Chapter Sixteen

"Why do I need to be out here?" Juliana whined.

Vicente Ferrer wanted to backslap her. But then she'd collapse into a crying mess and be *completely* useless.

"Because I enjoy your pleasant company," he said instead.

Juliana missed the dripping sarcasm. She gave her long black hair a nervous twirl between her fingers. She wore the usual micro shorts and a camisole over her obvious implants. The air conditioning was on high. Chill bumps up her legs and arms.

"Cente," she said. "It's so dark and there are things out there in the swamps."

It was pushing midnight and the two of them were in Vicente's big four-wheel-drive pickup on a side road south of town.

"Yes," Vicente said. "Things like several hundred pounds of coke. Things we need to find before daylight."

The truck bounced as it left the paved road for a sandy trail through the scrub. The drop coordinates were a hundred yards ahead, but that guaranteed nothing. After half again that distance Vicente stopped and doused the lights. Same shit every month.

"Well, it's out here somewhere," he said. "Let's go find it."

Juliana gave a horrified look. Her stilettos were at least three inches high.

"No, Cente," she said. "I'm the lookout. I can't go slogging around in a swamp dressed like this. These shoes cost $250!"

Vicente knew exactly what they cost. He bought the damn things. He slapped a flashlight into her midsection.

"Then leave the goddamn shoes here and go barefoot. We need to find the drop."

He exited the truck to preclude any more of her whining. If the bitch hadn't been such a hot moaning whore in bed, he'd have no time for her. But he hadn't gotten enough twenty-year-old action way back when he was twenty, so he'd bear the burden associated with doing a woman half his age.

Vicente stood a solid six feet tall, with a chest and abs chiseled hard with a weight set in his dealership shop. He wore his short hair slicked straight back to purposefully accentuate the close-cropped goatee on his strong jaw. He flicked on his flashlight.

The truck's passenger door opened and Juliana heaved a resigned sigh. He knew she'd come around. His motivation to find the pallet of cocaine out here was financial. Hers was stronger; personal addiction. He passed his flashlight over the soggy ground at the edge of the Everglades.

"You sure they dropped it last night?" Juliana asked.

He'd stopped answering her more idiotic questions and had found it a great time saver. The Colombians never missed a drop. They'd flown over in a tropical storm to deliver the monthly shipment of cocaine on schedule. The Colombians were all about cash flow, out from the wallets of indulgent Americans and into their pockets.

Citrus Glade might no longer produce a legal white granular product, but it was perfectly situated to distribute an illegal replacement. Just a short swampy hop from the Gulf of Mexico, a low flying plane could skim the unlit treetops between the two populated coasts and arrive undetected. A dropped bundle needed no airport, so the vast empty space outside the town fit the bill as a delivery site. Thank God and the Federal Government for GPS.

Vicente's flashlight played across something big. He spotlighted it and exhaled in exultation. One enormous cube of shrink-wrapped crystal gold, one-third buried in the muck. He could always count on the Colombians.

"Get over here," he commanded Juliana.

She approached in a tiptoeing slog, face pinched in pain at each step. She passed Vicente without a word.

Vicente returned to the truck and pulled it within a few yards of the shipment. A shooting star arced across the sky as he returned to the bundle.

Juliana slit the shrink wrap with the tip of her manicured fingernail. She punched a hole in one five-kilo plastic-wrapped brick and extracted a fingernail full of coke. Halfway up to her nose, Vicente slapped it away. She whimpered a protest.

"What the hell? You aren't out here to get fucked up. Toss me those bundles."

She heaved one in Vicente's direction. He caught it like a running back. He slid it into the truck's open tailgate under the black tonneau cover and turned in time to field the next bundle.

"When does this go north?" Juliana said, trying and failing to make the question nonchalant.

Vicente knew she was far less concerned about the business than for her personal access to the blow. "A few days," he said. "Only six wrecks on the back lot but I've got a line on a few more."

For a small dying town, Vicente Ferrer ran a surprisingly thriving car business. He moved a serious amount of used steel off the main lot, most of it to out-of-towners. The big draw was his *push/pull* promise. Any vehicle you could roll into his lot by any method was worth three grand. *Push in a Pinto, leave in a Lincoln.* The sales gimmick brought in a regular supply of lead sleds down CR 12 every week and Vicente took them all.

With the last of the bundles in the truck, Juliana sat in the passenger seat while Vicente tamped the abandoned shrink wrap down into the muck. She gave her muddy feet a look of despair and cradled her shoes on her lap. Vicente returned to the driver's seat and they headed back to the shop.

Vicente's window was down and he let the brief moment of tolerably temperate air blow back through his hair. Once at the dealership, he'd stash this stuff in the tool room and dole out Juliana's powdered allowance. She'd be in la-la land in fifteen minutes, he'd give her the once over, boot her ass out the door and be home before dawn. A solid night's work all around.

Soon all this would be behind him. He had bigger plans than to be a dope-smuggling middleman, always looking over his shoulder for the DEA or some state trooper too dumb to take a payoff. This week he'd tap into a mother lode of cash. And it would be adios Juliana, adios Citrus Glade, hello house on Key Biscayne.

It couldn't happen fast enough.

Chapter Seventeen

The next day dawned and Andy started it with road kill. Mrs. Martinez called in a dead gator out in front of her yard on south CR 12. Andy could handle that. As long as the gator wasn't moving. Afghanistan had permanently satisfied his need for excitement. County Animal Control took care of the ones that could still bite off a hand.

Mrs. Martinez stood at her mailbox waiting as Andy pulled up in the city's white strip job Chevy pickup. The dumpy widow wore an amorphous rose house dress and dark glasses so wide they looked like a visor prop from an *X-Men* movie. Her hair was a shade of red not known in nature. She fanned herself with a supermarket advertising insert.

Andy stopped at the curb. He opened the door to a thick blast of humidity. The truck didn't have a radio but thank God it had air conditioning. He ambled over to Mrs. Martinez.

"It's right there," she said. Her non-fanning hand pointed to the fifteen-foot alligator carcass in the road, as if Andy could miss it. One of the cars passing by apparently had not. The gator's head was crushed flat.

"I'll take care of it, Mrs. Martinez."

"I knew you would come," she said. Her Hispanic accent made the *you* sound like *Jew*. "We count on the town's war hero."

Andy cringed and turned away. He hated the undeserved description. Anyone back from the Middle East was a hero, no matter their record. Mrs. Martinez would have had a whole different outlook if she knew Andy's.

He pulled the truck up behind the dead gator. He dropped the tailgate and slid a ramp out of the bed. He locked it on place on the tailgate, donned a pair of gloves and began to unroll the cable from the bed-mounted winch. Mrs. Martinez shuffled up to gawk.

"Seen this fellow before?" Andy asked. Some of the gators were regulars with their own favorite ponds to haunt.

"No. There's been no gators around here for years."

Andy wrapped the steel cable around the gator's rear legs and under the abdomen. He gave it a test yank.

This thing had been dead for hours. It was odd to have a gator out here, so far from water. And especially strange to have it lying in the road at night. Contrary to their generally torpid demeanor, the creatures could move fast when they needed to. One that grew this big learned long ago to stay off the roadways.

Andy flicked the switch and the winch ground to life. The gator began a slow scrape across the asphalt with a sound like someone sanding leather. Mrs. Martinez went back to her house. The winch dragged the gator up the ramp and into the truck bed. The shattered head hung a few inches off the tailgate's edge. Close enough for government work. If wouldn't fall off before he got it to the dump for disposal.

He pulled off his gloves, turned and nearly walked over Mrs. Martinez. She had returned with a can of generic orange diet soda in her hand. Beads of condensation rolled down its sides.

"For you," she said.

Damn, Andy thought. *I'm over thirty and here she is handing me a soda like I'm the teenage kid who just cut her lawn.*

"You get rid of that thing," she said. "You are a savior."

Andy shivered in response. *Yeah, that's all it takes to be a savior here. Clean up road kill.*

"Thanks, Mrs. Martinez. Glad to help."

He got back in the truck. In the few minutes he'd spent retrieving the deceased reptile, the cab had turned oven-like. Andy started the clattery diesel and flipped the A/C fan to high. The soda can felt cool in his hand.

Diet orange soda. Probably fifteen cents per can. It was worth a laugh. In a state that grew much of America's oranges, someone sold this soda which contained no orange products at all. And to add insult to injury, it was diet. He tossed it on the seat and dropped the truck into gear.

A mile down the road his growing thirst got the better of him. He grabbed the soda can and popped it open. He downed a big slug of it. It managed to taste worse than he had expected.

There were a few perks to being what amounted to the town handyman. Diet orange soda wasn't one of them.

Chapter Eighteen

Autumn Stovall stood calf-deep in the still waters of the western Everglades. Marsh grasses brushed against her knees just over the top of her boots. Tiny fish darted in and out among the stalks. The chorused drone of buzzing insects filled the air. Off to her right, a large white wood stork shuffled in the shallows in search of breakfast among the reeds.

She nudged her broad-brimmed hat back from her forehead and wiped away sweat with the back of her hand. Sure it was eighty degrees before noon and fire ants had attempted an uphill march along her boots earlier, but all was harmonious. Mother Nature was taking her course, right on schedule.

These acres had been Apex Sugar's farmland for decades. But the government had bought them out and turned the deed back over to the original owner. All man-made improvements had been stripped away, the land leveled and access restricted. The first rainy season hit and the acreage went underwater, just as planned. Plants and animals exploited the new habitat with a vengeance. Just a few miles from Citrus Glade, the Everglades was making a comeback.

And the government paid Autumn to watch the show. Witnessing the advance of wilderness was a biologist's dream job. Every day she documented the return of a new species or the bloom of a plant long absent. She'd never felt so attuned to nature.

And the job offer came as she was completely out of tune with humanity. Years of graduate lab research had left her burned out on the hard science half of biology. After graduation she wanted to get back to the aspects that happened above the cellular level, to be immersed in nature. The job near Citrus Glade was about as far south as she could go without getting wet, and as far from civilization as she thought she wanted to be. So she graduated, spent a week in her New York hometown of Sagebrook with her mother, and then headed to Florida.

She pulled her smart phone from her pocket, typed in some observational notes and turned for home. The commute was the best part of the job.

Her small RV was parked at the end of the road. Porky, as she called the van-based camper, was her first post-graduate investment. The brochure said that it slept four and that was as accurate as the "servings" count on most packaged foods. In reality, it was perfect for one person with a minimalist lifestyle. Six years of college had her well prepared for a minimalist lifestyle. She'd traded her car at the dealership, tossed her clothes in the back and piloted the RV south on I-95. She hadn't looked back.

She slipped out of her boots, stepped into home-sweet-home and tossed her hat on the table. Her light red hair had always been at least shoulder length but she'd cut it short for the hot south Florida field work. She gave it a quick, cooling fluff with both hands. A generous helping of freckles still dotted her cheeks, despite her mother's prediction that she would grow out of them. Sweat soaked her shirt and shorts but the wet clothes did not reveal much of a figure. She called herself a lean, mean observational machine.

Her schedule was about three days in field and then a trip into town. Satellite TV and radio made the isolation much more bearable than the average person would think. Plus, she wasn't really alone.

"Where's my Oscar?" she called.

A big orange tabby lifted a sleepy head off of the small sleeping bunk. He blinked twice, assessed that Autumn was no threat, and returned to the land cats spent most of their day.

"Good job, Watch-cat," Autumn said. Oscar had joined her south of Richmond. On a whim she visited a shelter and rescued the old codger. At ten, all the annoying kitten traits were long gone. He was housebroken and trained to travel. Plus he had climbed up into

Autumn's lap when she sat down at the shelter. Experience told her redheads had to stick together, so she liberated him for a life on the road.

Today was the day to run into town. Fresh food, new water, top off the gas. She started up the RV and slipped it into gear. It rocked like a ship at sea over the rough sand road before it hit smoother sailing on CR 12. Minutes later she was in Citrus Glade. When Porky pulled into the Food Bonanza supermarket parking lot, she parked him next to an aging white pickup with county exempt tags. The truck didn't pique her interest. Its cargo did.

The gator that hung across the tailgate had to be fifteen feet long. This specimen was to gator length what Michael Jordan was to human height: a major outlier. Of course her length estimate was more of a guess than usual. The head had been crushed flat. She reached down to open the jaws and inspect the teeth.

"Hey, hey. You don't want to do that!"

She turned to see a man in a city DPW uniform jogging up to the truck.

"It's okay," Autumn said. She pulled out her ID from the National Parks Service that listed her name with her Ph.D. "My name's Autumn. You can trust me. I'm a doctor." She winked at him. "This is a hell of a gator you have here."

"He was my morning project," Andy said. "I'm Andy Patterson, by the way."

"Road kill your specialty?"

"One of my many areas of expertise," Andy said, voice tinged with sarcasm. "It's a small town with a small-town budget. Gator's your specialty?"

"One of *my* many areas of expertise," Autumn said. She ran a finger along the gator's ridged dorsal scutes. "I'm monitoring the old Apex farms as the Everglades reclaims them."

"Maybe you can tell me what this bad boy was doing on CR 12 in the middle of the night."

Autumn paused her inspection. "Really? That's odd. There's

abundant new habitat with the Apex land flooded. He should not have had to travel that far for good hunting, especially this time of year. Even juveniles haven't seen any habitat stress."

Andy gave the dead gator a sad look. "It's a shame."

Autumn was impressed. The universal description locals had for an alligator was invariably either "pest" or "profit" depending on whether you were a poodle-loving homeowner or a hunter. They walked back to the front of the vehicles. She pulled a business card from her ID case.

"Well, I'll tell you what," she said. "If you come across one without a Firestone tread pattern, let me know. A nice dissection will sure add to my survey results."

Andy tucked the card into his shirt pocket. "Will do."

Behind Autumn, Oscar surfaced in the RV's driver's side window, two white-tipped paws on the door edge. He eyed Andy with suspicion and let out a low meow.

Autumn's face turned red. "Sorry. He thinks you are keeping me from restocking his personal food pantry."

"And apparently I am," Andy said. He reached up and touched an index finger to the glass. Oscar sniffed it as if he could smell it through the glass. He closed his eyes and rubbed the side of his face against the window.

"Looks like you're forgiven," Autumn said in shock.

"I've got to get to the dump before Tick-Tock here starts to ripen," Andy said. "Nice to meet you."

"Same here," Autumn said. The white pickup pulled away and Autumn turned to face Oscar, who was still in the car window. "And what's with Mr. Anti-Social being so friendly all of a sudden?"

Oscar managed a small exculpatory meow.

She turned and watched the truck drive off. "And what's with a guy who can reference *Peter Pan* off the cuff?"

It might be time to spend more time in town.

Chapter Nineteen

Mayor Flora Diaz was sure the latest addition to Citrus Glade was a good thing. Reverend Rusty Wright of the First Baptist Church was certainly no fan. But Flora wasn't one to look at any new business in her withered town with too jaundiced an eye. Other than Vicente Ferrer's car business, Citrus Glade had the commercial traffic of a ghost town. After the minor orange and grapefruit harvests, everyone kind of hunkered down for the rest of the year. This could be the first of dozens of shops that refill the shuttered stores on Main Street, the start of a regular renaissance after the NSA embarrassment.

And that return to small town greatness was her dream. She had been raised here, back when Apex money sloshed around town like swirling water in a bucket. She missed the place when she lived in Coral Gables. When she inherited her mother's house, she moved back and friends convinced her to run for mayor. The job was mostly PR and she didn't mind the tiny pay to do her part to try and resuscitate her hometown.

She and Reverend Wright stood outside the refurbished Magic Shop. Reverend Wright was a good half-foot taller than the mayor. He had thin angular features with high cheekbones and deep-set eyes. His full head of silver hair was all that kept him from looking cadaverous. He wore a shiny light gray suit with a bright yellow tie. Reverend Rusty was always dressed like the TV preacher he'd longed to be, no matter what the weather dictated. He pointed a long finger at the Magic Shop window.

"That there is the work of Satan," he said. He spit the last word out like it left a bad taste in his mouth. "Witchcraft has come to town and we need to crush it before it spreads."

Flora looked at him askance. She had the elected political power, but Reverend Rusty had an hour-long weekly conduit to most of the townspeople. She had learned how willing he was to fan the flames of public opinion when something ran afoul of one of his Biblical interpretations. When he'd called her about the "abomination" in the center of town, she knew better than to ignore him.

"Reverend," she said. "It's a magic shop. Kids' toys."

"A conduit to the Devil himself," the Reverend said. He clutched a black leather-bound Bible to his chest.

The excess drama made Flora sigh. "Now, Rusty. He's just a normal shop owner. He did a benefit show at the retirement home for Pete's sake. We'll talk to the man."

They entered the store with the ring of a bell. A big brass cash register from the 1920s sat on the end of a poorly stocked display counter. There wasn't much inventory on display elsewhere either. A set of shelves along the back wall held boxed kids' magic sets and several different books on stage craft. A mannequin stood in the corner wearing a black silk top hat and a short black cape with a bright red lining. Lyle Miller stepped out from the back room, artificial smile already in place, hand extended.

"Welcome, welcome," he said. "I'm Lyle Miller."

"Mayor Flora Diaz," Flora said as she shook his hand. "And Reverend Rusty Wright."

The Reverend shunned Lyle's proffered handshake. The magician's eyes narrowed and he pulled back his hand.

"What can I do for you this morning, Mayor?"

"We're just checking out your store," she said. "The opening was kind of a surprise."

"Yes, well, I did all the paperwork over the phone. The owner was happy to find a tenant."

Flora didn't doubt it. The buildings on both sides of the street were mostly vacant.

"The Reverend here has some concerns," Flora said, voice tinged with dismissive sweetness, "that you will be directing our youth to the dark side."

Lyle laughed with a bit too much emotion. "No, no. Rest assured, good Reverend. Everything here is just stage magic."

"Stage magic?" the Reverend said.

"Of course," Lyle said. "Illusion, prestidigitation, sleight-of-hand. Simple tricks made amazing with a bit of showmanship. Allow me."

Lyle stepped behind the counter. He pulled out three cups and a red ball. He placed the ball under the center cup.

"We all know where the ball is," he said. He gave the cups a lazy shuffle in a figure-eight pattern. "And it seems easy enough to follow. In fact right now..." He paused the shuffle. "...it should be in the center spot again. But through the use of stage magic..."

He raised the cup. No ball. He stacked the three cups. The ball was gone.

"...it has vanished."

The mayor raised an eyebrow. The corners of Reverend Rusty's mouth drooped in boredom.

"But we know the ball didn't vanish," Lyle said. He flipped one hand over and the ball popped out from the wrist of his shirt. "It's just a little trick. Hand-eye coordination and audience misdirection."

Flora turned to Reverend Rusty and batted her long eyelashes. "See, children's toys."

The Reverend appeared unmoved.

"Kids learn that practice makes perfect and that there's an art to showmanship," Lyle said. "All clean fun."

"And the kind of magic that *isn't* stage magic, Mr. Miller?" the Reverend asked.

"Ah, ritual magic," Lyle said. "Witchcraft and wiccans. Conjuring the powers of nature, practicing the black arts. None of that happens behind these doors."

"All clean fun," Flora repeated. "Happy, Reverend?" She already knew the answer.

"I'll keep my eye on you," Reverend Rusty said to Lyle.

"I look forward to it," Lyle said. There was a look in his eye that Flora didn't quite like, but it disappeared in an instant.

Lyle offered the Reverend his hand again. The Reverend looked down in derision. Lyle offered it to Flora instead.

"A pleasure to meet you, Mayor." He gave her a true politician's handshake, firm grip with the right, his left hand at her wrist.

"Good luck, Mr. Miller," she said as she directed the Reverend to the door. "I love to see new business downtown."

As soon as they were outside, she turned to the Reverend.

"Please, Rusty. This fellow has just invested more in this town than anyone else in years. His place could be the start of something wonderful. More shops could follow. People traveling between Miami and Naples will start to see Citrus Glade as a destination."

Reverend Rusty looked back at the storefront window. The sun's glare masked the narrow view of the store beyond it. He drew himself up and gripped his Bible.

"I'll be watching him," he said. "The good Lord will be my guide and I shall watch Mr. Miller."

From inside the shop, Lyle had a perfect view of Reverend Rusty, the sanctimonious bastard. He'd seen his type over and over through the centuries. Whether following Jesus or Osiris, they were all the same. He was just the kind of pinprick that tended to become infected. If the old man began to act on his convictions, Lyle would need to respond.

The mayor, on the other hand, would be no problem at all. Her dim *whapna* wasn't worth his worry. She had the eternally sunny disposition that blinded her to the kind of work Lyle liked to do. She'd blithely smile as the whole world collapsed around her.

Lyle couldn't wait to watch her do it. But for now he had to gather one more unwitting recruit for the Grand Adventure.

Chapter Twenty

An hour later, Lyle pulled his long black convertible up to the front door of Ferrer Motors. He could feel that the *whapna* he sought was inside.

The four boys in town would only wage half the battle to come. They would generate the magic his plan needed. But if experience told him anything, and he had thousands of years of it, a little defense never hurt. When he was deep into the incantations, he had no time to man the gates against any do-gooder town folk. Ah, for the days when mercenary knights were a dime a dozen or brown-shirt storm troopers were free. Why in the Dark Ages, he could spin a whole village of peasants into loyal defenders. He'd need nothing so grand in Citrus Glade. By the time they sensed he was a danger, they would be too preoccupied saving their own lives. Lyle would not need a large quantity of minions, just high quality. The *whapna* of Shane Hudson had that dark powerful quality. The man now walking out the front door of Ferrer Motors had it as well.

Vicente approached with a broad, fake smile that Lyle truly appreciated. He flashed back the same empty grin and stepped out of his car.

They introduced themselves and shook hands. Lyle could feel that this was his man.

"1975 El Dorado," Vicente marveled as he eyed Lyle's car. "That is one fine ride. Don't get me wrong, technology has advanced since then, but for its time, wow. I can make you a great deal on trading it in."

Right to the high pressure, Lyle thought.

"That newer Cadillac caught my eye," Lyle said. He pointed at a glossy Escalade SUV with enormous chrome wheels.

"You have great taste. This car is here for you and you alone. Low mileage, one owner. Decent on gas. A real head turner."

All lies. Centuries among mortal humans had enabled him to spot a lie the way a hawk spies a mouse in a wheat field. But the prevarications rolled off Vicente's tongue with impressive conviction.

They walked over to the vehicle. Lyle feigned interest and ran a finger along the top of the fender.

"I need to cut my inventory and I'm ready to make a deal today," Vicente said. "I can take two thousand off this baby this afternoon to get it to move. I'll also do right by you on your trade." He offered Lyle less than half the El Dorado's value. "I can even finance you right here at a competitive weekly rate."

"This will be a strictly cash deal," Lyle said. "And I'll need you to leave the title paperwork blank for me."

Vicente nudged Lyle in the ribs with his elbow. "Say no more. The taxman makes more than his fair share anyhow. I sell you the car and what you do with it then is none of my business."

Lyle liked his ethics. But his *whapna* was too black, too rich to be sustained with mere cheating of customers. This business fronted something much more sinister. Trafficking illegals. Trafficking drugs. Prostitution. Perhaps all of the above. Whatever it was, it earned a place on Lyle's team, whether he knew he signed up or not. Lyle clapped him on the shoulder.

"That sounds interesting," he said. "I'll give it some thought."

As he pulled his hand away he pinched two hairs from the shoulder of Vicente's shirt. Vicente did a poor job at masking the disappointment generated by his escaping pigeon.

"Sure you don't want to drive her? Is there anything else I can tell you about the car?"

Lyle clenched the hairs in his palm. "I've got everything I need, thanks."

When he pulled away, he watched a faded red truck pull in behind him, a real rust bucket beater with Lake County tags. Vicente pounced on the new victim and steered him straight to the Escalade that moments ago had been the car for Lyle alone.

Lyle slipped the two black hairs into an envelope with the two silver strands from Shane Hudson. He began to hum a song he learned as a boy, about excited hoplite soldiers approaching battlements on the eve of war.

Chapter Twenty-One

Autumn returned to the Everglades, but to the next spot in her rotation, a few miles south of where she had been before. She pulled off CR 12 and through the rotting fence that had once enclosed acres of Apex sugar cane. She particularly liked this location. A flat patch of white concrete surfaced where some building had once stood. The RV fit perfectly on it and she never feared that rain would mire her tires in the muck.

Oscar manned his co-pilot position. Back paws in the passenger seat, front paws on the dashboard. He swayed with the motion of the RV, as if his head was gyroscopically leveled. Though, or perhaps because, his previous life had been with a homebound senior, the big boxy tabby had taken to travel, provided that Autumn didn't make him leave his home on wheels.

"Damn it," Autumn said. She jabbed the brake and the RV crunched to a halt on the gravel road well short of the concrete pad.

A brown and black Burmese python stretched out on the sunny pad. The snake had to be a dozen feet long. The middle of the snake bulged like the weak spot in a garden hose. This snake had just eaten something big.

Autumn loved all animals, but she loved the Everglades more. The python was an ocean away from where it belonged in southeast Asia. Stupid people bought them as pets, unaware that the little reptiles would grow to eight feet within a year. A snake that could wrap around your wrist was cute. A snake that could wrap around your waist was scary. Panicked owners released the snakes into their backyards and they found their way to the Everglades, where an absence of natural predators and an abundance of prey created a population explosion. Wildlife officers killed hundreds a year, but the consensus was that the genie was out of the bottle.

"Keep an eye on things, Oscar." Autumn pulled on some blue latex gloves, grabbed a square-tipped shovel and exited the RV. The humidity draped her like a hot, wet blanket.

The torpid snake lay motionless as she approached. Its scales reflected the sun and fostered an illusion of wetness. Like a guest at Thanksgiving dinner, the snake had seriously overeaten and was resting through the digestive process, recharging its internal heat pump with solar power. With the ability to unhinge its jaw, there was little limit to what the big snake could swallow after it crushed the creature to death.

The python could strike with speed when it hunted from its coiled ambush. In its current bloated state, that wasn't going to happen. Autumn approached from the rear. The snake was bigger than she had thought, at least sixteen feet, and the bulge in its midsection was easily three feet around. This snake was a pig. It had to go.

She raised the shovel over her head, sharpened edge pointing down. The snake flicked out its tongue to give her a sensory once over. Too late. Autumn brought the shovel down like a guillotine. It caught the snake a foot behind its head and severed it. The snake's jaws made one spastic snap and went still. Blood puddled in the gap between snake parts.

She reached down and inspected the head. It was so large it took both hands to lift it. This one had been years in the Everglades. She tossed the head aside and pulled a large knife from her belt.

"Let's see what damage you have done."

She rolled the snake over on its back. Female. At up to thirty-six eggs per clutch, this one had probably added over a hundred invaders to the struggling Everglades. Autumn pierced the lower end of the snake and slit the skin up to where the head had once been. She peeled away the scales like she was shucking a huge ear of corn.

"Well, I'll be damned..."

Curled up inside the snake, as if ready for the reptile to birth it, lay a deer. The snake's digestion hadn't fully kicked into overdrive and the deer was complete. Autumn yanked it out and guessed its weight at seventy-five pounds. She had heard that a python could take down a deer, even alligators, but hadn't seen it herself. All the more reason to eradicate these invaders.

She stood and surveyed the mess. It looked like an Animal Planet crime scene. She could bury the two pieces, but why do what Nature would better take care of? Scavengers would be on this feast minutes after she left, starting with ants and working their way up to vultures. Even buried, the scent would draw all sorts of creatures that would skew her observations. There were other waypoints she needed to check, anyhow.

She reentered the RV. Oscar peered around the side of the passenger seat, round head like a giant creamsicle tennis ball with whiskers.

"Hey, puffball. Did you catch all that action?"

She extended a gloved hand to Oscar. He sniffed the glove and then gave a violent shake to eradicate the scent. He bounded onto the dashboard. Autumn snapped off the sweat-filled gloves and tossed them in the trash.

"You said it," Autumn said. "Snakes give everyone the creeps."

Chapter Twenty-Two

The NSA tower rose from the abandoned Apex plant parking lot. Vicente Ferrer sat on a folding chair in the stripped-out cargo area of an idling, windowless white van beside the tower. Piles of computer components and assorted other electronic junk littered the rusting floor. The sliding door was open. Sweat made his silk shirt stick to him in the oppressive humidity. He wouldn't even be out here for this, but he'd learned years ago, if you wanted something done right, you might not be able to do it yourself, but you'd damn well better supervise the person who did.

An open manhole yawned close enough to the van that Vicente could have stepped into it. Squirrelly Wilson stuck his head out. His tangle of long blond hair gave the young man the aura of a 1970s rock star, but a mouth full of crooked, stained teeth put any teen-idol impression to rest. He tossed a handful of plastic connectors onto the pavement.

"That should do it," he said. "Spliced and diced and checked on twice."

Even at this distance Vicente could smell Squirrelly's breath, a rank combination of cigarettes, coffee and tooth decay. He wrinkled his nose. A man should have standards.

"Then get back in the damn van before someone drives by," he said.

Squirrelly climbed in and Vicente cleared a way so he could get to the driver's seat. He rolled the door shut. Blessedly cooler air blew across his arms from the front vents.

"There's no way to track what we're doing, right?" Vicente said.

"Can't see how," Squirrelly said. He gave his head a shake like a dog trying to dry itself. "We aren't rerouting any of the information. We're just reading it as it passes. Data mirrored on the fly as it goes by."

Vicente was about ready to punch Squirrelly in his mismatched teeth if he uttered one more moronic rhyme. But the loser had been arrested for just this kind of scam, so he'd endure his jabber to access his skills.

"Then we send the info wirelessly to your computer," Squirrelly said. "Even if someone finds the skimmer, they don't know where the data's going."

Data flowed through the NSA tower like water through a fire hose. The project was supposed to monitor overseas communications, but there was a healthy flow of domestic information as well. Bank transfers, credit card purchases, cell phone call records, airline reservations. All the little details that NSA supercomputers would piece together to create the mosaic of future terrorist attacks. Vicente needed but a trickle from that information torrent. Credit cards and social security numbers would be more than enough. A few tapped from one bank's data stream, a few tapped the next day from another's. Never enough to warn of a major security breach, but cumulatively enough to sell for a good price. His connections in Colombia had connections in Kiev and the connections in Kiev had cash. Who knew a thumb drive of zeroes and ones would be worth so much money?

"And to review," Vicente said. "If anyone finds out what you've done?"

Squirrelly's face went dark. His earlier skimming scheme he'd been caught for had earned him some lengthy prison time. "Violation of probation," he said. "A bad situation, a hallucination."

"Probation will be the least of your problems," Vicente said. "Our Ukrainian friends will make sure you never see the inside of a cell. Trust me." He rolled the door back open. He stepped out and around the open manhole cover. "Now put this cover back on and then get the hell out of here."

He turned on a heel and left for his car. Squirrelly's usefulness was about to run its course. Once the system proved out, his Ukrainian friends might need to tie up that loose end early. Someone like Squirrelly wouldn't be missed.

Chapter Twenty-Three

Later that evening, oil dripped on the bridge of Vicente Ferrer's nose and splattered into one eye. He spewed a stream of curses and rolled out from underneath today's old Dodge pickup trade-in. He groped until he found a rag and wiped the stinging liquid from his eye.

He was alone in the shop behind Ferrer Motors. The neon lights gave everything within a fuzzy edge, a faded color treatment. The soft lighting didn't do much for the dilapidated Dodge. The red paint had faded to a rusty rose and a gash ran down one side of the pickup's bed like someone had attacked it with a chain saw. The prior owner had nursed the pile of crap down from Eustis that day. Vicente gladly took the trade and finally unloaded that lemon Escalade.

He wasn't smiling at the damn truck now. Smaller cars were so much easier to turn into drug mules. The parts just weighed less.

He pulled the oil pan with him as he rolled back under the truck. He'd finished the modifications to it. He'd pulled it from the bottom of the engine, put a load of shrink-wrapped cocaine in it, and welded a false bottom above it. Once the pan was bolted back on and the tired engine refilled with used oil, the contraband would be undetectable, hidden in a sealed container, surrounded by a noxious mélange of petroleum-based scents no drug-sniffing dog could penetrate. His repertoire included hollowed-out transmissions and fake gas tanks, but the oil pan trick was his favorite, because the vehicle still ran, making it less suspect.

Vicente spun the oil pan bolts on with two hands. He was way behind. In a perfect world the mule cars would have all been prepped and ready to load when the coke shipment arrived. But Vicente did not live in a perfect world. Creative as he was, he still needed at least one more car, unless he was going to duct tape the shit inside the fenders of the ones he had. And the cars he did have weren't quite ready. He was supposed to prep them last night but—

"Cente," Juliana called from the doorway to the office. Her voice was slurred and guttural, her brain just reviving from a catatonic dose of the same thing Vicente just secreted in the bowels of the Dodge. She looked smoking hot in tight denim shorts and a red tube top. Her long hair looked like she had just crawled out of bed, and for good reason.

She staggered toward him with half-closed eyes and a dreamy look. "Cente, that is some excellent blow." She sniffed back a trail of mucous into her damaged sinuses. "How about some more to keep the party humming?"

Vicente didn't have time for this. Juliana had performed her required duties with the usual enthusiasm. She had been paid in kind and promptly inhaled her fee. He didn't have time for a second round with her and he sure didn't have more coke to send her way. There was only so much he could safely skim off the Colombians. The bastards weighed everything twice and had no concept of inventory shrinkage.

"You're done for the night," he shouted up through the Dodge's engine bay. "Beat it."

"No, no," she whined. She knelt next to the truck. "I'll make it worth it." She reached underneath and gave Vicente's crotch a sloppy tug.

He startled at her touch and banged his head against the underside of the truck. A shower of rust flaked down into his face.

"Son of a bitch!"

He blindly kicked out and his boot caught Juliana in the chest. She went flying backward and crashed into a rolling toolbox. He launched himself out from under the truck and onto his feet.

"Beat it, you drugged-out bitch! I've got work to do here. When I need you, you'll know."

Juliana looked up with the confused, contrite look of the chronically battered. "*Lo siento*, Vicente. I didn't mean nothing. I'm sorry. I just—"

"Go!" he yelled.

She rose and teetered off on her red stilettos.

He grabbed a rag and wiped the rust from his face. The scrap yard south of Macon expected the mules in a few days and the Colombians were big believers in just-in-time inventory. One more trade-in tomorrow and he'd have what he needed. Someone was going to get the deal of a lifetime.

Chapter Twenty-Four

Barry was the last to join the other three Outsiders in front of the Magic Shop Tuesday afternoon. He huffed and puffed with each labored pump of his bicycle pedals, white knees poking through the holes in his jeans. He coasted to a stop in front of the store.

"Late," Zach said, "for everything but a meal, as usual."

"I couldn't help it," Barry said. "My mom—"

"No one cares," Zach said. "Get your asses inside before Lyle cancels class on us."

Each of the boys had their school backpack slung over a shoulder. Each pack carried the owner's magic purchase. A gold coin lay nestled in the bottom of each boy's pocket. They entered the store to the falsetto ring of the door's bell. Lyle leaned against the back wall of the empty shop, arms folded across his chest, a look of profound satisfaction upon his face.

"Apprentices!" he said. "Come to master the craft that has thrilled and confounded man for millennia. Enter!"

He stepped before the beaded curtain that covered the entrance to the back room. The boys gathered round. Lyle held up a finger to pause their advance.

"Here is a last chance," he said. "Magic is not for the weak, the confused, the uncommitted. Through this doorway you will find secrets others will never know, powers others cannot comprehend. But when you cross the threshold, you cannot go back. This is the moment when you commit to complete this education in the Dark Arts, and then reap all its benefits. No one will think less of you if you are not up to the task."

Ricky was reminded of the signs at the entrance of the rides at the county fair that warned pregnant women and people with heart conditions to stay the hell off. His judo teacher and his Cub Scout pack leader had never given such an ominous warning before an event. He caught a tiny tremble in his knees, a little knot of dread in his gut. Barry's slack-jawed look telegraphed similar feelings.

"What's the hold up?" Zach said, chin thrust skyward. "We're not afraid. Let's go."

"Hell, yeah," Paco said. "Let's do it."

A little flash of fear crossed Barry's face, like he was about to be left alone in some cave without a flashlight. "Yeah, yeah. I'm pumped." He stepped closer to Lyle.

All four turned to look at Ricky. He took a half step back. A voice deep inside of him shouted that he needed to run, fast and hard, as far from here as he could. He needed to throw the deck of cards in a fire. Whatever was on the other side of that curtain of beads was on the other side of the line between good and evil. He could practically feel it breathing.

But if he walked out, he walked out alone. And he was sure that the cards, if he kept them, would never be magic again. He felt the tug of a current that had the other three in its grip, a current that rushed toward Lyle. Ricky stepped forward.

"What are we waiting for?" he said.

Lyle led the four through the beaded curtain. It sounded like rain as the strands brushed each other. The other side of the shop was everything the front half was not. Magic tricks were stacked against each other. A box to saw a woman in half. A glass booth with a hose at the top and a water drain at the bottom. Cloaks. Multi-colored strings of scarves. Hoops. Straitjackets. Lengths of chain. In the center stood a black oak table, thick enough to weigh a few hundred pounds. At its center was a crystal ball the size of a basketball atop a solid gold plate. Plywood blocked the room's windows from the inside.

Lyle led them into a circle around the oak table. The boy's eyes flitted from amazing item to amazing item around the room.

"Apprentices," he announced. The boys all focused on Lyle. "Look down and take your position on a point."

A five-pointed star within a circle circumscribed the oak table. Lyle stood on one point. The boys shuffled to the other four.

"Now you will be sworn in to the brotherhood," Lyle said. "Repeat after me."

Lyle recited the following oath, pausing after each phrase to allow the boys to repeat the section back to him.

"As a practitioner of magic, I promise never to reveal the secret of my power to a non-magician, unless that one swears to uphold the Magician's Oath in turn. I promise never to perform any magic for any non-magician without the consent of my master. I shall follow the orders of my master without question. In return for the powers I practice, I pledge my eternal soul."

The last word withered as Ricky spoke it. His soul? The Reverend said the soul made humans special in the eyes of God. The soul would live forever. What had he just traded it for?

A blinding, glaring light exploded from the crystal ball. The lines of the five-pointed star lit up like the script on a neon sign. Ricky went flash blind. His feet hummed. The coin in his pocket blazed without burning.

The light died down. The crystal ball sparkled from within like a snow globe filled with silver swirling flakes. Ricky's vision faded back in. His fingertips tingled, as if some power danced at them, ready to be used. The others had similar looks of stunned amazement. Paco had a double-strength version of the crazy eyes he got when he set something afire.

"Magic is all around us, apprentices," Lyle said. "It surrounds all living things. Early man felt this, but attributed it to spirits. Through training, you will be able to unbind it from its host, draw that energy to yourself. That is the power you feel now."

Zach pulled the rings from his pack and held one in each hand. They sang with an almost musical hum as they vibrated in Zach's hands.

"Each of you has his own phrase," Lyle continued, "his own key to unlock the magic from the world around you, and use it with your talismans."

"*Bakshokah shuey,*" Zach said. He brought the two rings together and they joined with a chime.

Lyle's eyes lit up. The sapphire ring on his finger glowed. "Now you are channeling the power. Push it. Feel it. Release it."

Zach let the rings go. They hung suspended in the air. The boys gasped. Zach grabbed them where they joined and they dropped together with a musical note.

The other boys grabbed their tricks. Paco had his wand out first. Lyle made a circle with his wrist and a small white ball appeared. He rolled it toward Paco across the tabletop.

"Vanish it," he said.

Paco stopped the rolling ball with his wand. "*Bakshokah korami.*"

The ball disappeared in a puff of white smoke. Another appeared at Lyle's fingertips.

"Again," he commanded. "In the air!"

He lobbed the ball upward. Paco locked the ball in his bug-eyed gaze and pointed the wand at it. "*Bakshokah korami.*"

The ball flashed into a tiny white cloud and never hit the ground.

Barry already had his magic hat out and opened on the table, his mother's red silk scarf across the top. He needed no prodding from Lyle. "*Bakshokah apnoah.*"

He flipped away the scarf and reached in. He pulled out a yellow parakeet perched on his forefinger. He laughed and flicked his hand in the air. The parakeet fluttered off.

Paco didn't miss a beat. He tracked the flying bird with his wand. "*Bakshokah korami.*" The bird evaporated with an audible pop of yellow-tinged smoke.

Adrenaline surged through Ricky's veins. He pulled his cards from their case. The entire deck moved in his hand, dancing to some unheard beat. "*Bakshokah serat,*" he said.

He put his hands palms up and the cards ran in an arch from one hand to the next like a Slinky going down steps, then reversed course. He spread the deck out across the table and he held one hand above it.

"One-eyed jack," he commanded.

A card floated up out of the deck and rolled face up into his hand. The one-eyed jack of spades.

"Excellent," Lyle said. "Talismans down."

Three of the boys put their tricks on the table. Paco eyed a painting on a far wall and pointed his wand. Lyle's eyes narrowed. His hand shot out in Paco's direction. The ring glowed bright blue and he snapped his wrist to the right.

Paco screamed in pain. The wand flew from his hand and bounced on the table. He tucked his right hand to his chest.

"Remember your oath," Lyle said. "Follow my orders without question. You don't want to feel the repercussions."

Paco nodded rapid fire.

"You will practice for two days," Lyle said. "Never together. Never in front of others. Doing nothing that will arouse suspicion. You will master feeling the flow of the power. On Thursday you will return to continue your education. Now scatter."

The boys grabbed what Lyle had called their talismans, loaded them into their packs and scrambled for the front door. They winced at the bright sun as they exited the darker shop. A few stray cars rolled down Main Street but pedestrian traffic was nil. They formed a huddle around their bikes.

"That was radical," Zach said. "Could you feel the magic run through you?"

"I felt like a super hero," Barry said.

"When you dropped the wand..." Ricky asked Paco.

"It felt like someone snapped my wrist," Paco said. "I swore it was broken. Do not screw with that guy."

"Then follow his rules." Zach said. "Home and practice. In secret."

Lyle told the boys only half the truth. They did indeed draw magic from the world around them. But like atomic fission, the tearing asunder of the magic released another type of residual energy. A huge burst of it had just rolled from under the Magic Shop along the water mains beneath Citrus Glade. It followed the path of earlier pulses and ended its run in the vast underground cavern beneath the sagging Apex Sugar plant. The cavern now glowed with the illumination of the energy echoing back and forth within its walls, far more powerful than when those first weak pulses arrived days ago.

Lyle could never fill the cavern in time by himself. But now, four times faster, it would be completed right on schedule.

Chapter Twenty-Five

Later, Zach was alone in his room, door shut behind him. He said the magic phrase for the second time and joined the third ring to the other two. He gave the chain of three a twist and they stuck together.

The feeling of exhilaration was beyond anything he'd experienced. Not just the amazement at completing the impossible, though that was part of it. It was the power. The rush of energy though his body, the way the magic made his heart race and made every nerve ending buzz and kick. He'd never felt so *good* before, so *alive*. He said the magic phrase and separated one of the rings.

Perhaps there was more this ring could do. He pressed the ring against the bedpost.

"Bakshokah shuey."

He closed his eyes and pushed. The ring passed through the bedpost like a knife through butter. He opened his eyes and it was linked to the bed's frame.

"Awesome."

He pulled it back through as slowly as he could. He closed his eyes again. His fingertips tingled as the ring moved through the bedpost. He could feel the atoms shuffle themselves and then realign. He stopped the ring halfway through and let go. It remained embedded in the bedpost. He grabbed it again and extracted it.

"Wicked cool," he whispered. This little trick had to be good for something.

He got up and flipped the lock on his bedroom door. He pressed the ring against the wood at the base of the knob. He closed his eyes and pushed. The ring started to pass through the door. He stopped it midway. In his mind he saw the ring pass through the lock cylinder, filling the space between the tumblers. He let his control of that part weaken and it went solid. He twisted the ring to the right. The lock popped open.

That opened his eyes to a world of possibilities. Suddenly nothing was off-limits. And the coolest off-limits item in the house was...

Zach entered his parents' bedroom and pulled a shoebox-sized gray metal lockbox from under their bed. A dust bunny rolled off the top. He put one ring against the lock cylinder and said the magic phrase. The ring phased into the cylinder and he gave it a nudge to the right. The lock clicked open. Zach extracted the ring.

He flipped open the lid. Inside was his father's pride and joy, a sleek black Beretta 9 mm pistol. Perforated cans littered the backyard where his dad had put the gun into service. Of course Zach wasn't allowed to even touch the thing. Not until he was "a man" according to his father. Well, fourteen and able to diffuse solid matter seemed man enough.

He picked the gun up from the lockbox. It was cold. And heavy. Cops in the movies swung these things around like they were weightless. He wrapped both hands around the grip and leveled the gun at a picture of some flowers on the wall. He lined the sights up on one petal.

"Bam," he said and jerked the gun back in mock recoil. Oh, yeah. The fun was just beginning.

A car crunched up into the driveway outside the house. Zach dropped the pistol back into the lockbox, slammed the lid and slid it back under the bed. Now wasn't the time to reveal the secret of his access. But soon, his father's little friend would come in handy.

Chapter Twenty-Six

Paco had the power back. The list of crap he was going to make vanish was long and he needed to get to work before the energy ebbed away again.

Ritalin was top of the list and he went straight to his mother's bathroom. The evil little pills had cheated death once, but a second time was not going to happen. He set the bottle on the edge of the sink. One chant, one tap, and poof, no meds.

The little flash and pop made him tingle. Inspiration hit and he went to the carport. Next to the lawnmower sat its red plastic gas can. Now if a bottle of pills made a flash, what would a can of gasoline do?

Paco's eyes lit up in excitement. Visions of red fireballs danced in his head. He grabbed the gas can. It was at least half full.

"Jackpot."

He took the can around to the backyard and dropped it on one of the many sandy spots. He'd caught the house on fire once and wasn't about to live through a beating like that again. This would be far enough away and no one was home in the neighborhood to witness the display. Perfect.

Sunlight flickered off the can's glossy red surface. The sides had a slight bulge from the pressure of the expanding fuel. Even better. He could not stop grinning.

He pulled the wand from his pocket and snapped it around so the white tip faced away. He sat as far from the can as he could and put the tip to its surface.

"*Bakshokah korami.*"

He barely had the words out of his mouth when the can vanished in a flash of light. But this time there was a palpable rumble along the ground. An orange ball of flame blossomed from the center of the flash and moved outward in all directions. Heat washed over him in a brief, beautiful, searing wave.

The flames evaporated and left a charred circle on the ground. An acrid smell of burnt gas and sulfur filled the air. The fine hairs on Paco's arms were singed into black little coils. His skin felt thick and he wiped at his face. Soot covered his fingertips.

In this perfect, glorious, wondrous moment, Paco lay back flat on the ground, stared up at the blue sky and laughed. And the laughter bounced back and forth within him and multiplied. What came out was a high-pitched uncontrolled cackle that any passerby would no doubt judge insane.

Chapter Twenty-Seven

"Barry!" Judy Leopold banged on her son's bedroom door with her fist. She had on her Burger World uniform. It was a size too small but all they had was a large. "What are you doing in there?"

Her commanding tone belied the fear that gripped her. What could he, a teenage boy, be doing for hours in there that she would want to find out about? Drugs. Sicko video games. Internet porn. Masturbation? God, if she walked in on him with his pants down, she would die of embarrassment before he did. But she needed to find out what went on in her house, even if she hated knowing it.

Books rustled and drawers slammed within Barry's room. She twisted the knob again in vain. Her face went flush with anger. Locked doors were forbidden in the house. She pounded again. The flabby skin on her arm swung like a pendulum with each pass.

"Open this door now!"

The door opened a crack. She shoved. Barry had already retreated in anticipation of the onslaught. He looked guilty as hell.

"What are you doing in here?"

"Nothing."

"Why did you lock the door?"

"I don't know...just some privacy, I guess."

"Well, you can have privacy when you are an adult on your own," Judy said. "Sit down."

He parked himself on the bed. She marched over to his computer and punched up the browser history. The first piece of good news was that it wasn't deleted. The second was that she recognized all the sites and they were porn-free.

Something was still up in here. She rummaged through his desk drawers. No skin magazines, no drug paraphernalia. Oh, she'd been to the PTA meeting and knew just what to look for. The drawers were clean.

She glanced at his dresser. A sock poked out of one drawer. Barry winced. Bull's-eye. She yanked open the drawer. She pulled out a black silk disk.

"What in the world?"

"It's just a hat," Barry said. "A top hat."

Judy looked at it like it was from Mars. "Who are you now, Fred Astaire?"

"It's from the Magic Shop. A prop. Abracadabra, that kind of stuff."

Judy passed her hand into the hat. Barry's eyes went wide. She popped the hat open and put her hand inside. When she pulled it out, Barry finally exhaled.

"And this is what you were messing around with? You have to do that in secret?"

"You have to practice to get good," he said. "I'm not good yet."

This didn't add up. "So you're going to pull things out of a hat?"

"It'll look that way."

She tucked her short brown hair behind her ears and bored into him with her maternal truth detector. The reading wasn't good.

"Well, if you think I'm letting a rabbit live in the house, forget about it now." She popped the hat closed and tossed it on his bed like a Frisbee. "Get your homework done before you mess around with that, Houdini."

She made an event out of leaving his bedroom door wide open against the springy doorstop and headed for her car. She had the night shift at Burger World. Her husband was out on his two-month stint on the oil rigs. Two jobs kept a roof over their heads, but did not leave the time to know what went on under the roof. The American Dream.

That Magic Shop gave her the willies, and it wasn't just her.

Several other church members thought something unholy was going on within its walls. Her husband was going to have to get to the bottom of it when he came home next month.

Barry followed his mother's departure from his room with a sigh of relief. He dreaded that she was going to take the hat with her when she left. If she'd known its power, she surely would have.

As soon as he heard her pull out of the driveway, he popped the hat open and took a seat at his desk. He slid open his bedroom window a few inches. He draped a handkerchief over the hat. He held the gold coin in his left hand this time. The lining of his pants pockets dampened the warm thrum of power after the incantation, and Barry wanted to feel every bit of it.

"Bakshokah apnoah."

The coin practically danced against his closed palm. The rush of exhilarating power coursed through him with every pump of his heart. It felt like sparks exploding inside his head. He reached in and pulled a tawny field mouse from the hat. It blinked its big black eyes at him and sniffed the air with a twitch of its whiskers. Barry stuck his hand out the window and dropped the mouse to the ground to follow the trails of its dozen brethren who had preceded it.

Barry slumped back in his chair to savor the moment, the sweet afterglow of the rush of creation. He'd never experienced anything so...completing.

This was the time of day he usually grabbed a snack, something nice and sugary in the snack cake family. His stomach called in a reminder, but his brain sent it to voicemail. The hat beckoned. One more trick. Just a little lizard. No effort at all.

An hour later he'd set seven of them free.

While Barry's drama unfolded, Ricky made his cards do wonders. He had the house to himself as his father had Angela with him doing errands. He sat at the kitchen table and propelled the magic cards through the air and around the room with casual flips of his fingers. The gold coin hummed warm and happy in his pocket. The cards returned to the table and formed into the shape of a circle. A few cards slid to the center in the shape of a star.

Ricky paused. The power, the pleasure, which thrummed through every muscle in his body, left him in a state of euphoric exhaustion. He gathered the cards in his hands and clutched them to his chest. Had he really let the Reverend's paranoia worry him about accepting these? He rolled his head back against the top of the chair and sighed.

From under his house, and three others in town, energy traced the water pipes of Citrus Glade. Not flashes and flickers like before, but steady streams as the boys peeled away magic from the world around them. It coursed over the network of pipes, coalesced in town, then ran hard and fast through the main line to the Apex sugar plant.

Under the plant, the limestone cavern glowed half full.

Chapter Twenty-Eight

The abandoned Apex plant moaned as the wind blew by, the kind of groaning noise an old man makes when he battles gravity to stand erect. Loose corrugated steel slapped the building's side and the breeze whistled through the smattering of broken windows in the upper floors. Rats skittered within the walls in search of shelter.

Lyle stood alone in the vast, vacant main processing room. Creditors had torn out all the salvageable equipment and left rough potholes in the concrete floor. Electrical power streamed to the tower outside to power cell phone transmissions, cable TV and the NSA's search for terrorists, but the plant buildings weren't connected. Instead, a set of twin torches lit the area in a figure eight of flickering yellow light.

Lyle stood at the center of a five-pointed star within a circle spray painted on the floor, a cruder copy of the one in the back room of the Magic Shop. With the second circle complete, his teleportation spell could send him from the shop to here and back. And he was about to begin frequenting the plant far more often.

Incense smoldered in conical tarnished bronze censers at each of that star's points. But the smell wasn't the sweet floral fragrance incense usually delivered. The aromatics of the censers smelled of char and seared fat, for the offerings Lyle made to tap into the great magic were dried entrails and organs. A rank haze filled the room.

Lyle might not have needed so retro a setting for his incantations. But his master taught him sorcery this way two thousand years ago on the Mesopotamian floodplains. To pull in the magic power of nature, Lyle felt he had to be closer to it, without the insulation of technology.

Perhaps the spells would still work using microwaved meat and halogen floodlights, but he was certain that it worked without.

For this true start of his Grand Adventure, Lyle wore the Sacred Stole. Wide as one's hand, it wrapped around the back of his neck and hung down across his chest in two parallel strips that ended just past his waist. The stole clinked with each of Lyle's movements, for the vestment wasn't made of cloth, but of bones, threaded with tendons dried centuries ago.

Torchlight danced across the bones, polished by the handling of ten thousand rituals. The oldest bones at the top were of creatures long gone; the canines of great saber-toothed cats, molar chips of wooly mammoths, spiraled horns of beasts forgotten to man save in myths. Other, less exotic animals completed the stole's center, adding their power to the sorcerer's own. The tips of the stole were finished in tips themselves, a delicate fringe of human finger bones, the bones of the sorcerer master who sired Lyle's entrance into the black arts. The master's noble, involuntary sacrifice to add his *whapna* to the ancestral garment had bought Lyle his immortality.

A cast-iron bookstand stood before Lyle and on it rested the thick tome of collected incantations, another posthumous donation from his former master. The parchment pages were open to the spell Lyle needed, one so infrequently used, and so specific in nature, that he did not have it memorized. Years had faded the thick, black-inked proto-Aramaic lettering to a washed-out gray.

"*Leshanoa, baklah devopah,*" Lyle began.

As he read the text aloud, the torchlight flared. It began to burn sideways instead of upward and then reset into a rising, counterclockwise swirl. The smoke from the censers puffed thicker and followed the torchlight's lead.

With each line of text he recited, the earth beneath him began to tremble. The great cavern below him, emptied of the water that created it, now hummed with the energy released by the magic in town. Lyle's incantation focused these random flashes into a single, cohesive energy mass that began to mirror the counterclockwise rotation of the growing haze above Lyle's head.

He chanted in a slow, rhythmic fashion, focused on forming each word with perfection. So long ago, this was the language of millions, now only he understood it, he and the magic that surrounded the world. Certainly, he taught his four apprentices some phrases, but did they know each one of them chanted their own portion of *darkness falls, darkness enlightens, darkness enriches, darkness frees*? Hardly. But they understood the impact, felt the power, comprehended in some way that the door they opened went somewhere man should not go. That was plenty for them to know.

The power churned below him and rose to a level demanding release. Right now, he was the path of least resistance to the rest of the world, a position he would never survive.

"*Seelak gorshna eridatu*," he said and stretched his hands toward the communications tower in the parking lot.

The spinning, glowing mass below him sent a runner out to the tower. It bounced along a power cable conduit until it hit the tower's base. Then it sent a surge up the superstructure like radiant blue creeping vines. They wrapped around the tower's tip and bloomed like a flower in the sky. Threads of azure energy snapped and sparkled from the tower's peak, the powerful byproduct of the apprentices' magic.

Inside the plant, the incense in the censers vaporized in a puff of black smoke and a flash of neon blue. The ground went still.

"Let the games begin," Lyle said.

No one notices the fall of an avalanche's first grain of sand.

At Miami International, the barometric pressure had been on a slow, steady rise after a weak front passed through and was at 30.55 inches. The forecast called for a continued increase as high pressure rolled in from the north. Instead, the needle paused, wavered, and nudged back to 30.54.

Lyle's Grand Adventure was on.

Chapter Twenty-Nine

It was the strangest thing.

Big rectangles of mildewed concrete paved the old DPW parking area. Time had widened the expansion gaps between the slabs. The department's few vehicles, the pickup, a street sweeper, a light-duty tractor and the long-idled garbage truck, each had their own parking space and that still left room galore within the chain-link fence.

All summer, the lot had been a flat gray desert. But last week, weeds had sprouted along the expansion gap in the center of the lot. These unwanted volunteers hadn't just poked their heads through the crack. Almost overnight, they shot up a half foot and kept growing. A few were palm fronds and several were budding pin oaks.

The oddest thing was that the strip of green did not go straight across the lot. Two-thirds of the way through, it took a right angle along another expansion joint and headed west toward Memorial Park. The rest of the joints remained barren as desert dunes.

Andy was used to spraying the lot once or twice a year in response to a few stray sprigs of green. But this profusion of plant life was unheard of. This Wednesday morning, he was giving it a double-strength shot of poison. That had to kill it.

He sprayed around the tires of the dump truck, big tires that stood well past his waist. He did not like the feel of being next to them. The big wheels reminded him of the trucks he drove years ago in Afghanistan and the fewer memories he reviewed about that place the better.

Andy had grown up in the south Florida heat, but even that hadn't prepared him for his final summer in Kandahar. Each day peaked at one hundred and four degrees in the shade and there was no shade to be found. He once watched another soldier fry an egg on the hood of his M51 five-ton tractor. Sea breezes regularly cooled Citrus Glade's summer days, but any puff of wind that crossed southern Afghanistan felt more like the rush from an open oven.

He'd enlisted and chosen this specialty, 88-Mike, officially a Motor Transport Operator, and rationalized that it was an applicable skill in the civilian world. There weren't many want ads for 11-Bravo Infantry on the *Miami Sun-Sentinel* jobs site, but long-haul truckers were always needed. At least that's what he told everyone.

He'd wanted to be a soldier since he was a kid, watching in awe as John Wayne tread the sands of Iwo Jima and Robert Duvall announced that "Charlie don't surf." But when the time came to enlist, when he sat in that office full of the real Army, knowing that he'd be deployed into combat zones in southwest Asia, he flinched. That infantryman, whose job was, as the recruiter said, "to close with and kill the enemy," faced an opponent with the same mission statement. He could find something just a bit safer, not embarrassingly safe like computer programmer, but something with a more reasonable level of danger. Big-rig driving seemed like the ticket.

As Specialist Andy Patterson bounced along the rutted highway his last week in country, he wished he'd had more foresight. In this war, he hadn't picked something safer. The most common enemy they faced were hidden IEDs and Andy drove a big target. Every run from Point A to Point B, no matter how short, was a nerve-wracking experience, a constant scan for fresh-dug earth and exposed wires. Everyone he passed was a potential trigger man for a buried explosive charge.

He felt cocooned wearing the defensive implements of war; helmet, flak vest, gloves and glasses. But all these safety items never made him feel safe. He still rode in the flimsy cab of a truck riding over a tank of diesel fuel.

The fateful day, with a week before he rotated home, he hauled a tanker of water, as inoffensive a cargo as there could be, and one he hoped the Taliban would ignore. After all, the deliveries were to villages in the province, clean water to keep kids healthy. But he and the Taliban rarely thought alike.

He rolled into one of the destination villages. Escort vehicles filled with infantry and topped with swivel-mounted machine guns bracketed his truck. When he stopped at the destination point, soldiers scattered to provide a perimeter.

The arrival drew a crowd and crowds made Andy nervous. Worse, the wizened village elder was on hand to take credit for the arrival of fresh water. A local leader's show of American support was too often a magnet for Taliban retribution.

He rushed through the setup for the water drop, connecting the pump hose from the truck to a big rubber blivet the Army had stationed in the town. He opened the valve.

Kids materialized, as they always did, to watch this amazing process. They played around a spray of water from the blivet coupling. A few men of dubious loyalty stood along the crowd's edge. Andy looked down to check the flow rate and when he looked up again, the men were gone. His heart skipped a beat.

A civilian woman dressed head to toe in a black burqa passed through the crowd like a cancer cell among the healthy bright colors. She closed on the village elder. Just her eyes showed.

Her eyes. Andy would never forget her eyes. They positively burned, two hot black coals focused on a target, immune to distraction, looking out from deep within the evil side of being human. He stood frozen at the tail of his truck.

The rest happened in slow motion, and each time he relived it, those replayed seconds ran like minutes. Only Andy had the angle to her actions. She reached the village elder. The children were too engrossed in the waterworks to pay her any mind. Her hand extended from beneath her future shroud. She held a black cylinder with two wires at one end, a red switch at the other. Her thumb hovered over the button.

Soldiers shouted in deep elongated syllables. Weapons snapped as riflemen brought them to bear. The slow-motion thump of his heart pounded like a countdown clock.

He was closest to the woman. In a few strides, he could have been on her, and wrenched her thumb from over the red harbinger of death. He could have brought the rifle slung across his back to bear and with one bullet ended her misguided mission. He could have shouted to the world that she had a bomb.

Instead, he ducked. He whirled backward and plastered his back against the cool steel of the water tank. His calves hit the big trailer's tires and he held his breath. The world went back to full speed.

The sound of the explosion rolled though Andy and made his organs vibrate. The body of the suicidal woman vaporized. Nails and screws that surrounded her charge pinged against the water trailer like stones into a steel can. A wave of brown dust washed under and around the trailer, rushing by his legs like some polluted sea. Bits of bloody flesh sprinkled the ground in a hellish rain. For two eternal seconds, all was silent.

Then came the screams. Children wailed in inconsolable pain. Parents cried in horror and rushed to retrieve their dying futures. Soldiers shouted orders and radios crackled with emergency calls. One of the infantrymen lay on the ground, right leg sheared away at the knee.

The head of the suicide bomber lay on the ground near Andy's feet, the headdress torn away to reveal the face of a young woman his age, jaw torn away, tongue exposed. The eyes that smoldered with hatred were now glazed and vacant. A woman the age to be caring for children somehow driven to kill them. It was all insane.

Around the other side of the truck, small bodies lay in pieces. The village elder was a ragged torso. Blood splattered the tanker's side. Water spewed through shrapnel punctures in the blivet's thick rubber and the bladder slowly deflated. In the shock of it all, Andy remembered to do the strangest thing. He shut off the truck's water valve.

He owned this scene. He could have intervened, and these children would not be dead. He checked his hands, his feet. Undeservedly unscathed.

But outside damage and inside damage were two different things. Andy was back in the States in a fortnight and shredded his re-enlistment papers. He wanted to get as far away from the visions of carnage and the humiliation of his cowardice as he could. He bullshitted his way through the cursory outprocessing psych evals, left everything he owned in a barracks dumpster and came home to Citrus Glade and the DPW.

Standing amidst the newborn weeds in the DPW lot, he gave the dry-rotted tire of the dump truck a kick with his toe. When the town had been more of a town, the dump truck had made rounds once a week and picked up oversized items. That service disappeared years ago. The dump was strictly do-it-yourself.

The idea of putting the big truck back to work as a fee-based service surfaced, but Andy topped the list of those who opposed it. He had no desire to climb back into a cab any higher up than the pickup truck. The thought of it make his hands shake. His excuse was that the beast had two forward gears and no reverse. Transmissions weren't cheap. The mayor agreed.

As he sprayed the final few feet of resurgent weeds, he noticed that the greenery pointed like an arrow across the street and to the small park around the World War I memorial, which bloomed like it was springtime.

There was something familiar about the pattern on the ground, the bend in the parking lot that crossed to the memorial. He couldn't quite place it.

There wasn't time to sweat it now. Some kids had yanked a stop sign out off CR 12. He had to replace it before someone decided to exercise their newfound right-of-way and got killed.

Chapter Thirty

Dolly felt fresh as springtime flowers.

She'd gotten eight solid hours of sleep last night, the first time in ages. But there was more to it than that. The world seemed to have more…clarity. Things looked sharper. Things felt sharper. *She* felt sharper. Her right knee didn't hurt when she got out of bed in the morning. For whatever reason, today was going to be a great day and she was going to take advantage of every minute of it.

She called Andy and he picked up his cell on the second ring.

"Are you at work already?"

"Such as it is," Andy said. "What's wrong?"

Of course he would jump to such a conclusion. She rarely called him. Since she'd moved to Elysian, she had felt like a burden. She felt guilty calling him, taking him away from his glowing life to support the dying embers of her own.

"Nothing's wrong," she said. "Just the opposite, in fact. How about lunch today?"

"Let me check my schedule. I can wedge you in. Where do you want to go?"

"Somewhere cheery," she said. "Pick me up here at noon and don't be late."

"Not one minute," Andy said. She could hear the smile in his voice.

She hung up and went to the day room. Walking Bear had his usual seat at the picture window. She came up behind him and placed a hand on his shoulder.

"Good morning. What do the birds tell you today?"

Walking Bear grabbed her fingers. His hand was rough, calloused, strong. He looked up and straight into her eyes. She could not remember the last time they had such direct, intense, unnerving eye contact. His brown eyes seemed to go on within him forever.

“It’s all wrong,” he said. “Fall is almost here and this is all wrong.”

Dolly’s hand started to hurt.

“The birds are too active. Rabbits scamper and don’t rest. There is no balance.”

Every sentence Walking Bear said got progressively louder and his grip on her hand tightened. She began to be afraid. He was a big man and if he got out of control...

“Walking Bear, please,” she said as she tried to squirm her hand free of his.

“Look!” he shouted. “You’ll see it if you look!”

His voice had already carried to the nurse’s station and Nurse Coldwell had come at a run. “Walking Bear!” she yelled. “Let Dolly go!”

Walking Bear released Dolly. He stood and turned to face Nurse Coldwell. He towered over the shorter nurse, his shoulders still powerful despite his age. His face was a confused mixture of fear and anger. “I’m sorry. But the animals... there is something wrong.”

Strange outbursts from patients were just another part of the day at Elysian. While Walking Bear wasn’t one of the regulars, the staff’s training kicked in no matter who was involved. Two other, larger male nurses followed in Nurse Coldwell’s wake. Walking Bear’s jaw went slack, and he looked like a child who realized his last tantrum had crossed the line. He raised his hands waist high.

“I’m okay, I’m okay.”

The male nurses stopped on either side of him. Their eyes darted from Walking Bear to Nurse Coldwell and back, waiting for the order to restrain.

“Why don’t we go back to your room to relax, Walking Bear,” Nurse Coldwell said. Her tone was a command, not an invitation.

“No problem,” Walking Bear said. He left the day room, head hung, with the two male nurses in tow.

Dolly watched the episode with distress. Walking Bear might have had a few delusions about his pseudo-Indian heritage, but in all her time at Elysian, she had never seen him agitated or even hint at becoming violent. His perception of a connection with the local wildlife's consciousness was harmless. Walking Bear was one of the few here she could count on to have a clear head.

Why did he have to do this on a morning when she felt so wonderful? Was there some fixed amount of mental health available at the home? When she felt great, did someone else have to feel bad? She certainly hoped not.

Shane Hudson missed all the morning's day room excitement. Normally, he'd have been there by now, but this morning had unfolded as anything but normal.

Progressive nerve damage was a bitch. The affected extremities didn't hurt or feel any different. As far as Shane could tell, his legs were as good as they had been when he played wide receiver for Citrus Glade High and when he stalked the humming factory floor at Apex Sugar. He just couldn't move them well. His brain sent the command, but his damn legs screwed up the reception. At first it was weakness, then he needed the cane, then the goddamn chair. The quack doctor said it was just a matter of time before the dying nerves withered away completely and he would need to be lifted out of bed, unable to make the short walk to the bathroom or his chair. Then he'd be back where he started eight decades ago, laying in a bed, pissing into a diaper. Screw that.

This morning he pulled back the covers and stared down at his legs. Atrophy had worked its evil spell on the muscles and his legs were a shadow of their former glory. He reached down to swing them over the edge of the bed and to his shock, they beat him to it. The message to move got through and the two happy volunteers slid out over the side of the bed.

Shane stared in disbelief. The worthless sons of bitches were finally reporting for work? He reached down and felt the muscles in his calves. The flaccid little bastards had a little spring to them for once. He massaged them and felt a tingle, like when a limb wakes up from being asleep.

He scooted off the edge of the bed and gingerly stood, putting most of his weight on his arms. His legs didn't do the usual spastic shudder. He lifted his hands from the bed, and shifted his weight to his feet. It wasn't the normal, panicked, temporary return to verticality, but a stable, confident stance. He stretched to his full height and gave his knees a little flex.

Shane smiled. The old legs felt *good.* Not ready to kick the shit out of a lazy Apex employee *good* yet, but a hell of a lot better than yesterday, or even last month. Whatever brought this improvement on, he'd take more of it.

In the privacy of his room, he paced the floor with steady steps, reacquainting himself with life from five-foot-nine point of view. With every liberating stride he relived some slight he had to endure trapped in that goddamn wheeled prison of a chair. No more of that shit.

But when he left his room late that morning, after Walking Bear had returned to his, Shane rolled out as he had the day before, black oak cane across his lap. He wasn't about to share the news of his rejuvenation with the inmates, or the staff of this dump. He'd nurture this cure on his own, hold the news to himself until the right moment to awaken the others to the triumphant return of Shane Hudson, and the distribution of some serious payback. With accrued interest.

Chapter Thirty-One

It wasn't possible.

Felix Arroyo held an orange in his hand that could not be. This little green ball had been shriveled and undersized the day before yesterday, the leaves around it curled inward from the lack of moisture. If someone wanted pictures to define a failed crop, his acreage was the model grove.

But the fruit at his fingertips now was something completely different. The plump sphere had a healthy, waxy feel. The robust, dark green skin shined in the morning sunlight. The tree's leaves opened wide, speckled with the daybreak's dew. Felix ducked his head between the branches and drank in the tangy scent of ripening citrus. It had to be a dream.

The three-row swath of rejuvenated trees swept across his grove west of CR 12 to the far end of his property. Two-thirds of the way down, another north/south band of brighter green trees intersected the first at a right angle. In all, a quarter of his crop looked as healthy as an Ag college demonstration plot.

Carlina approached from between the verdant rows of trees. She carried a handful of bright wildflowers in her gloves.

"These are from the field across the property line," she said. "Our good fortune spreads."

"I don't understand it," Felix said. "I'm happy about it, but I don't understand it."

"How can you not understand? You see the healthy trees. They form the cross." Carlina raised her flowers to the sky. "God is the source of our gift. Our prayers are answered."

It was a miracle, Felix knew that. And as far as he knew, the Lord was the only source of those.

Reverend Wright awakened to his own religious epiphany that morning.

Years ago, a member with extra concrete and the skills to use it had built a little fountain in front of the church. Water poured over a low precipice and into a narrow white pool. It was supposed to represent the River Jordan, home of St. John's baptisms, praise Jesus, but lately it looked more like a soupy green gash between the concrete walkways. The pump was weak and the level of chlorine it took to keep the algae down made entering the church akin to walking through a bleach factory. Dissolved minerals had stained the waterfall an ugly rust red.

When he arrived at the Congregation of God Church that morning, the water in the small fountain at the entrance sparkled crystal clear. Water flowed over a bone white waterfall and danced all the way to the drain at the pool's end before its return trip. Reverend Wright had tried every remedy at Glades Hardware and nothing had restored the old fountain to its former glory. Yet somehow, overnight, it turned pristine.

As the Reverend stood in admiration of God's wonders, Maribel Wilson walked up beside him. She added her off-key contribution to the choir each Sunday, but her collection basket contribution more than made up for it in the Reverend's eyes. She only came up to the Reverend's shoulder. She wore a wide straw hat and big sunglasses, the uniform of her morning constitutional.

"Reverend," she said. "You cleaned the fountain."

"As always," he answered, "I cannot take credit for the work of the Lord. It was that way when I arrived."

Maribel edged her glasses down her nose and gave the area a closer inspection. "Really? Wait, there's something else..."

The Lord's bounty did not stop at the fountain's edge. The flowers along both sides of the walkways were in full bloom. The ornamental yews sprouted bright green growth. Between the fresh water and the budding bushes, the air had the sweet smell of spring.

"God has blessed us," the Reverend said. "Just this Sunday the congregation prayed for the health of our church and our prayers have been answered."

Maribel looked unconvinced. The Reverend knew even the most devout usually were. This backsliding society had so conditioned everyone to scientific explanations. The search for a rational, though reaching, alternative hypothesis always blunted the acceptance of miracles. Nonetheless, he certainly would not look at the Lord God's handiwork as anything but divine.

"I am already filled with the fire of the spirit for this Sunday's sermon," the Reverend said.

Maribel voiced some encouraging words and continued her morning march through downtown.

The Reverend looked at the war memorial across the street, a bronze statue of a doughboy that paid honor to the county's fallen dead in the Great War. The sparse grass at the statue's sandy base had turned a luxuriant green. And it may have been his imagination, but the statue's head had lost most of that mottled patina that made the soldier look like a leprosy victim. It shined with a ruddy, brown color.

The meaning could not be clearer. Like manna from heaven, like the destruction of the walls of Jericho, the condition of the memorial was a sign from God. Clearly the Congregation of God Church was the epicenter of the Lord's blessing and from here it was spreading across town, first to a symbol of the righteous defenders of freedom, then further on to the current keepers of the faith. Even the most unrepentant would be unable to deny what their eyes saw. A great awakening was being visited upon the town, and Reverend Wright would be here to lead it.

He looked down toward Main Street and thought of the first change the upcoming awakening needed to sponsor. The eradication of the blasphemous Magic Shop.

Chapter Thirty-Two

Shane Hudson rolled into the day room. Chester Tobias and Denny Dean had the usual table with a mass of dominoes spread out between them. Shane took his spot at the table's head.

"Doing okay, Shane?" Denny ventured. "Little late to the game this morning."

"Never better," Shane said. He meant it more than the two could know. He gave each a visual once over. "How you two feeling today?"

Chester gave his right shoulder a roll and winced. "Damn bursitis lit into me this morning. Woke me up about three a.m. Asked for a shot of something, but you know how that works around here."

Shane turned his head to Denny, who looked flattered that he cared. "Not bad. Something in the breakfast gave my stomach the usual roll but the rest of me is fine."

Well, whatever mojo Shane tapped into last night apparently wasn't universal. He gave the room a quick sweep. Chief Stupid Bear wasn't at his post for some reason, but a half dozen of what Shane called the Drool Patrol were out and about. Three of them looked, for the first time in ages, alert. Their eyes didn't stare off into space. They moved from object to object, as if some long dormant recognition routine had been reactivated. One of the old geezers was actually watching TV, his head rolling in sync with the game show's big flashing wheel as it spun for prizes.

So there were winners and losers in this recovery lottery. As long as he was one of the winners, he didn't care about the rest of them. Well, he cared about Dolly Patterson. He'd be happy if she was on the loser list. That smug bitch could use a shot from the head of his cane, and once he was back on his feet, he'd be sure to give it to her.

At the far end of the room, Janine, spokesgirl for the New Age, surveyed the Elysian day room in triumph. She had two leather laces braided into her hair this morning. She polished a crystal with a soft white cloth.

"Now if I can see the difference," she said to Nurse Coldwell, "you *must* see it."

Nurse Coldwell had her hands crossed across her broad chest, fingers barely touching her elbows. Condescension dripped from her voice as she answered.

"The fact that several patients seem a bit more alert might look like a big deal to you," she said. "But we see random changes like that all the time. Plenty of residents move up or down from day to day. It's natural, not supernatural."

"Ah, ah, ah," Janine said, finger raised and wagging. "I can feel the amplified energy level in the room. You would not have invited me in if you didn't think the crystals would work."

"I didn't invite you," Nurse Coldwell said. "The owners did. And to keep my job, I'll refrain from any comment on that decision. But I will tell you that the fact that Mr. Bingham looks like he's watching *Take a Spin* on the television isn't a great breakthrough."

Janine flitted to the next crystal, unfazed. "You'll see. Soon you won't be able to deny the changes." She dusted the final crystal in the room. "When I come back next week, you'll see what's happening."

Nurse Coldwell shook her head as Janine floated out of the building. Nut job. Certifiable nut job. If she herself spouted all that New-Age garbage, the staff would sign her up for a room here with daily supervision.

Nothing rejuvenating was going on here. Yes, a few of the worst cases were having a good day. And Dolly was in a fine mood, but she was universally up when she was coherent. But Walking Bear had to be given a mild sedative, and he was never a problem. Did the crystals want to take credit for that?

This place was the last sad stop for many. The owners were misguided fools for letting the false hope of moronic pseudo-science through the front door. Of all those who checked in here, none ever checked out. No hunks of rock were going to turn that success rate around.

Chapter Thirty-Three

Carlina Arroyo blew in through Reverend Wright's office door like a barely contained tornado. She beamed with the enthusiasm of the newly converted, an enthusiasm the Reverend rarely saw.

"Reverend!" she said. "We have a miracle in our groves!"

Normally the Reverend would have a jaundiced reply for such a proclamation. But in light of the transformation of the church fountain, his curiosity piqued.

"Sit down and tell me about it."

But Carlina was not in a sitting mood. She stood and fired off a description of the renewed harvest hanging from the trees on her property, her story punctuated with a flurry of wild arm gestures and stray bits of Spanish.

"And the sign from God," she finished, "is that the blessed trees are all in a cross." She made two sweeping gestures with her right hand in case the Reverend had forgotten the shape of the Christian symbol.

Coincidence? Coincidence was an atheist's code word for the hand of the Almighty. Reverend Wright rose and went to the other side of his desk. He grasped Carlina by the shoulders and looked down into her glowing brown eyes.

"Follow me, child."

He led her through the door to the church and out the front door of the building. He raised his hands over the rejuvenated fountain like a temple priest over the Ark of the Covenant.

"The Lord has also blessed the church and renewed the memorial across the street," he said. "His hand has touched your groves in response to the prayers of the righteous and penitent. This is just the beginning, the sign that others can believe in, so their faith can restore our town."

"Amen, Reverend," Carlina affirmed.

The Reverend cast a contemptuous glance in the direction of Main Street.

"In the midst of all this benevolence," he said, "that Magic Shop brings evil into our community. Am I the only one who sees it?"

Then divine inspiration struck the good Reverend. He would spread this miracle across town the way the Good News spread across Judea. He could see it, plain as day, but as the Good Book said, others had eyes but could not see. The time had come for an awakening, for the Rev himself to open those eyes to the wonders of God's coming salvation.

"Praise God for his inspiration!" he said.

Carlina followed him as he went to the storage shed at the rear of the church. He spun the combination lock and yanked it open. The doors swung out with the creak of disuse. The musty smell of mold and dry canvas wafted out. Carlina helped him extract a dusty white canvas bundle. The Reverend rolled it out on the ground.

"Carlina, child," he said. "We are going to spread the word."

Bold red letters on the banner read *REVIVAL.*

Chapter Thirty-Four

Andy spent the morning taming the explosion of greenery at Memorial Park and delivering the cuttings to the dump.

As he drove back to the DPW, he noted something familiar and strange. The same stripe of weeds that surfaced in the DPW parking lot had ripped through the intersection of Main and Tangerine. And blossoms festooned the magnolia at the corner. Some bizarre green thumb had taken a haphazard swipe through Citrus Glade.

He thought of someone who might know why Mother Nature had randomly run amuck—Autumn, who he had been looking for an excuse to call. The cute redhead. The embarrassingly *younger* cute redhead. He pulled out his wallet and fished through an assortment of receipts. He couldn't find her card.

He was half relieved. It would be a lame excuse. They would be talking about mostly weeds here.

It was pushing noon and he'd promised his mother they would do lunch, if she remembered. He took out his phone and dialed Elysian Fields for a weather report.

Andy stood in the doorway of his mother's room without trepidation. Nurse Coldwell's prognosis had been more than good, it had been excellent. He gave the open door three knocks.

Dolly turned and delivered an enormous smile. She wore her paint-dappled apron and was working on a canvas that faced away from the door. She held a palette in one hand and a brush in the other. A second painting of a seascape was at the far end of her work table.

"Andy! Is it lunch time already?"

Andy gave her a loose sideways hug to avoid any wet paint. He nodded at the seascape.

"That looks beautiful," he said. "Really vibrant."

"Ooh," Dolly said. "I had a brainstorm to make the light really dance off the whitecaps." She took a spray can up off the table. "Clear lacquer sprayed at the wave tips. They actually look wet!"

Andy gave the can a circumspect look. "Geez, Mom. You gotta be careful with that stuff. Flammable with toxic fumes. You need more ventilation and the windows in these rooms barely open."

"Bah," Dolly said with a dismissive wave. "Compost heaps smell stronger than that stuff."

Andy turned from the seascape to the canvas on the other easel. It could not have been more different. The vibrant seascape hosted an active mix of blues and greens that captured the waters so unique to the Keys and Biscayne Bay. The other work was all blacks and grays, an Impressionist rectangular outline with some kind of conical mast at one end. The unfinished painting gave no hint of what the finished product would be.

"And this one is...?"

"Well," Dolly said. "I really can't say. I woke up this morning with a picture of it in my head. The image wouldn't go away. I figured that meant it wanted to be painted out of me."

Andy cocked his head sideways to see if an adjusted perspective was the key to understanding. It was not. "It's not as...bright...as your usual work."

"And now you're an art critic," Dolly said. "The spirit moves me and I follow its path. For all I know, that painting may be done as it is. We'll see tomorrow."

She pulled her apron off and tossed it over the canvas.

"So did you come down here to critique my work or to get your feeble old mother a decent meal?"

Within the hour they were seated at The Chew and Chat, the last man standing in the battle against the fast-food onslaught. The population exodus had long ago doomed the mid-level seafood and steak houses that Citrus Glade used to support. The Chew and Chat, with its mix of country-fried everything and homespun dĕcor, still hung on, though whether because the clientele was devoted or desperate was anyone's guess. The booths were full and Andy and Dolly had a table on the main floor. Their paper placemats had *The Sunshine State* emblazoned over a map of the state. It had to be vintage mid '70s because a dozen long-shuttered Mom-and-Pop roadside attractions were still listed on it.

"Monday, we had two visitors," Dolly said. "A New-Age free spirit in the morning and a creepy magician in the afternoon."

Andy paused with the fork halfway to his mouth.

"Lyle Miller was at the home?"

"Yes, enthralling us all with Cub Scout card tricks. He made Shane Hudson look foolish so I guess it was worth it."

"But you were not impressed."

"Honestly?" Dolly said. She shot conspiratorial glances right and left and whispered, "He kind of gave me the chills. Of course, I felt silly about it afterward."

"It's not just you," Andy said. "The Reverend is all wound up about him opening a 'shop of evil' on the town square. Flora thinks the Rev needs to chill. But to tell you the truth, I met him in passing downtown one morning and he sent my blood running cold. Probably all part of the persona he wants to create."

"If it isn't the Gator Slayer," a woman's voice said.

Andy turned to see Autumn at his shoulder. A wide-brimmed straw hat framed her face like a painting. Andy grinned in recognition.

"And if it isn't the Gator Doctor," he replied. "And to clarify, I think I'm more of the Gator Scraper than Slayer."

Dolly gave Andy a little kick under the table.

"Oh, Autumn," he said. "This is my mother, Dolly."

"Nice to meet you," Autumn said.

"Nice to meet you," Dolly answered. "Joining us for lunch?"

Andy blanched. Autumn missed his reaction.

"Oh, thanks, no," Autumn said. "I'm just picking up an order to go. I had a hankering for fried eggplant and this place does it better than I ever could. Just saying hi." She turned to Andy. "Remember, your next road kill's mine."

"I'll gift wrap it," Andy said. He watched every step of her retreat.

"And she is?" Dolly asked.

"A wildlife biologist studying the Everglades outside of town."

"She's cute," Dolly said.

"Mom, please. I just met her yesterday at the Food Bonanza."

"Who told you road kill is the way to a woman's heart? You didn't get that from me."

"Who says I'm looking for a way to her heart?"

"Your smile when you saw her says it. I've seen that look before, though certainly not recently."

Andy realized that there had been a little twinge there when he saw her. Something special about the way the sunlight lit her red hair...

"You're imagining things, Mom."

She nailed him in the chest with a pack of sugar and smiled. "Don't contradict your mother."

The waitress delivered two steaming plates of food to the table. "Anything else you need?"

Andy thought about Autumn again. Maybe there was. "Excuse me a second."

He left the restaurant and caught Autumn as she unlocked her RV.

"Say, can you give me your opinion on something this afternoon?"

Chapter Thirty-Five

"Yeah, that is weird," Autumn said to Andy.

They both stood in the DPW parking lot, one on each side of the strip of weeds that had defied Andy's attempted extermination. She plucked a few sprigs and sniffed them. She and Andy walked across the street to Memorial Park.

"These blooms are all out of season," Andy said. "This is a springtime growth. And the grass shouldn't grow so fast I'd need to cut it twice a week."

"Well, growth cycles need water, nutrients and sunlight," Autumn said. "Daylight hours have been a constant so there has to be a boost in one of the other two."

"Water?" Andy scratched his chin. "Let's check something out."

He led Autumn inside to his office. There were four desks in the room but three were empty.

"Run off the other employees?" Autumn asked.

"When this was a real town," Andy said, "there was a real staff. Most of the work is farmed out to the county now. DPW is a staff of one."

"I like a man who is indispensable," Autumn said.

Andy went straight to the town maps and pulled out the butcher-block-sized sheaf of water main maps. He spread out a sheet on his desk and pointed to the DPW parking lot.

"I thought the growth strip patterns looked familiar," he said. "A waterline runs right through the DPW lot, with a dogleg over to Memorial Park." He flipped to another sheet. "The spurts of springtime growth around town followed the path of the main waterlines through Citrus Glade. Three join under the jungle that sprouted at Memorial Park. There's one wide stripe of green heading south. "

"A leak would water the ground around it and encourage growth," Autumn said. "But could the whole system all of a sudden be leaking?"

"Well, no," Andy said. "Pressure would be down and people would be getting sand in their sinks."

"I guess something could be leaching out of the pipes," Autumn said. "I'm not sure what."

"But whatever it was would have to be in the water as well, right?" Concern darkened Andy's face. "And everyone drinks that water."

"I'll get some plant samples," Autumn said. "I can test them for nitrogen, phosphorous, contaminants. I can let you know if it's anything dangerous. But since no one's sick, I doubt it."

"And I guess a big growth spurt is less worrisome than a massive die off, right?"

"I'm sure whatever's going on won't hurt anyone," Autumn said.

Neither of them sounded at all convincing.

Chapter Thirty-Six

Walking Bear could not sleep that night.

The nurses had given him the Calm Down pills that morning and one more in the afternoon. The Calm Down pills always made him tired, and he'd spent most of the day in bed. He'd tricked them on the evening dosage and hid the pill under his tongue. The nurse didn't check such a cooperative patient too closely. Now midnight approached and he was wide awake.

He sat in the darkness and watched the tree line from his window. He was not imagining the things he saw that morning. Over the years he learned the rhythms of the animals outside Elysian Fields. Gopher tortoises did not come out in the pre-dawn cool. Rabbits did not chase each other in the heat of the day. Storks and egrets did not do mating displays in the fall. Something was turning the balance of nature on its head.

He cracked the window open. The sounds of the night filtered in on a wave of warm, heavy air. The chirping of crickets, the hum of small insects. The underbrush in the tree line rustled as stout animals waddled through it.

Back when he was a boy, before he had embraced being Walter Connell, the song of the night sang him to sleep. The nights he spent with his Anamassee grandmother in her shotgun shack at the edge of the Everglades had been filled with this same calming melody. She taught young Walter the ways of the natural world, how to become part of it, instead of trying to stand above it.

He was six when his grandmother died, much to his father's relief. Her embrace of their anachronistic Anamassee heritage had been a lifelong source of personal humiliation for him. His father left the shack to rot and kept Walter well within the Miami city limits.

Walter prospered within man's concrete canyons off the white south Florida beaches. A chain of dry cleaning shops put his two children through college and on to lives of their own along the West Coast. When cancer took his wife at age sixty-two, he was left alone, physically and mentally. Walter dove into community service projects, but he could not assuage his growing spiritual solitude. In the unnatural quiet of his empty house, he wanted to hear those night sounds of the Everglades again.

He returned to his grandmother's old home. The acres had never been sold, deemed too worthless by his father, and later too priceless by Walter. Hurricane Andrew had leveled the house to nothing but a floor atop pilings of concrete blocks. Walter pitched a tent on the remnants of the hardwood floor he once raced Hot Wheels across. Darkness fell and the cooing trill of the Everglades evening enveloped the tent.

At midnight, he awoke nose-to-nose with a sniffing armadillo. He didn't move. The armadillo didn't move. But Walter Connell heard it speak. Inside his head, the armadillo announced that he was Walter's spirit guide, sent by his grandmother and his Anamassee forefathers to rescue him. He had traveled alone for far too long. He had a great destiny to fulfill and his name from now on would be Walking Bear.

It was surprisingly easy to shed the existence he had taken a lifetime to build. He sold the shops, sold the house, cut his ties. He met with the few tribal elders that still remained and immersed himself into the ways of the Anamassee.

A year into his journey of renewal, he had a small stroke. The doctors recommended a rest and caregivers at the ready for the likely event of another onset. Walking Bear had never been to Citrus Glade, but Elysian was the closest home to his beloved Everglades. He never regretted the move.

Something rustled the bush outside his window. Walking Bear leaned his head against the mesh screen. Two tiny black eyes looked up at him. The armadillo waved its armored snout back and forth.

“You have news for me, Spirit Guide?” Walking Bear asked.

The armadillo sniffed the air and then scratched at the ground. Something snapped in the woods across the lawn. The armadillo froze and its ears rotated that way in response. It turned and skittered away.

Walking Bear knew he wasn’t crazy. His spirit guide felt the disturbance. He focused on the tree line.

A dark shape slunk low between the bushes. It ventured out into the clearing and became distinct, a dull brown in the faded indirect light. A feral hog, several hundred pounds large with four robust tusks.

The hog swung its head with a snort and returned to the woods. Walking Bear gripped the window sill. What he thought he saw had to have been a trick of the light, a reflection from the moon. There was no way a hog’s eyes could shine blue like that.

Now he’d never get to sleep.

Chapter Thirty-Seven

The next day, the bell on the Magic Shop door rang multiple times. That told Lyle the boys were early. Which meant they were right on time.

He entered from the back room and all four apprentices stood in the empty shop, spent magic props in hand. Red-rimmed eyes stared out from wan skin. Their clothes were wrinkled and dirty. They looked like hell. To Lyle, they looked wonderful.

Barry Leopold pushed his way past the other three. Fingerprints smudged the edges of his glasses. Lyle wasn't surprised the low man on the Outsider totem pole took the lead. He had the most to lose.

"It's not working," Barry said with a wave of his hat

Lyle suppressed a cringe at the whine in the boy's voice.

"The power's gone again. We can't do the magic."

Lyle feigned surprise. "Why, none of you have the magic?"

Four wearied heads shook no. Ricky rocked back and forth in place. Paco rubbed his right hand up and down across a nasty-looking burn on his left forearm. Zach pulled his coin from his pocket and held it out for Lyle to see. His hand shook like a quaking aspen.

"It's not working," he said. His voice was dry and cracked. "There's no power."

"Only the most powerful apprentices could drain so much magic so quickly," Lyle said. "Nothing lasts forever."

Zach rushed forward and grabbed the front of Lyle's shirt. He tugged at it with a weakness disproportionate to the desperation in his eyes.

"You gotta pump us up!" Zach pleaded. "You gotta!"

Lyle flashed a mock sympathetic smile and then backhanded Zach so hard the boy careened across the room. His rings flew from his hand and pinged against the floor. He hit the wall and slumped to the floor. Blood seeped from where Lyle's blue ring sliced Zach's cheek.

"You make demands, apprentice? The rest of you have demands to make?"

The other three shrank back under the sorcerer's gaze.

"Better," Lyle said. "The next step opens the door to greater power, if you have the courage to step through it. But you have to be willing to commit. Are you willing?"

Zach slunk back to the others and all four nodded at Lyle in distressed affirmation. Lyle never doubted they would. They had drunk from the great fountain of power and now without it they would die of thirst. Lyle returned to the back storeroom, the four apprentices in tow.

Without command, the four took up positions around the black oak table, each on a point of the star painted on the floor. They lay their talismans on the table. The crystal ball that had sat at the table's center was gone, replaced with a black iron chalice. A string of amethysts circled the base and a band of gold encircled the cup's lip.

"*Corundi metaba celesqui,*" Lyle chanted.

The chalice rose from the center of the table. The boys' eyes all focused on the cup.

"*Gusti verato hubnis.*"

The chalice began a slow rotation.

"Apprentices, you stand here ready to commit yourselves fully and completely to the power of this world, to the magic that brings you strength. Through the essence of your life, you will bind yourself to me and receive all that this world has to offer."

The four boys stared at the glossy black cup with frantic anticipation, ready to pay any price for the power and ecstasy of performing magic.

Lyle drew a large knife from the small of his back. Intricate designs covered the pewter-colored blade. The white handle was carved from a human femur.

"Corobungi jakad."

The knife levitated out of Lyle's hand. The chalice hovered in front of him. He extended his hand over the chalice, palm down. The knife passed under his hand and the blade cut a crease in his palm. Blood ran down into the chalice. The wound closed.

Each boy extended his hand as Lyle had and watched the chalice's advance with pleading eyes. The knife followed and at each boy's station sliced an outstretched palm. One by one they added their precious blood to the dark cup. It returned to Lyle and he grasped it with both hands.

"Corobungi wakad."

He raised the chalice to his lips. The thick liquid poured down his throat like wildfire.

As the last drop left the chalice, the four boys' heads snapped back in unison and they faced the ceiling. Spasms wracked their bodies but their heads stayed motionless, transfixed by something far beyond the room's ceiling. Then their bodies went still and their heads lolled forward again.

Their eyes had rolled up so far that only the whites were visible. When they rolled back down, the pupils glowed neon blue. A wicked grin crossed each one's face.

"Gather your talismans and return home," Lyle said. "Make magic without ceasing."

Each boy held out a hand. His talisman flew off the table and into his grasp. Without a word, they left the back room. The doorbell's jingle signaled their exit.

Now Lyle felt them. The same way he felt sensation at the tips of his fingers, so he sensed the four boys as they silently split up to go home. Their essence was bound to his, three stronger than the fourth, but all more than strong enough. In this state, the boys would supercharge the power flow to the Apex plant and the Grand Adventure would shift into high gear. He just needed to cast two more spells and

Chapter Thirty-Eight

With the boys gone, Lyle set about the rest of his business.

The test of this spell had gone perfectly when he tried it a few nights after his arrival on a single alligator. He'd gotten the thing to march right out one night and attack some oncoming traffic on CR 12. The alligator losing the contest validated the magic. The time had come to go wide open.

He brought out an open pottery bowl of small harvested organs; an alligator brain, a python esophagus, a hog gallbladder. He sprinkled the carcasses of a variety of dead insects on the top. Herbs and scorpion tails finished the mix. He held the bowl above his head and said the incantation. The bowl grew warm in his hands. The organs slithered inside of their own accord. A puff of black smoke arose from the bowl. The organs stopped and sizzled.

Suddenly, it was as if Lyle could see through thousands of eyes at the same time, eyes that dotted the landscape for miles around Citrus Glade. Snakes, alligators, wild hogs. With a thought, he could plant a single overriding command in each or all and the order would become their sole directive.

Lyle turned down the connection and kept it open at only the lowest level. Now was too early, but soon he would need these creatures at his command to help make the Grand Adventure a reality.

Lyle leaned forward and rested against the table. He was completing the equivalent of a sorcerer's triathlon. Sparking the storm, tapping the animals in the Everglades, each would have individually been a day's work for most. Channeling so much power was demanding and draining. Even Lyle, with thousands of years of there would be no stopping him.

Ricky was just a hazy passenger on his bicycle. Buildings raced by on the way home, but he wasn't making it happen. His feet pumped the pedals and his arms steered the bike, but it was as if he was inside a marionette with someone outside pulling the strings.

He didn't feel quite right inside this body. Ricky had a sense of dread, like he was riding a train that was heading for a washed-out bridge. But he couldn't keep a hold on that feeling. The bliss of the power of magic crowded it out. And if that wasn't enough, there was the anticipation of more. Because as soon as he got home, it was going to be him and his magic cards all alone in his room. And that was going to be wonderful.

practice, felt the strain of two such exertions. But there was one more spell to cast so that the Grand Adventure would continue unimpeded.

He brought out the gold plate that had held the crystal ball in place. He made a bed of wheat chaff and dusted it with ground human bone. He arranged the hairs of Vicente and Shane Hudson into a pile. He chanted an incantation over the plate.

He struck a match and touched the plate's edge. Yellow fire licked across the wheat chaff. He uttered a second incantation and the flames turned blue. The hair in the center caught fire.

Lyle began his third, more lengthy spell. The coins he had given the Outsiders were antennae that attracted magic and redirected it to the boys' talismans. The boys would be caught in the slipstream, but without access to Lyle's incantations, could not direct the power they felt. Those whose hair he had collected and set afire would have so much more. The black *whapnas* of these individuals were ready to absorb the dark power the magic created and make them apprentices the likes of which the four boys could never become.

So Lyle commanded that some of the malevolent power he drew from the magic stream divert to those whose hair burned bright before him. The flames flashed cobalt blue and winked out.

His minions did not know it, but now they awaited his call.

Chapter Thirty-Nine

Inspired by miracles, the Congregation of God's revival preparations went full-speed ahead.

Carlina Arroyo activated the call list and recruited a dozen of the most faithful to spend the day in the service of the Lord. Given the heat and the expected overflow crowd that night, using the sanctuary was out of the question. In the tradition of revivals that stretched back to the 1800s, this event would be outdoors. First things first, the canvas tent had to go up in the Congregation of God's backyard.

It was more of an undertaking than anyone remembered. The great white tent rivaled ones from the glory days of the circus and raising it took a lot of muscle and some trial and error. But by midday, it stood tall and proud, a snowy beacon announcing the arrival of the Word of God. Reverend Wright's chest swelled with pride at the sight of it and then he chastised himself, quietly, for the sin.

The worker bees assembled the stage and set the podium at the center. Uncomfortable metal folding chairs faced the platform, ready to direct the attention of the congregation on the preacher's words. The sound system and other pilferable items could wait until tomorrow evening to be set out. The Reverend had tremendous faith in human spirit, but little in the weaker human flesh.

Spouses of the participants organized a potluck dinner in support. By dusk the setup was complete and the volunteers had full bellies.

"We are so blessed," Carlina said to Reverend Wright as she tied down the last corner of the revival banner. It hung across the face of the church and the red arrow underneath pointed to the tent in the back. "My orchard, the church fountain, the memorial. Tomorrow night we will give thanks for the miracle."

"Indeed," Reverend Wright said. "We will offer much up to the Lord."

But the Reverend had plans to offer up more than thanks. He would offer up a revelation, a public exposé to show the Lord that the people of Citrus Glade were worthy of this great miracle he wrought among them. Until now, the town had done little to warrant God's favor. For redemption, he would unmask Lyle Miller.

Carlina followed the last few volunteers home and left the Reverend alone at the church around nine-thirty p.m. He could wait until later to undertake his clandestine mission, but now was more than late enough. Downtown Citrus Glade rolled up the sidewalks after five p.m. By this hour, it would be still as a morgue. Besides, at his age, midnight excursions were something left long in the past.

Reverend Wright pulled a flashlight and a crowbar out of the shed. He tucked the flashlight into his pants and tried to hold the crowbar along the length of his arm to keep it unobtrusive, just in case he did cross someone's path. He walked a jagged route behind businesses and along the edges of empty lots. He paused across the street from his target.

The corner traffic signal had reverted to its nighttime pattern, abandoning the three-color sequence for a four-way flashing red. Each flash bathed the building below it in a bloody spotlight and illuminated the words in the window: *MAGIC SHOP*.

The shop was dark, the sign on the door read *CLOSED*.

It was now or never.

The crowbar slipped against the Reverend's suddenly sweaty palm. His pulse pounded in his ears. His plan had seemed simpler in the daylight. Break into the shop, find the evidence of evil that he was certain was there, and expose it to the town once the revival reached fever pitch.

He swiveled his head and scanned both sides of Main Street. Deserted. As it would be at this hour. Still, he suffered a touch of paranoia, a certainty that as soon as he stepped out to cross the street, the road would be filled with members of his congregation wondering why their shepherd was running through town with a crowbar in his hands.

He took a deep breath and broke for the other side of the street in a gangly, arthritic shuffle of a jog. He crossed over and tucked into the alley along the side of the Magic Shop. He gave the street one last look.

Still empty.

But he did not want to press his luck and get caught trying to open the front door. Every store had at least one rear entrance. The Magic Shop's would be here in the dark somewhere.

He took a few deep breaths to calm his racing heart. He pulled the flashlight from his pants and snapped it on. He played the beam along the building's side. No door. He killed the light.

He inched down the alley. He wrinkled his nose at the smell of urine and dog feces. He worried what he might step in, but kept his flashlight extinguished, more worried more about attracting attention. At the rear corner of the building he paused again. The Magic Shop backed up to the solid brick wall of the former Citrus Glade Fine Furniture, the perfect shield from prying eyes. He flicked on his light for a moment and lit the shop's back door.

He ducked into the doorway. The old wooden door felt a bit spongy. There was no deadbolt. This was going to be easier than he thought. He wedged the crowbar between the door and the frame just above the knob.

He froze. He was about to trespass into a building, and he had the intention of stealing something once inside. That was one broken commandment and two steps on the wrong side of morality. He was a man of the cloth. What devil's temptation got him out here in the dark of the night?

He shook his head. His was no devil's work. The evil in the town brewed within that building, not within him. Sure he was using some questionable tactics, but in the pursuit of a righteous goal. The ends always justified the means when working in the name of the Lord. He braced his shoulder against the door and gripped the crowbar.

On a whim, he first reached for the door knob. He twisted it and the tumblers clicked to grant him entrance. Like parting the Red Sea for Moses, the Lord had removed this far smaller obstacle for him. Praise God.

He pushed the door halfway open and sidled into the pitch-black back room of the Magic Shop. He closed the door without a sound. He trembled with anticipation.

He clicked on the flashlight. Lyle's smiling face lit up, just inches from his own.

"Hey, Rusty!"

A baseball bat slammed into the side of the Reverend's head and darkness returned.

Chapter Forty

Rusty Wright awoke to a splash of cold water and a flash of bright light. His arms and legs were bound together. His head pounded like a bass drum and there was a ringing in his left ear, the one the bat crushed.

As his eyes finally focused, he saw he was still in the back of the Magic Shop, surrounded by tricks and props. From his neck to his ankles, he lay in a narrow wooden box on some kind of gurney.

"Wakey, wakey," Lyle sang. He had an empty plastic cup in his hand. "Sorry to interrupt your slumber, but time is of the essence. My time, that is. Yours has about run out. Sorry about the bat. I could have done something more magical, but, honestly, you had it coming. Breaking into someone's place of business. You sinner."

The Reverend struggled against his bonds. "You're crazy. Let me out of here!"

Lyle gave Rusty a condescending, downward glance, like when an adult hears a child say something utterly clueless.

Rusty looked around the room as well as his limited mobility would allow. The box was in the center of the floor pentagram.

"I was right. This shop is the work of Satan!"

Lyle shook his head in angry exasperation. He yanked Rusty's head back by the hair and shoved a rag in his mouth.

"Two thousand years and you Christians still get it wrong," Lyle said. "Sorcery isn't witchcraft, isn't Satan worship. Three different animals. This..." He circled his index finger around the room. "...is *sorcery*."

The cloth absorbed every drop of moisture in Rusty's mouth. He wanted to scream but it took all his concentration to breathe through his nose and keep from suffocating.

"Now tonight's trick," Lyle said, "is a classic. Sawing a woman in half." He pounded on the box like an auctioneer. "I just need a volunteer from the audience."

Lyle bent his head next to Rusty's. "You sir? You'd like to volunteer?"

Rusty mangled a muffled reply of "drop dead" through the gag.

"What's that?" Lyle said, hand melodramatically cupped to his ear. "You say I promised to saw a woman in half? Well, sir, in some circles, you would qualify."

Lyle grabbed the end of the long box and pulled. The box began a fast counterclockwise spin around a central axis, staying centered on the pentagram.

"Notice, ladies and gentlemen, no mirrors, no wires, nothing up my sleeve."

Rusty's head did some kind of rollercoaster ride. The spinning box and his major concussion vied for the right to make him deathly ill. If he threw up into the gag, he'd choke on his own vomit and die. He closed his eyes and prayed.

Lord though I walk through the valley of the shadow of death...

Lyle stuck out a foot. The gurney wheel hit it. The box jerked to a stop. Rusty's head snapped back and forth like it was on a spring. His swelling brain felt like it was going to burst through his skull. He let out a whimper.

Lyle reappeared with a long metal saw in his hand. It looked like a prop from a silent movie about lumberjacks, with a heavy wooden handle and a row of jagged, uneven teeth along the silver blade. Lyle flexed the tip back and forth with his free hand. The saw made an oscillating warble.

"Now, ladies and gentlemen, note the saw. Completely real in every way. Sharp enough to slice through steel, so our mushy volunteer here should be no problem."

Rusty made another wriggling, futile attempt to force open the box.

"Normally such physical trauma would send the subject unconscious with pain," Lyle said. "But through the wonders of magic…"

He pointed to each tip of the pentagram on the floor. As he did he chanted "*hakeesh alasim*". The tips glowed. When he completed the fifth, the entire drawing blazed with light. A shudder ran through Rusty and every muscle in his body locked.

"…our volunteer won't have to miss a thing!"

Lyle slid the saw's blade into a slot in the center of the box. It dropped down and hit Rusty just above the waist. His stomach muscles flinched under the heavy impact. Sharp metal teeth punctured his shirt and gouged his skin. Warm blood trickled across his belly.

Oh Lord, my savior, he thought. *Save me from this devil of a man.*

Lyle looked into Rusty's eyes. "Smile. You're the star!"

He gave the saw a vicious, rearward yank. The blade tore through Rusty's skin with the finesse of a feeding great white. A wet, ripping noise echoed inside the box. Pain, white and hot as the center of the sun, exploded within him. Tears burst from his eyes and he screamed into the stifling gag, a wailing high-pitched shriek only torture could elicit.

The next forward thrust of the blade dug deeper. Organs caught on the irregular teeth, and when the blade yanked them to the right, the shudder inside him ran all the way up to the back of his throat. A second wave of pain, somehow, unbelievably worse than the first, rolled up into his pounding head. His cry came out in a wailing stutter. At the end of the stroke, the saw blade penetrated far enough that the teeth rested midway down his frozen forearms. His chest deflated as his shredded tissues oozed away.

Two rapid strokes hacked through his arms. He felt his hands disappear as they separated, heard their twin thumps as they fell lifeless into the wooden box. His bones splintered as the blade dragged through them. Daggers of scorching pain pierced the base of his skull. His head rolled back, wide eyed, the sensation too horrible to allow him to scream.

The final stroke tore through his spine. The serrated separation rocked his torso against the sides of the box. Something warm and thick puddled up around his shoulders. Blood filled his throat and he choked.

"And, *voila*," Lyle announced. "One man is now two!"

Lyle rolled the two boxes apart. Blood and organs hit the floor with a thick splat. Rusty's hands followed with two dead, wet thuds.

Sweet Jesus, this can't be real, Rusty prayed through the torrent of pain.

"And our volunteer has experienced it all!" Lyle said. "But he hasn't quite seen it. Let's show him what he's missing!"

Lyle pivoted the top half of the box up, raising Rusty's head. The box went fully vertical and the bottom hit the floor with the gushy crush of Rusty's spleen. The rest of the organs in his torso dropped to the ground and yanked his head forward like a puppet's.

Rusty stared straight into the bloody empty cavity of his lower body. It smelled like shit and piss and copper. An intestine flapped over the edge like an undigested sausage.

His mind snapped, unable to fathom the incomprehensible. He did not hear Lyle's last victorious taunts. He did not feel the saw blade against his neck. He only knew when it cut his spine for the final time and the world went forever dark.

Lyle sighed, smiled and leaned back against the wall. Blood dripped from his hands and speckled the legs of his pants. The Reverend's entrails seeped to the edge of the floor pentagram. He propped the preacher's severed head back up on top of the box, glazed eyes looking across the room.

It had been a long time since he'd killed with his own hands. The magic made it so easy to do it remotely, like the stupid waitress's heart attack or the animals swarming from the swamps. Ah, but what a liberating experience using the saw had been. He missed that physical contact, the sensation of having life seep away through his fingers.

Across the millennia he'd been alive, that was the one true constant. From his youngest days he'd found the death of any creature pleasurable, and killed any insect or animal he could overpower. As he grew older, he loved the days when the calves were slaughtered or the hunts brought down deer and bison, because he could openly indulge his bloodlust to the praise of others, a far cry from their reaction if they saw him when he silenced family pets in the night.

Would his master ever have taken him on as an apprentice if he knew the cold, dark current that ran though his heart? Most certainly not, and Lyle had hidden his inclination from his instructor until their last night together, when their roles reversed and Lyle taught the old man a few things about the art of ending life.

As a boy he'd liked kicking over ant mounds. He'd watch the stupid creatures scurry in panic to save their young and right their world turned inside out. Now every hundred years or so, when the ennui of immortality set in, he did the same thing with mortals. He'd plan a Grand Adventure.

And now the time was ripe. His last obstacle was removed. The cavern under the Apex plant hummed with the power the magic had unleashed. Lyle's own apprentices were hard at work topping off the tank. His two unwitting assistants with the clouded *whapnas* were about to be summoned.

The Grand Adventure was about to shift into high gear.

Chapter Forty-One

Autumn Stovall awoke to the unaccustomed sensation of Oscar's soft, insistent head butting. She stirred in bed with great effort. She had been up late analyzing the plant samples from the green swaths around town. She'd found no reason for their rapid growth. It was as if someone had just turned on the "springtime" switch all plants have buried in their genetic code.

She opened one eye. Oscar acknowledged her change in consciousness with a plaintive meow. She reached out to pat his head and he bounded away.

"Fine. Be that way."

Sunlight flashed in under the camper's thin shades with each flap from the morning breeze. Strange item Number Two. The Everglades' air was usually still as death each morning until the sea breezes worked their way in.

Oscar trotted the length of the RV floor, leapt into the passenger seat, transited the dashboard, jumped down to the driver's seat and started a second lap. Autumn checked his food and water, but both were full. In fact, they looked untouched from when she filled them last night.

"What's the matter, Osc?" There wasn't a cat less likely to be agitated than Oscar. He slept through south Florida thunderstorms.

Oscar stopped on the dashboard and stared out the window.

Autumn exited the RV to total silence. No splashes of water, no drone of insects. All the vibrant sounds of Everglades life were gone. Strange item Number Three.

The deep blue sky above made her feel like she could see up into space. But the rising sun burned crimson in the east. Black puffy cumulus clouds enveloped all horizons. Falling rain made gray curtains beneath the clouds. Both coasts were getting hammered by thunderstorms. That was usually an afternoon event, and usually only on one coast or the other.

She turned to see Oscar peer out at her through the RV windshield. She probably anthropomorphized her cat way too much, but she was certain the look in his eyes said "Get back in here!"

Carlina arrived at the Congregation of God at eight-fifty a.m., brimming with enthusiasm for the revival's start. The rest of the volunteers would be there soon and they would spend the day scrubbing the church and working the grounds. The burst of life around the fountain needed a bit of trimming to keep the walkway clear. Inside and out, the church would look its best. If the revival went as planned, plenty of new folks would be in attendance, and you know what they say about first impressions.

She first checked the tent and mini-stage at the side of the church. She'd last seen it in the darkness and in the daylight it was much more impressive. The tent shone like a mountain snowcap in the bright morning light. The edges ruffled in the soft morning breeze. The *REVIVAL* sign's big red letters could be read from across the street. Great advertising, but also she had a few members of the congregation posting notices around town. Wilbur Garrison, the Citrus Glade postman, would even drop flyers in mailboxes today. Delivering items without postage was against regulations, but Wilbur felt the Spirit move him to bend the rules a bit.

Carlina checked the front door of the church, but it was locked. Odd, since Reverend Rusty would have already been up and working by now. She went around back to his parsonage and knocked on his door. He didn't answer.

Strange. His car was in the driveway. Worst-case-scenario thoughts ran through her mind. Heart attack. Slipped in the shower and unconscious. Stroke. She fumbled for the spare key hidden in the potted palm by the door. The door creaked as it opened.

"Reverend?" she called from the doorway. When no one answered, her concern doubled. She bustled through the living room, arms pumping with each shift of her stocky frame. "Reverend!"

There were no dishes in the sink. Coffee wasn't brewing. The Rev never started a day without coffee, what he called God's natural stimulant. The Reverend could be dead. She rushed down the short hall and threw open his bedroom door.

The bed was made. A set of dark blue pajamas lay draped over the back of a chair at a small desk. He never went to bed. Sometime after she left last night, the Reverend disappeared.

Where would be go? Did he need to spiritually prepare for the evening, spend time in isolation like John the Baptist? Surely he would have told her. Wouldn't he?

She left the parsonage and ran into Eric Thompson. The retired schoolteacher wore a faded old golf hat and carried a pair of long garden shears in his gloved hands, ready to give the shrubbery a haircut.

"Reverend Rusty in there?" he asked.

Any answers she had would only breed more questions she *couldn't* answer. The Reverend would return from wherever he went. She hoped. She couldn't divert her volunteers from their mission readying the church for the revival.

"He'll be by, Eric. He mentioned having the bushes trimmed out front."

Eric gave the shears two quick snaps. "I'll cut them down to size. Amazing how they kicked into overdrive this time of year, isn't it?"

"One of God's gifts," Carlina answered.

Chapter Forty-Two

"And we'll get the weather this morning from Chuck Randall," the WAMM anchor said. "Chuck, what's going on out there?"

Whitney had the day off, at a minimum. The local news knew how to play up any story, to spread a little panic and bump up some ratings. This was not one of those times. They hadn't brought the trusted Chuck Randall in early to make a ratings point. They thought his gravitas might save lives.

"Reggie, what we are seeing is unprecedented," Chuck said. A map of south Florida with an isobar overlay filled the screen behind him. It looked an awful lot like an archery target. "Low pressure systems like this usually form in the Atlantic Ocean. But we have one forming overland, centered off Alligator Alley near the town of Citrus Glade. Barometric pressure has dropped to 28.2 so far."

The screen switched to radar. Huge swaths of green arced across the Miami area, across north of Sebring, down through Naples and south across the Keys. Patches of red flashed within the green where violent thunderstorms hammered away.

"This system is drawing energy and moisture from the sea surrounding us. In the past dozen hours, a tropical storm formed right over the south end of the state. Normally such a system would move either north or west, but what has just been named Tropical Storm Rita hasn't moved at all. Both coasts and the Keys have already seen several inches of rainfall and winds of over forty miles per hour.

"This storm has stymied most of our prediction models, but the consensus is that it will grow to hurricane strength. Evacuations of the Keys and all coastal regions have been ordered. Southbound lanes of the Turnpike, I-95 and I-75 have all been switched to northbound traffic."

The camera closed on Chuck until he nearly filled the screen. He looked straight out of millions of televisions across the state.

"This will become a killer storm," he said. "Do not wait. If you live along the coast or in a high rise or have special needs, head north now."

Chapter Forty-Three

Mayor Flora Diaz slammed down her office phone in frustration. The county supervisor had been worse than useless. He'd been useless and insulting.

She wasn't surprised when she called Florida Division of Emergency Management. Tallahassee was as shocked by the arrival of Tropical Storm/Hurricane Rita as anyone. Help was coming, but it was a long way away and would be there in time to help in the aftermath. She hadn't expected much more.

But the county supervisor not only could spare no deputies or resources, he confessed that he didn't know Citrus Glade had a mayor. He thought the dead town had been re-incorporated into the county years ago. He said he had coastal population centers to worry about and didn't have time to worry about "the boonies" as he put it. When he hung up, Flora felt lost.

A killer storm was more than she had bargained for as mayor. She had no real leadership experience, not for something like this. The mayor's position was supposed to be mostly PR, cheerlead for getting a few businesses started up, manage the micro budget, organize the Fourth of July fireworks with the Elks Club. Life and death decisions were for someone else, somewhere else.

Andy knocked on the door and entered.

"The weather's supposed to go to hell in a handbasket soon," he said. "FPL has repair crews stationed in Sebring ready to start repairing downed lines as soon as the storm passes. I've pulled all the trash cans from the parks and all the vehicles are secure in the parking lot."

"There's no help coming," Flora blurted out. "No sheriff's deputies, no FDEM, no National Guard. Stuart tells me the Food Bonanza is being picked clean down to cocktail onions and canned beets. We are going to get pounded and we are not prepared."

Andy sat in the chair by her desk. "Citrus Gladers are pretty resilient, used to standing on their own. The fact that the Food Bonanza is cleaned out means that they have taken their safety into their own hands."

"But many can't," she said. "Mary Wickersham out in her little trailer. Jenny Bingham here in town with no car and using a walker. Someone needs to help them. I need to help them."

There had to be some way for her to shelter the townspeople in need. Her eyes lit up.

"The bomb shelter," she said. "We could open that."

The bomb shelter, like all the infrastructure of Citrus Glade, was a remnant from another decade. In the 1960s, the Cuban Missile Crisis had the country on edge, but it put the fear of the Apocalypse into South Florida. Citrus Glade had gone whole hog on Civil Defense and hollowed out the basement of City Hall into a bomb shelter, complete with hermetically sealed doors, air conditioning/recirculation and a generator that was also a backup for City Hall. Those townspeople were going to survive the bomb so they could slowly starve to death in America's radioactive remains. Access was through ground-level storm shelter doors against the building's east side.

"It's ready," Andy said. "I cleaned it up last month. MREs and water and first aid supplies are still stockpiled from when Hurricane Katrina brushed the area. I kicked on the generator and it checks out."

Flora sat up straighter in her chair. She could make this happen. She just needed to let everyone know the shelter would be open. She punched a button on the intercom on her desk, another technological leftover.

"Serina?" she asked her receptionist/clerk. "Can you set up a reverse 911 call for me?"

Serina clicked back amid some background static. "Sure. And tell

Andy that Pete McNichol just called with two gator carcasses for pickup."

"Well," Andy said as he stood, "looks like we both have a busy morning ahead."

Pete McNichol's house was out past the town limits, north on CR 12 but south of the canal. Technically he was out of Andy's limited jurisdiction and the county should have hauled away the gator carcasses. But Pete told Serina that the county was too busy with hurricane prep to help him out and there was a duo of dead gators there. Andy knew that at seventy-eight, the frail man wasn't going to have someone else to turn to.

He pulled up in front of the concrete-block bungalow and there wasn't a carcass in sight. Well, Pete didn't say they were in the front yard, but if they weren't by the road, did they die of heart attacks?

He opened the door of his truck and the front door of the house flew open in response. Pete McNichol stood there barefoot. He looked even smaller than he was in blue jeans and a baggy white shirt. He wore a pair of large, thick glasses. He waved at Andy like he was shooing gnats away.

"Hurry! Hurry!" he shouted in a reedy little voice.

Dead animals had a pretty flexible schedule, but Andy put a little spring in his step to accommodate the panicky man. Some people got so itchy around a carcass.

He stepped into the house. Pete slammed the door behind him. The place smelled of mothballs, something Andy was sure the government had long ago declared toxic.

"Thank God," he said. Pete pulled Andy toward the sliding glass doors that faced the backyard. "They are in the back. You have to take them away. They ate my poodle Alice. They stared at me all night after that. They've got to go."

"Whoa, whoa. These aren't dead?"

"Not yet. See, look at them out there."

Pete pointed to his backyard. The yard backed up to a small lake. Two ten-foot gators lay on the grass between the house and the water. They looked asleep. A thin rope ran from a pole in the ground near the house to a spot a few feet from the sleeping reptiles. The end of the rope was freshly frayed. Adios, little Alice. Who leaves bait like that tethered outside by a lake in Florida?

"Mr. McNichol, I don't have anything to kill them with. You told Serina they were dead."

"They will be," he said. "Wait."

He stepped into the living room and walked back in with an M-16 assault rifle. Andy jumped back.

"Hey! What are you doing with that? Point that at the ground!"

Pete frowned and lowered the muzzle.

"I know how to handle a weapon, boy. Got this one after I got back from Nam. I'll go out and blast 'em, then you can haul them off. That'll keep the sons of bitches from staring at me."

The old man's hands shook as he held the rifle. He squinted at Andy though his glasses. Pete couldn't hit the pond, let alone the gators, especially being so upset about his dog.

"I'll take care of it, Mr. McNichol."

Pete looked Andy in the eye, then out the door at the gators. He handed Andy the gun. Andy hadn't touched an assault rifle in a long time. By choice. He remembered the familiar plastic feel of the butt stock and hand grips. It did not feel good.

Andy did have the state permits to shoot nuisance gators. He had to for the DPW. Of course he'd never done it. The county boys had too much fun with it. He really didn't think he'd have to do it now. If he went out there and made a ruckus, the gators would shuffle off back into the pond and everyone would be happy. He checked that the rifle was on safe. He noticed a lot of rust around the trigger. He stepped out the back door.

The gators were adults, a bit smaller than the one Andy pulled off the road a few days ago. Only folks near the top of the food chain could rest so easily in the open. Time to shoo them home.

"Hey gators!" Andy yelled. He stomped his feet on the ground. He slapped his hand against the rifle's butt stock.

The gators' eyes stayed shut.

Alligators could move fast as a horse when they wanted to, especially short distances. Andy wasn't going to get any closer. He did have a very expensive noisemaker in his hands. He flipped off the safety. He checked the chamber. The crazy old man had already chambered a round. Andy brought the rifle to his shoulder.

Multiple flashbacks flipped through his mind. Basic training, qualification ranges, arms room details, dusty desert roads, ambush responses. Sweat beaded on his brow. His heart hammed out a rapid beat. He sighted down the barrel at the ground a few feet in front of the gators. He exhaled and squeezed the trigger.

The rifle popped and he caught the familiar, unwelcome smell of burnt cordite. The round punched the ground in front of the gators and sprayed their noses with sand. Their eyes popped open. They blazed bright aquamarine.

"Holy shit," Andy gasped. The rifle barrel drifted downward.

"Told ya they stared at me!" Mr. McNichol yelled from the doorway.

The gators bellowed and charged. Their mouths opened to reveal pink tongues surrounded by rows of gleaming white teeth. They moved fast.

Andy reacted before he could think. He brought the rifle to bear and fired. One round right, one round left, back and forth. Chunks of flesh flew from the gators as bullets hit the mark. A bullet hit one gator in the foreleg and blasted it clean away. The gator lurched downward and its momentum dug its jaw into the sand. Andy drew down on the second one and sent three rounds into its midsection. The impact rolled the gator on its back and it fell still.

The first gator raised itself up on three feet and opened its mouth with a hiss. Andy sent a round down its throat. The bullet tumbled through the animal's body and exited at the other end, severing the back half of its tail in an explosion of blood and flesh.

Andy took a few steps back and rested against the side of the house. What in the hell was that?

Mr. McNichol walked over to the tailless gator carcass and gave it a kick. "Serves you right for eating Alice, you son of a bitch." Tears welled in his eyes. His hands shook.

Andy felt sorry for the old man, living out here in the middle of nowhere, wife gone on to whatever was beyond our mortal horizon, and now his dog, *their* dog eaten by some leftover from the age of dinosaurs. He cleared the rifle and snapped it to safe. He handed it back to Mr. McNichol. The old man shook his head.

"Hell, you had better keep it. I shot a hole in the wall with it last night. Why do you think I waited for you to get here to shoot the damn things?"

Andy slung the rifle across his shoulder, a move that felt more familiar and far less foreboding doing it than he'd expected. He headed back to the truck and wondered if the two carcasses would fit in the bed.

In the short time he had been here, the sky's horizons had filled with dark, bellicose thunderheads.

Chapter Forty-Four

Vicente Ferrer stared out the shop window at the worsening weather. He'd lived his whole life around the Caribbean and had never seen a storm this strong blow up so fast. His mother would have blamed a vengeful God.

Vicente had woken up this morning fully wired. Well before coffee could take credit, his mind had hit full speed. He was amped up on something and ready to get things in order. There was something under his skin, some itch he couldn't define that needed to be scratched.

Vicente's big concerns were about the damage the hurricane might bring. Not the damage to Ferrer Motors and his inventory, but to the government property he had a special interest in. The NSA tower was rated for hurricane strength winds he had been told, but that promise was a bit too vague. If something went wrong out there, the NSA would have repair crews on it before he knew, and those crews would surely find the little modifications he and Squirrelly had put into place. He didn't want to put a kink in that new revenue stream.

His cell phone rang and displayed a blocked number. He gritted his teeth. His unlisted cell only got calls from one blocked number.

"Hello."

"Vicente, amigo." Raoul's voice had the usual cheery familiarity to it. Like the playful yip of a pit bull before it clamped on your arm.

"Raoul. Good to hear from you."

"Our delivery had better be on time."

Way to cut to the chase.

"Boss, Hurricane Rita's beating us to death here." A premature assessment, but Raoul was on another continent.

"Hurricane Rita don't mean shit," Raoul rumbled. "You don't need to worry about that storm. You need to worry about the storm we'll unleash if our shipment is a minute late in Macon. And the storm will double if the shipment is light again."

Son of a bitch. That shit couldn't have been light. Unless that twat Juliana made a personal withdrawal from the Bank of Colombia after hours.

"No problems, Boss. It will be there. On time. All of it."

"It better be or the driver won't come back in one piece." Vicente was always the driver. The line went silent.

This was ten pounds of shit in a five-pound bag. The Colombians needed that coke to roll to Georgia. The Ukrainians had already put a deposit down on the data that was about to flow their way. He needed a clone. Instead he had...

"Juliana!"

She wandered in from the shop office. She had abandoned her trailer for the relative safety of Ferrer Motors' concrete-block construction. He marched over to her, pulled the truck keys from his pocket and shoved them in her hand.

"You're driving to Macon."

"Cente, no!" she whined. "The weather, it's so bad. I cannot drive that truck. I don't even know where to go."

"Bullshit. I taught you to drive it and you drove it fine when we went up there last time. You've seen the route three times. Get in the cab and go."

"Northbound traffic will be hell..."

"No, our lives at the wrong end of the Colombians will be hell." He raised his arm as if to back-hand her. "Get the fuck out of here. Now!"

"I need some clothes," she surrendered. "Cente, let me get a bag. I'll be back. I swear."

"Pack a bag and get going," he said. This was one of the times he wished she'd pack a bag for good.

Juliana slunk out of the shop.

Vicente paced the garage floor and fumed at the idiot girl. She'd stolen from the Colombians. Could she do anything stupider? We'll if she'd skimmed a bit off the top this time, she'd be there to pay the price when the Colombians weighed it up. They'd get retribution. He'd get rid of her. He'd be square with the syndicate. South American problem solved.

Next issue, the tower. He dialed Squirrelly's cell phone. Voicemail picked up.

"Dude, it's Squirrelly. Rita's on her way, so I'm heading north today. Leave a message."

Vicente pounded the *end* button before the annoying beep sounded. The weasel had skipped out ahead of the storm. He was the only one who could pull the skimmer off properly.

Did everything have to be such a problem? When he finally blew out of this town, he was hiring better help.

Chapter Forty-Five

The firmament foretold a horror story to come.

By the afternoon, Autumn saw all the signs. Clouds raced across the sky in great counterclockwise bands like phantom cars on a tight circular track, darkened with the growing energy they absorbed. Then there would be wind and rain and darkness. Irregular gusts of wind already blasted her Everglades outpost. They would get worse before they got better.

She had caught fuzzy pixelated snips of the Miami TV weathercasts and the weathermen were shooting straight. This storm was going to be major and it was going to be local.

Oscar sat on the steps just inside the open RV side door. His eyes were closed, his mouth slightly open as he sniffed the air. He spit out a half-sneeze and settled down into a compact little hunch, fur stiffened. He took up watch over the swaying wetland grasses.

Autumn thought her location would be okay to ride out the storm. It took a lot of rain to raise the water levels of the broad shallow swamp and the rise she was on was several feet above the waterline. There were no large trees to come crashing down on her little metal shell of a home and she could reposition it into the wind as the storm shifted. Better to ride it out here.

As she uploaded the morning's observations, Oscar let loose a low defensive growl.

"Oscar?" She rose and stuck her head out the door. The cat was hunkered down on the stoop, the fur along his spine bristled like a feline Mohawk, ears back against his head and streamlined for combat. His tail snapped back and forth.

An enormous python lay coiled at the base of the steps, head raised in striking position. Its black tongue flicked through the air to taste the range to its feline target. Autumn caught her breath when she saw its eyes. They were a piercing bright blue.

Her maternal instinct smothered the scientist in her. She grabbed the shovel by the door and leapt over Oscar. He dove behind her into the trailer.

The snake hissed. Autumn hit the ground and the snake rocketed forward like a brown/green comet. She flicked the shovel up just in time to shield her neck. The snake's head hit the spade with a clang, like it had been struck with a hammer. The impact bent Autumn's wrists. She sidestepped and lowered the shovel, expecting to see a dead snake.

Instead it lay coiled for a second strike. Its mouth gaped open to expose needle-sharp fangs. Blood poured down from a gash between its eyes, unfazed and burning blue. It struck again.

Autumn swung like a baseball player. The shovel rang as it struck the snake's skull. The upswing sent the snake's head in a wide arc. It dropped down on its back, lighter belly exposed, head cocked at an unsurvivable angle. Its eyes were dark.

Oscar wailed and Autumn whirled in his direction. A second snake girdled the cat's midsection. Orange fur stuck out between the tightening coils. Oscar snapped in vain at the scaly tail that writhed out of reach. To his rear, the python's head rose to strike, blue eyes focused on the back of the cat's neck.

Autumn launched the shovel like a javelin. The blade struck the snake below the head and then pinned it to the side of the RV. Its coils unraveled and the freed cat sunk its teeth into the snake's underbelly. The python's head, not quite severed by the blade, snapped back and forth in a futile search for revenge. Its eyes went dark and it dropped with a thump on the steel blade.

Oscar gave the carcass a hiss and bounded through the RV door. Underbrush rustled behind her. Autumn spun around. Seven snakes slithered in her direction, fourteen blazing points of blue locked on her and closing fast.

She yanked the shovel from the gash in the RV's side. The severed snake head lay in the shovel. The scientist in her surfaced for a split second and she flicked the head and the shovel through the doorway. She bounded in and slammed the door behind her. A python hit the tiny door window with a crack. The glass shattered but held.

Autumn scrambled into the driver's seat. Through the panoramic front windows she saw that pythons surrounded the RV. If some suicidal snake did break any of the glass...

She flicked the ignition key. The dash lights dimmed with each labored turn of the starter. The gauge said the batteries were fully charged. She pumped the accelerator and tried again. The motor turned even slower.

Not now, she thought. *C'mon, Porky! You always start first try!*

A snake pounded against the side of the RV. Out the left window, a python coiled for a puncturing strike at the RV's front tire. Autumn's heart raced.

She jammed the ignition key toward the dash. The starter uttered a long loping moan with each labored turn of the engine. The cranking wound slower and slower. The dash lights went dark.

Suddenly, the engine roared to life. A wet ripping sound splattered under her feet. Twin red sprays of python vomited from the RV's front wheel wells as the fan blade shredded an under-hood snake. Autumn threw the shifter into drive and floored it. The RV spun a plume of sand behind it and lumbered forward. Autumn cut the wheel and the behemoth lurched sideways as it headed for the highway. The front wheels hit a python the size of a speed bump and Autumn slammed against the steering wheel with the impact. But momentum carried the day and the RV made its escape to the highway.

Autumn swung the RV south to hit Alligator Alley and civilization. She came to an immediate stop at the small truss bridge over the canal. Pythons with glowing blue eyes covered it.

She'd seen collections of snakes before, often coiled together for mating or warmth. But these giants weren't a writhing mass. They were a concerted collective, wrapped around the trusses and intertwined like bread bag tie-wraps. The snakes contracted and the trusses buckled inward with the shrieking wail of shearing metal. The trusses went horizontal and the bridge collapsed with a crash into the canal. Thirty feet of air separated Autumn from her escape.

She piloted the RV through a swaying U-turn and went with Plan B. She headed north into Citrus Glade.

Oscar jumped up into the passenger seat and meowed. He put both paws on the dashboard and scanned out the front window. Python blood matted the white bib on his chest.

Chapter Forty-Six

Autumn didn't see another car on the deserted streets of Citrus Glade. When she passed the Food Bonanza, she knew why. The lot was full to overflowing, everyone in town stocking up on supplies. The WAMM weatherman's warnings had not fallen on deaf ears here. Rain squalls had blasted her on the way into town and the sky had grown noticeably, ominously darker.

Autumn was better stocked for the inevitable power outages and foodstuff shortages. The RV powered itself and she had food laid in for at least a week, if canned would be okay. She didn't feel the need to fight that crowd. What she did want to do was take a better look at the snake head on the floor of the RV. Something had made it go homicidal.

She rolled down Main and looked for a parking spot with a bit of privacy to examine the snake's severed head. One big lot had a street sweeper and a rusting dump truck in it. The space between the dump truck and a building wall looked pretty secluded. She spun the wheel and nosed the RV into its temporary home.

Once they parked, Oscar left his co-pilot perch and trotted back to the python's head just ahead of Autumn. He gave it two perfunctory sniffs and a low growl. He looked up at Autumn.

"Thanks, boy," she said. "I can take care of myself from here."

Oscar retreated to an overwatch position on the kitchen table. Autumn scooped up the python head and set it on the countertop. She pulled her dissection kit from one of the drawers and rolled it open.

The snake's neck was a ragged bloody mess where the shovel blade had worked with less than surgical skills. The jaw hung partly agape.

Its eyes were open, but the lenses concave, as if the blue fire within them had boiled something away when it departed.

She removed a scalpel and flipped the head upside down. She cut away the lower jaw and what was left of the trachea. With a few slices through the upper pallet she exposed the snake's brain.

She'd seen plenty of snake brains in her studies, usually about the size of a grape. She'd never seen one like this. The organ was black, like a tiny charred lump of coal. Snakes didn't do much thinking with this undersized organ, but in this condition it wouldn't do any. It looked like something had supercharged the brain from the inside and smoked every synapse.

Three sharp bangs on the RV door broke her concentration. She opened it to see her friend from the Citrus Glade DPW.

"I wondered if you would find some shelter with the hurricane brewing," Andy said.

"This is a cozy little spot for Porky, but I hadn't planned on staying here long."

"Well, technically it's illegal to park in the city lot," Andy said. He gave the lot a dramatic inspection. "But there may be an extra space I can spare." He gave her blood-striped wheels a sideways look. "What happened here?"

"You wouldn't believe it," Autumn started.

Attacks by pythons. Snakes destroying a bridge. *She* barely believed it. But that didn't make it untrue. She relayed the story of her day, showed him the remains of the snake. He didn't call her crazy.

"You might want to check these out," he said. "Bring the tools of your trade."

Autumn followed him to the tailgate of his pickup truck. A gust of wind delivered a spray of thick raindrops. Two gators lay in the rear. Andy told her his story. She was relieved that she wasn't the only target of Mother Nature's apparent rampage.

"You want to check out their brains?"

"Hell, yeah! I'll be right back."

The weather wasn't conducive to a measured autopsy but all she needed to know was going to be right inside the skull anyway. She grabbed a small battery-powered saw and a rib spreader. By the time she got back, Andy had a blue tarp tied over the bed of the truck like a tent.

"Dead animals and a tarp shelter," Autumn teased. "You know how to worm your way into a scientist's heart, don't you?"

Andy's cheeks reddened a bit.

They both climbed into the protected bed. The claustrophobic humid air smelled like algae and blood.

Autumn flicked on the tiny saw. It spun into action with a high-pitched whir. She started at the top of the skull and sawed a stripe down the center to the tip of the snout. She inserted the rib spreader and twisted. The head popped open a few inches.

"Unreal," she muttered.

Andy stuck his head in under the tarp. "Prognosis, Doc?"

"See this?" She pointed to a mass of blackened tissue about the size of three olives. "That's the brain."

"In all that head?"

"Alligators are all sinus," she said. "This is all they have to think with. And this one's fried. Cerebellum, medulla oblongata." She prodded the inside with the screwdriver blade. "The pituitary looks like an exploded balloon, which would account for some of the behavior you saw. Something got inside this gator's head and pushed the overdrive button. Just like the pythons."

"Something like what?" Andy said.

Autumn gave the charred brain another poke. Rain pounded against the plastic over her head as the storm worsened.

"Like something I can't explain."

Chapter Forty-Seven

Gridlock.

From Key West to central Florida, the population's prudent retreat had descended into panic. Announcers said *Rita* on the weather reports, but people heard *Katrina.* Twelve lanes of I-95 through Dade County became a long thin parking lot as rain-induced accidents blocked entire sections. Evacuees switched to surface streets and the gridlock spread like blood poisoning to the smaller thoroughfares. A firefight broke out on a bridge from a barrier island when a man in a black and chrome Hummer tried for a quick return to his home around the police blockade. At noon, the governor addressed the state, but particularly the residents of the Keys. He told them to sit tight. A1A was a Gordian knot of vehicles, backed up all the way from the mainland when hundreds of cars ran out of gas. He warned them that if they walked the Overseas Highway, there was still no place to go. Even the shelters were moving north.

Tens of thousands were trapped in the evacuation. Millions more watched the chaos and opted to forego it. Stores sold out of everything, alcohol of course being the first to go. Customers fought over what remained. Some long timers remembered Hurricane Andrew and this one would be ten times worse. The mayor of Miami-Dade imposed a curfew. The collective clicks of rounds being chambered and dead bolts locking echoed across the state.

All along both coasts, boats tore from their moorings as absentee owners had no time to reinforce the lines. Epic winds drove waves ashore that tossed the boats into piles. Entire marinas ripped their pilings from the ground and balled up into heaps of shattered fiberglass and smashed planking.

Small power outages in the morning grew into major blackouts by the afternoon. Crews, daunted by the worsening weather and the frozen traffic, did not venture out to make repairs. People with battery-powered radios heard the boiled water alerts that every city issued. Errant candles started dozens of fires that burned until the hurricane's downpour quenched the flames.

An awful realization spread among the people huddled in dark corners of their homes or cowering under blankets in their bathtubs. No power. No water. No food but what they had on hand. Civilization had deserted them and if the storm did the damage everyone foretold, it would not return for a long time.

Chapter Forty-Eight

A curtain of rain fell and pounded the pavement outside. Juliana looked at that and then back at her livid boyfriend. She ducked her head and chose to face the elements. She ran though the downpour and climbed into the truck cab.

The diesel rumbled to life. The truck departed with a grind of the gears and a splash through a newly formed puddle. Juliana gripped the wheel so hard her knuckles went white. She was so good to Cente and in payment he told her to drive forty thousand pounds of steel through a hurricane.

Rain lashed the windscreen like intermittent cracks of a whip. Her eyes felt heavy and her arms were like lead. She'd been high most of the day and the resultant energy crash was on its way. She wasn't going to make it to Macon in one day at this rate. She was going to need a little help, the same help that had gotten her through so much in the past.

She pulled over and slipped a baggie from her pocket. The white powder inside was damn near pure. The Colombians might cut it with filler once it got into the states, but they weren't going to ship it in that way. There was no comparison between it and the watered-down blow she used to do in Liberty City as a kid. She tapped a line onto the truck's center console and rolled a scrap of paper into a tiny tube.

When she inhaled the powder, every synapse in her brain caught fire. Her senses amped up to max. Colors got brighter, sounds got crisper. Above all, she was flush with energy, a boundless unbridled surge so powerful she felt like she was floating. Now she was ready to drive.

Another wave of rain pelted the windshield and she flicked the wipers on. The low speed was too slow, not for the rain, but for her senses and she switched it to high. She checked the side mirror six times, though the road was deserted, and pulled back onto CR 12. Her muscles jittered as the cocaine fueled them. She ground each gear as her left leg danced on the clutch.

CR 12 was a flat straight stretch north of town and despite the increasing rain, she hit sixty-five mph in no time. She thrummed her hands on the wheel in time to some beat that pounded in her head.

The rain picked up but it didn't register. Her mind raced. She saw the route up I-75, figured the miles, calculated the time. She could make it. She *would* make it. Nothing could stop her now at the wheel of the big rig. Cops would be busy with hurricane stuff. She would power through the weather, weave through the traffic, move like the wind.

She'd go so fast she could *create* time. Like that freaking movie with the DeLorean. She needed to do eighty-eight and, wham, she'd be flying. She pushed the accelerator to the floor.

Then when she got back, she would have proven herself worthy. She and Cente would blow out of this cesspool of a town. They'd live like royalty on the beach with a snowstorm worth of coke. Awesome.

She drove into a downpour and the windshield looked like a waterfall. Each frenzied sweep of the wipers cleared a split-second view of the watery road. No problem. She had it under control. She didn't need to see the road. She could feel it. She was one with it. The truck hit ninety.

The wheel tingled in her fingers. A swipe of the wipers flashed a yellow sign that said *Slow–Bridge Ahead*. That was the big canal north of town. She was making great time.

The truck powered over the little rise to the steel truss span. The wheel relaxed in her hands. Juliana thought how smooth the bridge surface was.

Then the cab nosed forward. The bridge wasn't smooth. It was missing, crushed like its sister on the south side of town. The cab splashed nose first into the rushing water of the rain-swollen canal.

She had a moment of hope when she hung horizontal by her seatbelt in the cab, still above the shallow churning canal. Then the trailer plowed forward and thousands of pounds of steel and plastic crushed the cab like an empty soda can.

Chapter Forty-Nine

Barry Leopold had lived the last twenty-four hours in and out of some blissful, hallucinogenic dream. Every minute he did magic shifted between crystal clarity and utter nonsense.

Yesterday, after Lyle's incantations, he felt like he'd floated out of the Magic Shop. He'd feigned illness when his mother got home. Her overprotective genes kicked in and she confined him to his room. As she slept that night, he used the hat.

Lizards, mice, turtles. The hat gave birth to a veritable ark of tiny creatures into the early morning hours. He collapsed into bed in ecstatic exhaustion.

His mother checked on him before she left for work. She let him sleep. The weather was turning nasty and she figured she would be sent home early.

Barry awakened later to a fuzzy recollection of recent events. But he knew he'd been on a magnificent high and the only way to continue it was with the magic hat. The more he performed, the better this flying carpet ride would be.

He locked the door behind him, a strict no-no in the Leopold household, but weren't they beyond all that now? He pulled the hat out of his desk drawer and popped it open. Just the sound of the hat snapping into place made him coo with pleasure, anticipating the rush about to come. He draped the first thing he could find, a dirty T-shirt, across the top.

He wondered what to conjure, what creature to call forth. He fell back to the cliché, a rabbit. A cute little bunny.

"*Bakshokah apnoah,*" he said as he waved his hand over the hat in a lazy oval.

A charge hit his heart like a bolt of lightning and telegraphed that the rabbit had materialized. He moaned in ecstasy. He pulled away the shirt and looked into the hat's black recess. Two aquamarine eyes glowed back from the darkness. The oddity of it did not register.

He reached into the hat. In his dreamlike state, all he felt was a bit of a pinch to his index finger. He extracted his hand and to his great surprise, his finger was gone. Blood burbled from the gash where something jagged had chopped away all below the first knuckle. He stared at his damaged digit with only the vaguest comprehension. Like a child with a boo-boo, he put his finger into his mouth. He cocked one eye and peered into the hat. Two bright blue dots stared back. The creature growled like gravel in a metal pan and leapt straight up. The rabbit cleared the brim of the hat before the dazed boy could react.

The mangy gray beast had ragged, asymmetrical ears. Twin rows of tiger shark teeth ringed its open mouth. It clamped on Barry's nose.

Pain exploded straight into his brain and swept Barry's confusion away. He shrieked. Blood spurted from both sides of the rabbit's mouth as its teeth dug deeper. Barry panicked, grabbed the hare from hell with both hands and yanked. The rabbit tore his nose from his face with a sickening moist rip.

Barry dropped the wriggling creature. He grabbed his face and his severed finger slid into the gaping hole above his mouth. Blood sprayed out like a fire hose. Barry stepped back, tripped and landed on his ass on the floor.

The hat spun two full revolutions and toppled on one side, the opening facing Barry. Inside a constellation of bright blue eyes bobbed and weaved. He screamed.

More rabbits charged. A half-dozen of them bounded out of the hat like a migrating infestation. They leapt straight for Barry.

The horde bowled him over, enveloping him. Each rabbit bared its serrated teeth and tore a chunk of flesh from his body. Before he could process the horror of it all, one rabbit clamped down on his neck and ripped his carotid artery free. Barry went motionless.

The rabbits did not mourn. In unison, they leapt from the floor, aimed at Barry's bedroom window. The glass shattered and the stampede burst out into the night, a fleeting mass of wet, gray fur lit with bright blue eyes. The swarm raced southward through the rain-soaked backyard in a beeline for downtown.

In front of the house, Barry's mother's car pulled up.

Wind whipped rain through Barry's broken window and the white curtains fluttered like twin spirits of the night. The drops rinsed the blood from the wounds on Barry's face and left the visage of a confused, nose-less boy staring up at the ceiling. One of the lenses of his glasses was shattered.

Two sharp raps sounded at Barry's door.

"Barry?" his mother called. "Are you alright? Open this door!"

The bedroom door burst open. Over the howling wind, none of the neighbors heard Mrs. Leopold's scream.

Chapter Fifty

Paco Mason hadn't been home.

He'd left the Magic Shop and wandered a random route through town, not fully aware of where he was or where he was going. Everything around him looked like it was shattered and re-assembled, a kaleidoscope of bits and pieces of a world he no longer inhabited.

He arrived back at his house that afternoon. This world of disjointed shards was strange, but familiar. He walked through his house with light, fluid steps. He flourished his wand in great loopy arcs as he flitted from room to room in a strange combination that was half modern dance and half orchestral conductor, all in time with some lilting, unheard music. Each time the intoxicating power that coursed within him waned, he tapped a passing object with his wand. *Bakshokah korami.* It vanished in a puff of flame and smoke. A release of magic flowed down and out from its home and a sliver of it reinforced the high that propelled him around the house.

His mother came in the front door out of the storm. He just saw her as slices, an eyeball here, a hand there, all flitting like a flurry of multi-colored snowflakes that never quite made a full design.

Her voice came as if it had been shattered and reassembled out of order. Random, choppy syllables. The phrases made no sense but he understood the tone. Harsh. Angry. Threatening.

Her anger intruded on the blissful world that encased him. If she didn't calm down she would ruin everything.

Suddenly her face reassembled from its fractured pieces and broke through his haze. Inches from his, she looked scared. She screamed his name as she shook the front of his shirt.

"Paco, what's wrong with your eyes? Stop this, now!"

Stop? He couldn't. He wouldn't.

He tapped her forehead with the wand.

"Bakshokah korami."

She vaporized and a thrilling rush consumed him. She was the biggest thing he'd vanished. Bigger felt better. He floated over to the couch and tapped it.

"Bakshokah korami."

He shuddered with the surge as the couch flamed and turned to mist. He tapped a table, a chair. Sulphurous smoke fogged the room. Paco's mouth hung open. Drool dripped onto his shirt. Oh, bigger felt *so* much better.

The whole house. What if he could vanish the whole house? He tapped the wand to the wall.

"Bakshokah korami."

Flames burst around him, the fire that he had always admired from afar. He was now part of it, within it.

The last second of his life was perfect.

The house and a good chunk of the ground around it disappeared in an orange flash and a pall of smoke, leaving a sandy crater behind. Rain splattered the sides and ran down to the bottom. Water collected and as it rose it covered a single gold coin and a black wooden wand.

Chuck Vreeland rolled over on the living room couch. Wind whistled through the eaves of the house. The damn storm wasn't over yet. His plan was to drink himself into a stupor for the whole thing. The plan wasn't working.

He swung his legs down and kicked a few empty beer cans across the floor. His distended stomach rolled onto his lap. His head spun a bit as he righted himself. Time to renew the fading buzz. He grabbed the open can on the end table and swallowed the last few flat, warm ounces. That wasn't going to cut it.

Lucky for him, he'd stocked up for the emergency. Two cases of beer and three bags of Cheetos from the Food Bonanza. No hurricane was going to starve him out. He wobbled to the kitchen to refuel.

Light shined out from all around the edges of his son Zach's door. The house had lost power before he fell asleep. If the kid had a way to power his computer for video games but his father had to drink warm beer... He lumbered down the hall and threw open the door to Zach's room.

"How the fu–"

He hadn't had enough to drink to explain this away. Three glowing silver rings floated in front of Zach as he sat at his desk. His head rolled in a lazy circle in sync with the spinning rings. His eyes were a solid blue milky haze.

In his alcohol-addled state, all these inexplicable components became background noise to a lone observation. His pistol lay on the desk. The gun that he kept locked up. The one that violated his parole. He charged in to retrieve it.

"Now boy, how the hell did you get my–"

As soon as he crossed the threshold, Zach turned to him with his unfocused, clouded eyes. He pulled the gun off the desk and fired at his father without aiming.

The bullet pierced Chuck's forehead between the eyebrows and the force threw him back into the hall. He was dead before he hit the floor.

Zach placed the smoking gun back precisely where it lay before. He stared back up at the spinning rings.

To the magic, Chuck's fleeting interruption was nothing of the sort. Power flowed unimpeded along the Vreeland house pipes and out to the cavern below the Apex plant.

Chapter Fifty-One

By afternoon the sky was black as coal. Gusty winds swept through Felix's orange grove and bounced the trees back and forth like a child would a rattle. Standing on the front porch, he worried that the wind would strip his renewed crop of oranges from the branches and leave him no better off than before the miracle had blessed him.

But his bigger worry was for his wife Carlina. She had left for the Reverend Rusty's revival early that morning and he had not heard from her since. The hurricane forming around them made the idea of an outdoor revival suicidal. He hoped the Rev would have enough common sense to call it off. After all, weather is an act of God. The Almighty couldn't be sending *that* mixed a signal.

He tried his cell phone for the third time since noon. Another fast busy signal. Every circuit was jammed. Cell service had overloaded as soon as the evacuation orders were posted.

The WAMM News at Noon showed evacuation traffic snarls that stretched up both coasts. The Overseas Highway from the Keys was one long parking lot. For once, it paid to be in the middle of nowhere. No evacuation traffic would run up CR 12. Citrus Glade was the focal point of what everyone was trying to escape, ground zero of hell.

He couldn't stand the waiting. He had a feeling Carlina was in trouble and he needed to get her home.

He entered the house. A gust of wind shook the rafters above him. The sky was almost dark as night. Power had been out for an hour and Angela colored by flashlight in the shadowy living room. She turned to face her father when he entered.

"Where's Mommy?"

There's the million dollar question, he thought.

"She's in town. Where's your brother?"

"In his room. As usual."

Dim blue light flickered out from under the doorway of his son's room. A hurricane rocked the house on its spindly foundation and Ricky was playing some hand-held video game, instead of out here with his sister. A sad day in the Arroyo household when the youngest daughter is the one with her head on straight. Enough was enough.

Felix threw open the door to his son's room and stopped dead in the threshold.

Ricky sat at his desk, hands in the air, eyes staring at and through his desk. Glowing playing cards moved across the desk unaided. A row of cards flipped over and back. Two piles shuffled in slow motion. The six of diamonds rose up on one point and pirouetted like a ballerina.

"*Santa Maria!*" Felix rushed in and yanked Ricky back from the desk. The boy did not react. Felix grabbed Ricky's face, turned it up to his and shook.

"Ricardo! What are you doing? *Mirame!*"

Nothing.

Felix grabbed Ricky at the shirt collar and raised his hand to strike some sense into him. Visions of his own father flashed through his mind, memories of this scene from the reverse point of view. He dropped Ricky like he was on fire, then wrapped him in his arms.

"Ricky," he whispered in the boy's ear. "It's your father. Wake up."

Ricky shivered in Felix's arms. Felix pulled back a few inches. The cards fluttered to a stop on the desk and the blue glow dissipated.

"Dad?" Ricky looked confused.

Felix swept the cards into a pile and held them in front of Ricky.

"What are these? Where did you get them?"

"Cards," Ricky mumbled. "The Magic Shop. Just a trick..." His eyes fluttered closed.

Magic. Real, dark magic. Like he'd heard that the *Santa Muerte* cult of the Mexican drug gangs practiced. There were miracles from

God and there were those that were not. God did not mess with playing cards. He shoved the deck in his back pocket and lifted his semi-conscious son into bed. The cards felt warm.

The Magic Shop. What had Carlina said about it? Something about the Reverend's bad feelings. Why hadn't he paid more attention? So worried about the harvest...

Well, he had his priorities straight now. He'd put a stop to whatever his son had dipped into. He needed his family back together, safe at home, now. He couldn't wait for Carlina's return. He went back to the living room.

"Listen," Felix said to Angela. "Your brother is asleep in his room. You two stay here. The storm will get worse and you do not need to be outside. I'm going to get your mother. I'll be right back. *No candles* until we get back." The last thing he needed was to return to a burning house. "Got it?"

"No candles, check."

He kissed Angela on the forehead and went out the door.

Felix saw three cars on the way into town, all heading south for an escape via Alligator Alley. But inside the dusky city limits, Citrus Glade was uninhabited. Food Bonanza was closed, but from the looks of the shelves through the window it might have been due to low inventory as much as the growing storm. Even the Zippee Mart was closed and that place was open on Christmas Day.

He pulled up to the Congregation of God Church just in time. Carlina and two other women were locked in a desperate rain-swept battle to keep the revival tent from going airborne. The wind had unstaked one end and now flapped the tent like a horizontal flag. The revival crew clung to the upwind ropes. Carlina's panicked face turned relieved when she saw Felix's truck.

The snapping canvas and the high wind made speaking impossible. Felix ran to the tent and dropped the remaining upwind tent poles. The canvas went flat and Carlina and her assistants wrestled it to the ground. The four of them rolled it up like a giant burrito. A wave of violent rain blasted across the lawn. With the tent under control, the other two women made a hunched dash to their cars in the parking lot. Felix followed Carlina into the church sanctuary.

Carlina wrapped her arms around her husband in a wet, appreciative hug.

"Thank God," she said. "We were trying to take down the tent when the far side broke free. We were about to ride that thing all the way to Sebring. Wait. Where are the kids?"

This wasn't the time to talk magic cards. He had those under control. He patted the back pocket of his jeans. Empty. He must have left them in the truck.

"The kids are home safe and sound," Felix said.

"Ricky and Angela alone? How could you think that was a good idea?"

"They're fine," he said. "You were the one I was worried about. Where's Reverend Wright in all this?"

"I don't know," Carlina said. "He wasn't here when we got here. No one had heard from him. Of course the phones *are* out..."

Something had happened to the Rev. This revival was his baby and there was no way he'd not be around for every step leading to its birth.

"Where would he go within walking distance?"

"The Magic Shop," Carlina said. "He was sure it was evil. He said there were secrets in there."

Felix knew the Rev was right about that.

Wind hit the side of the church hard enough to make the roof shudder. Rain lashed the windows.

"I'll go over and check it out," Felix said. "This storm will get worse long before it gets better." A fresh deluge hit the side of the church as if on cue. "Head home and take care of the kids. I'll be right behind you."

Back in the Arroyo house, Ricky opened his eyes. His mouth felt like a wad of cotton. His muscles ached. His temples throbbed in sync with his pounding pulse. Where was he? Why did he feel so...empty?

He closed his hand around the sharp edges of the magic cards. Oh, yes. The cards. He had been at his desk. Doing magic. The power. The ecstasy.

The coin in his pocket warmed. Ricky crawled out of bed and into his desk chair. He spread the deck of cards out on the desktop in one long, overlapping row.

"Bakshokah serat."

The cards stood on end like soldiers awakened to attention. Ricky's eyes turned an opaque blue and the cards began to dance.

Chapter Fifty-Two

Andy and Autumn had moved into the DPW office and out of the weather. Autumn watched rain lash the street through the window.

"How could they move?" Andy said.

"Who?" Autumn said.

"The snake, the gators. They had charcoal for a brain."

Autumn thought a moment. "Maybe only after they died. Whatever fueled them had no outlet and fried their gray matter. I'm guessing. None of it makes sense."

"Like the plant growth spurt along the water pipes."

"Or the sudden rise of a hurricane," Autumn said, "with the eye over Citrus Glade. Your little town here has issues."

"Only in the last week," Andy said. "This place has been listed under 'boring' in Wikipedia for years."

The office door opened. Felix stood there, soaked to the skin.

"Thank God you are here," he said. "I saw the truck in the lot. I need some help. Some backup."

"Doing what?"

"It will sound crazy."

"We're experts in crazy today," Autumn said.

Felix gave her a quizzical look.

"Autumn, Felix," Andy said. "Felix, Autumn. She's a biologist working the 'Glades."

Felix touched his hat and water splashed on the floor.

"It's the magician, Lyle," Felix said. "He gave my son magic cards.

Real magic. Float around and glow magic. It sounds nuts but I saw it myself. The Rev went to check out the Magic Shop last night and never came back."

"I can't believe he'd leave the church unattended in a storm like this," Andy said.

"Something bad happened," Felix said. "I want to check that shop and I need numbers on my side. And right now, you are the closest thing we've got to law enforcement."

Andy skipped adding some gallows humor about that confirming it was the end of times.

"Real magic?" he said. "You're sure?"

"I've seen it."

Andy glanced at Autumn to hear the voice of scientific reason.

"Hey," she said. "I can't explain the animals with the fried brains and glowing blue eyes, or the wild strips of growth along the water lines. I'm ready to call it magic."

"And all this started after Lyle Miller opened the Magic Shop," Andy said. "I met Lyle in passing and he made my blood run cold. Even my mother said he's creepy as hell."

"When all the probable answers are discounted," Autumn said, "you must consider the improbable."

"We'll check the place out," Andy said. He looked through the falling rain with concern. "But I don't trust the local wildlife."

"I'm their best friend, and I don't trust them," Autumn said.

"Wait one," Andy said.

Andy ducked out into the rain and returned with the M-16. Autumn looked impressed.

"Okay, John Rambo," she said. "*Now* I feel safe."

"I'm sensing you have a sarcastic streak."

"Really?"

"Ready when you are, Felix," Andy said.

They headed out and dashed through the waves of rain to the

Magic Shop's front door. Locked, of course. Andy shaded his eyes with his hands and tried to peer through the door glass. The low light made it difficult to see, but he swore the interior was empty. If the Rev thought there was something amiss, he wouldn't have seen it from here.

"This way," Felix said.

He followed Felix on a quick, splashing jog around back. The rear door stood open an inch. The buzz of flies echoed in the room. The hair on Andy's neck went to attention. He opened the door with the rifle's barrel. Rain splattered in and soaked the floor.

The darkened sky offered only the barest light and everything in the back room was little more than bulky shadows. He pawed at the wall until he found a switch. No power. He swung open the door to let in the waning daylight. He gasped.

A rectangular box about three feet long stood upright in a puddle of blood and organs. The Reverend's head popped out of the top of the box, though it was impossibly short for his body, like he was some twisted jack-in-the-box toy. His eyes had a cataract-like glaze of the dead.

"Oh, dear God." Autumn gasped.

"*Santa Maria,*" Felix said.

A duplicate box rested on four wheels to the left. The Reverend's feet protruded from one end. A large intestine snaked out of the other.

Andy averted his eyes. Horrific Afghanistan memories flashed by on fast forward. Bile rose in his throat like he was going to vomit. He sucked in a deep breath and spit the vile taste from his mouth.

He made a wide circle around the carnage in the room's center, Felix and Autumn right behind. Through the dried blood, he could make out the edges of some type of star painted on the floor. On a bench along the wall lay large yellowed architectural drawings. He flipped one over and then the next. They were floor plans. The legend on the lower right corner said APEX SUGAR.

"Oh God," Autumn muttered, transfixed by the Reverend's remains.

"Autumn," Andy said, "come check this out."

Autumn sidled over to the bench, eyes still glued to the two-piece body of the dead preacher. She finally cast her gaze to the drawings. "Apex Sugar. The stripe of growth heading south goes there. That could be it."

"Be what?" Felix said.

"The focal point," Andy said. "The birthplace of the hurricane and every other bit of hell this town has seen recently. From the looks of this place, Lyle Miller has been running some serious black magic through the town. I'm going to guess it's generating Hurricane Rita, the only hurricane to ever have no track. If the storm keeps building strength, it will scour both coasts clean."

"If Lyle isn't here, he'll be down there," Felix said.

"Then we had better go now while the roads are passable."

Movement in the doorway to the shop caught their eye and the three of them froze. A sheen of tiny blue dots were interspersed between the strings of beads. They pulsed, flickered and wavered, a narrow screen between the storeroom and the store floor. The dancing pointillist fabric shimmered and a high whining buzz overpowered the sound of the rain outside.

Autumn cocked her head with a look of vague recognition. She stepped to the doorway and extended a hand toward the opaque obstruction.

"If I didn't know better..." she said.

Two tiny blue dots, so close they appeared as one, broke formation from the doorway. They hovered and landed on the back of Autumn's hand. She pulled it back and up to her face to inspect it. Horror filled her eyes and she slapped the back of her hand. A drop of blood shot out between her fingers. Her head snapped around to face the others.

"Mosquitoes!"

Chapter Fifty-Three

If every dream was this good, Shane would never wake up.

He was back at the mill. The plant was in its prime and so was he. Stainless steel hoppers sparkled like new. Sunlight streamed in through crystal-clear polished glass. White tile covered the floor in alabaster precision. The wall clock said six-thirty and the wage slaves were about to start trickling in.

Shane felt as good as the mill looked. Not a joint ached, nary a muscle twinged. He saw his reflection in the side of one of the vats and guessed he was in his late twenties. The prime of his life.

The door to the main packing floor garnered his attention. A blue light pulsed behind it, a slow strobe that rose and fell in a familiar rhythm. There were no blue lights in the packing room. Someone was screwing around on his shop floor and he wasn't going to have it.

He marched over to the door. The pulsing light brightened. His ears throbbed. The familiar beat was in sync with his heart. He yanked open the door.

All the packaging equipment was gone. In the center of the room was that magician...Lyle someone. He stood inside a white star within a circle on the floor. The light behind him faded between light and dark blue. But there were no bulbs. Just the glow.

"How do you like it, Shane?" Lyle asked. His voice had a god-like reverb. "Are you enjoying my gifts?"

"Hell, yeah!" Shane gave his renewed arm muscles a flex. "You did this?"

Lyle reached out a hand and an aqua blue flame came to life above it. "Magic did it, Shane. Magic gives and also can take away."

He flicked his fingers at Shane and the flame leapt out at the renewed old man. It spun around his midsection like a living belt. Suddenly the grinding torment of osteoarthritis returned to all his joints. His knuckles swelled with enflamed pain. He winced and cradled his hands to his chest.

The flame split into two and raced down the inseam of his legs. It vanished into the floor. Then it felt like his legs vanished. Shane lost all sensation below the waist, the same familiar feeling that confined him to his hated wheelchair. A bone snapped like dry bamboo. He bellowed and collapsed on the floor.

"No," he shouted. His contorted face was rose-red with pain and rage. "I can't go back to this again!"

Lyle bent down and pulled Shane's face up to his. The magician's eyes were like opals.

"This is the source," Lyle said. "The Fountain of Youth flows right here. Get it while you can."

Shane woke up with a start, bathed in sweat. He sat up and touched his legs. Still felt 'em. Hot shit. He gave them a few test kicks. Still good as new.

That little encounter was no dream. It was a damn clear message. The pissant little magician was worth something after all. Whatever he had down at the Apex, Shane wanted more of it. A lot more.

He needed to get to the mill now, but first things first. It always paid to carve out a little time for some retribution. It just wasn't healthy to keep anger bottled up inside.

Time to get this party started.

Outside, Hurricane Rita raged. The emergency generator was all that kept Elysian Fields from being as dark as the rest of the neighborhood. Dispersed partial lighting lit the hallways.

Shane pushed the call button on the side of his bed. Just two quick beeps. Not enough to panic the reduced staff, but enough to get one to show up. He could imagine Dwayne the orderly leaving his hot coffee at the nurse's station, grumbling about having to help an old man to the bathroom. Jackass. Shane despised the night staff even more than the day staff. Any finger they lifted was such an inconvenience to them. Well, their permanent vacation was about to begin.

Dwayne stood backlit in Shane's doorway, white tunic a match for his pale complexion. The little pipsqueak had a pack of cigarettes in his shirt pocket, a transgression Nurse Coldwell would probably fire him for.

"What can I do you for, Shane?"

Shane cringed at Dwayne's familiar tone. Had some inversion of the world order suddenly made them equals?

"Give me a hand here," Shane said. "I just need to swing around to get out of bed."

"Sure thing."

Dwayne approached and passed out of the doorway's rectangle of light. Shane flipped back his covers. Dwayne grabbed Shane's calves and noticed Shane had on pants.

"Hey. How did you–"

The question got no further. Shane whipped one leg up and over. His foot roundhoused Dwayne with a crack. Dwayne's head snapped around and he dropped to the floor.

"Oh, what the..." he muttered as he touched the side of his face in shock.

Shane jumped out of the bed and whipped his oak cane out from under the covers. Dwayne raised his head into the open doorway's shaft of illumination. Shane smiled and gripped the tip of his cane like a baseball bat. Dwayne's head rose into the strike zone. Lyle swung for the fences.

The cane's heavy bronze hilt hit Dwayne's head with a muffled thwack. Teeth skittered across the floor. Dwayne's neck jerked to an abnormal, inverted angle. He hung there for a moment, then collapsed like an imploded building. Blood ran from his mouth and ear into a dark puddle. Pink brain seeped from a split in his skull. His chest didn't move.

Shane pulled the pack of cigarettes and a lighter from the departed orderly's tunic. He tapped one out of the pack and ran the white stick under his nose. Ah, that sweet smell of tobacco. How long had it been? He put the stick to his lips and lit it. He drew the smoke deep into his lungs. Ah, one of man's simple pleasures, denied by the do-gooder medical profession. He bent down and blew smoke into Dwayne's lifeless face.

"In the future," he said, "you will address me as Mr. Hudson."

He plucked a ring of keys from Dwayne's belt. He rested his cane on his shoulder and sauntered out into the hallway.

Shayla, the night nurse, looked up in surprise as Shane stepped behind the station counter.

"Mr. Hudson, what are you doing up?"

Shane brought the head of his cane down on her nose. Blood splattered all over her white uniform. She yelped and fell back in her chair. Shane flipped the cane around and plunged the tip through her heart and out through her back. She gurgled and gripped the cane's shaft. Blood darkened the front of her uniform in an expanding stain. Shane gave the cane an extra thrust. The nurse jerked like a hooked fish. Her hands fell to her sides and her head slumped forward.

Shane planted a foot against her chest and yanked his cane free. The bottom foot of the cane dripped the nurse's blood. He flicked a speck of brain off the head.

He dumped the nurse's pocket book on the counter and picked out her car keys. He was ready to make his escape from this prison. But until then...

He ran his finger along the switches at the nurse's station and stopped at the red one marked *LOCKDOWN*. He pressed it. A series of metallic clicks echoed from all around the building as the exterior doors sealed shut. The system was designed to keep any threat from entering, but Shane saw it as a way to keep any victim from leaving.

He pulled open the vestibule behind the station. He put on one of the long white lab coats within. The embroidered name on the chest said *Dr. Hal Griffin*. Shane grabbed a pen from the counter and overwrote the words to read *Dr. Death*.

He stood in the center of the hallway and twirled his cane like a drum major's baton.

"Elysian residents!" he announced. "The doctor has arrived."

Dr. Shane Hudson decided to start with some house calls. He had prescriptions to deliver. He unlocked the medicine locker and rummaged around to find something useful. He came across some amphetamines and popped one in his mouth. White Lightning they used to call it back when he ran the sugar plant and fourteen-hour shifts were the norm at high season. He put the rest in his pocket. Some for now, some for later. Wasn't that the slogan for some candy way back when?

He pawed through a box of pre-loaded syringes. Adrenaline. Hot shit. He wasn't going to mainline any of that himself. But he knew a few people who could really use the jolt.

Louis Webb woke up with fingers wrapped around his throat.

He choked and grabbed at his assailant. His feeble hands were no match for the powerful pair that threatened to close his windpipe. The ALS disease had taken too much of a toll.

In the dim light of his room, he tried to make out the face that hovered over his. Without his glasses it wasn't much more than a blur. He sputtered as he tried to choke out a question.

"Webb, you asshole," his attacker hissed.

There was no mistaking that voice. Shane Hudson. But he was standing over him. And strong as hell. That twisted bastard had been wheelchair bound for years.

"Shane?" he croaked.

"In the flesh," Shane answered. "Dropped by to repay a favor."

Louis' septuagenarian heart slipped a cog. He reached for the nurse call button and mashed it with his thumb. Shane laughed in response. He must have done something to the system. Or worse, to the nurses.

"So, Mr. 1st Federal Bank manager," Shane said. "Remember when the plant closed and your bank held my mortgage?"

Oh, God, no, Louis thought. *Not after so long.*

"I asked for a little mercy until I could get a new job," Shane said. His hand tightened as he spoke, as if the rising rage contracted his muscles. "Do you remember what you said?"

Louis gargled a few syllables. Shane shook Louis' head by the neck like a rag doll.

"You said, 'What goes around comes around.' Do you remember that?"

Of course he did. The whole town was happy to see the mighty Shane Hudson laid low.

"I thought you were a heartless bastard," Shane said. "Now I'm going to see if I was right. If I was, this won't hurt a bit."

Shane pulled a syringe from the lab coat pocket with his free hand. He bit the cover off the needle and spit it out. He twirled the syringe in his hand and drove it into Louis' bony chest.

A shaft of white pain ripped so deep into him that Louis was certain the needle had gone through to his back. Shane's iron grip on his throat stifled his scream. But his pain thus far would prove to be nothing.

Shane flipped his thumb over the needle's plunger and flashed a nefarious grin.

"Fire in the hole!" He laughed.

Shane squeezed the plunger. Louis' heart felt like it leapt out of his chest as adrenaline supercharged his tired muscles. The world went blank as his blood pressure spiked. His neurons went into mindless overdrive and spasms shot through his arms. A thousand memories flooded his mind, a rapid review before a fast-approaching final exam.

"Well, shit, I'm wrong," Shane said in a mock apology. He pinned Louis' neck harder into the mattress to keep his jerking body in the bed. "Looks like that adrenaline found a heart after all."

Shane kept Louis pinned to the bed for a good minute after his body stopped twitching, partly because he wanted to make sure he was dead, but mostly because it just felt good. Was there anything more satisfying than revenge?

Well, maybe one thing. And apparently after a several-decade hiatus, he was ready for that as well. The harder he choked Webb, the harder he'd gotten south of the beltline, and right now he was sporting a woodie to end all woodies. After years of disuse, he wasn't going to let that go to waste.

So now he had a serious to-do list. He had scores to settle with a lot of these inmates, first and foremost that world-class bitch Dolly Patterson followed by that big dumb Indian friend of hers, Chief Bear-Shit-In-The-Woods. He was going to need some help.

Lucky for him, he knew the two men for the job.

Shane kicked Denny Dean's bed hard enough that it slammed against the wall. Denny startled awake.

"Get up," Shane growled. "There's work to do."

Denny forced his eyes open. "Shane? You're standing." He saw Chester at Shane's side. "Chester. What time is it?"

Shane shoved two pills into Denny's hand. "Take these and get dressed."

"They're good shit," Chester said. His swollen pupils looked like black full moons. "Serious uppers straight from the nursing home stash."

This was like the old days. Shane used to hand out stimulants like candy when Apex ran overtime shifts. Denny popped them in his mouth and swallowed.

"Shane, how can you stand?"

"A miracle cure due to living a chaste life," Shane deadpanned. "C'mon. We're going to straighten a few things out."

Chapter Fifty-Four

Rain beat against the window and the wind made the cracks at the edge whistle when it gusted. But Hurricane Rita's upgrade to Category 2 wasn't what awakened Walking Bear from his light sleep.

He'd been dreaming of the wildlife around the home. Gators and wild pigs. They walked single file in step, like a giant animal conga line. Leg irons made of snakes bound each to another. Their eyes glowed blue like last night's hog visitor. They trudged toward a towering black building in the distance, where Walking Bear was certain they all would die.

It wasn't the dream, but a presence in the room that awakened him. He sat up in the darkness. Distant lightning flickered along the horizon outside his window.

An armadillo stood on the impossibly narrow window ledge. Rain coursed down its armor-like plating. It tapped the glass twice with its tail and hopped down.

Two times in two nights his spirit guide appeared to him. Walking Bear had never been so blessed. Or was it cursed. Something dark and evil had infested the creatures of the forest, and if he interpreted his dream correctly, was leading them to certain destruction.

But his spirit guide had awakened him so he would have the presence of mind to use caution. He took a deep breath and soaked in the auras around him. Some of the animals he sensed outside were torn, conflicted by a drive for vengeful violence that ran against their natures. But there was something wrong inside the home as well, a spirit half-dark with hate and half-red with rage.

As he stood up he heard the echoing thunk of the lockdown

latches on the exterior doors around the home. That could not be good. He dressed in the dark.

Walking Bear cracked open his door and peered out. Empty and quiet. He slipped out of his room. He crept down to the nurses' station. The night nurse sat sprawled in her chair. A slick, still waterfall of blood traced a path from her chest to the floor. Her face was forever frozen in a look of shock.

Something crashed at the far end of the hallway. Walking Bear crouched down and looked over the edge of the nurses' station counter. Denny Dean pushed Mr. Bingham's bed down the hallway at breakneck speed. Mr. Bingham was still strapped into it. Chester Tobias stood on top, riding it like a surfboard. He jumped off and Denny let go just before the gurney careened into a cart of empty dinner trays. The two broke out laughing like drunken high schoolers.

None of this made a bit of sense to Walking Bear. Those two were idiots, but they wouldn't go so psycho without...

Then his question was answered. Shane Hudson stepped into the hallway, wearing a doctor's lab coat and brandishing his infernal cane. Walking Bear did a double take to confirm that indeed the old rat was walking. More proof that something was very wrong with the balance of nature, both inside and outside of Elysian.

"Enough!" Shane yelled. His two accomplices straightened up like chastised children. All three ignored Mr. Bingham's moans from the crashed gurney. Shane pointed the head of his cane down the hall in the direction of Walking Bear's room. "Time to scalp the Chief."

The click of a closing door sounded as Shane led Denny and Chester around the corner of the nurses' station. The sound was too close to have been from any room but Walking Bear's.

No matter, Shane thought. *Awake or asleep. Even the big Chief can't handle three-on-one.*

The three stopped in front of Walking Bear's door. Shane tried the handle. Locked. He whipped out the nurses' master key and unlocked it.

"Time to have the Chief experience a personal Trail of Tears,"

Shane said.

He kicked open the door.

"Doctor Hudson making his rounds," Shane announced. His face screwed up in anger when he saw the room was empty. "Son of a bitch. Find that Indian."

Chester and Denny whipped through closets and peeled back the mattress from the bed. No Walking Bear. The three reentered the hallway. Shane planted a finger in each of his minion's chests.

"Go find him. He's a big bastard. He can't hide many places."

Shane gave the swelling in his pants a tug.

"I've got something else to take care of."

Dolly was lost within a vivid dream.

In it, she saw the black shape again. The one she had seen before. The one she had painted to get it out of her head. This time lightning flashed and she could make it out, the rusting hulk of the Apex Sugar plant with the NSA tower at its side.

The building flexed, like a great breathing lung. With each inhalation, blue light seeped from the expanded cracks in the walls. Inside, the wails of tortured souls echoed in the emptiness. Each contraction of the building exuded the foul stench of rotting corpses.

A hawk's feather appeared in one of her hands. Pruning shears in the other. She crossed them. The ground rumbled and she looked up to see the radio tower collapse onto the plant. It crashed through the roof and the building dissolved into a blue roiling mushroom cloud.

Her eyes snapped open to the comforting darkness and familiarity of her room. From down the hallway she heard laughter, mean, sadistic laughter in the unmistakable timbre of Shane Hudson's voice. Two voices twittered in response and she knew all three heads of Cerberus were up and at 'em. At this hour, that did not bode well.

She reached for her robe and thought better of it. Whatever was going on in the hall wasn't something to face down in pink terrycloth and fuzzy slippers. She slipped on a pair of jeans and a T-shirt.

Heavy sheets of rain pounded her window so hard it flexed in the frame. Things were heading south inside and outside of the Elysian walls. What a night.

She crept over to her door and cracked it open. She peered out in the hallway. Something crashed down around the hallway corner. Chilling laughter followed. She edged out of her room and inched down the hallway.

She hung her head into Shane's open doorway. Dwayne lay on the floor, a pulverized, bloody mess. Shane's wheelchair was still there. But Shane was not. How could he...?

Walking Bear's room was a few doors over. Something about being with that big quiet Anamassee felt really safe right now.

"Well, looky who's up to party with the big boys."

Chester stood in the hallway in all his splendid stupidity, pupils wide as sinkholes from whatever he was hopped up on. Blood splattered the front of his shirt. Denny stepped out from behind him and gave a lupine smile.

"Well, hello Dolly!" he said.

Shivers ran up Dolly's spine. These two were out of control.

Shane stepped between his two henchmen and pulled each back with a hand on a shoulder.

"No, no, boys. This bitch is mine."

Shane alone was more terrifying than the three of them together. Denny and Chester might have a shred of rational thought. Shane was psychotic. Without them to check him...

Dolly ran down the hallway.

"Nowhere to run," Shane called. He followed at a steady pace, long strong strides down the hallway. "It's an old-fashioned lock-in. A pajama party. Don't be antisocial."

Dolly had seen the tent in the sick bastard's pants. He probably hadn't had solid wood for years and she had a sickening idea what he'd be ready to do with it. She slipped on the floor as she rounded a corner and slammed into the wall. Something in her shoulder crunched and a flamethrower of pain raced through her right side.

“Don’t hurt yourself, Dolly,” Shane’s voice called from down the corridor. “That’s my job tonight.”

Dolly pushed off the wall and ran for her room. She slammed the door behind her and locked it. Shane might have had a miraculous recovery, but even in his prime he couldn’t break down that solid wood door. She leaned back against her work table and tried to stop hyperventilating.

The door handle rattled. Shane’s face appeared in the window like some twisted apparition. In the shadow she swore his eyes had a blue hue.

“Dolly, Dolly, Dolly,” he admonished her. “Fate can’t keep us apart.” He shook the nurses’ key ring in front of his face. “I’ve got the keys to your heart.”

She was trapped. The window barely opened and she couldn’t break it. Once he got in here...

Lightning flashed and something boomed outside the building, like a bomb exploding. The lights flickered and went dark. Emergency lighting far down the hallway kicked in.

“What the fuck was that?” Shane yelled down the hall.

Dolly could not make out the muffled response.

“Check the goddamn generator,” Shane ordered. Then in a quiet voice he whispered through the crack in the door jamb. “Dim lighting *is* much more romantic anyway.”

Keys jangled as Shane searched for the master. Dolly’s hand brushed against a cold metal cylinder. Clear gloss paint. She remembered the warning on the label:

Danger! Flammable!

She spun around and grabbed the can. She groped in the dark with her other hand, smacking away paints and brushes. It was here somewhere. She had just seen it.

The door behind her burst open.

“Say, bitch,” Shane said. He slapped his cane against one hand. “It’s time to party.”

Dolly felt it at her fingertips, a cool metal-tipped plastic cylinder. She snatched it and the spray can and spun around.

Shane was inches from her, a dark shadow backlit by the dim hallway lights. She aimed the lacquer at the dark recess of his face and sprayed.

“Fuck!” Shane halted. He flinched and spit as the spray coated his face.

Dolly brought the lighter up with her other hand and flicked it beneath the spray can’s stream. The plume exploded into a roaring torrent of yellow fire. Like dragon’s breath it lit the room and rolled toward Shane’s head. He raised a hand in weak defense from the sudden light and approaching heat.

Flames raced through his outstretched fingers. His face ignited into a sizzling yellow fireball. Shane screeched like a terrified child.

Dolly cut the stream. Shane pounded at his face with his hands, one of which was already a flaming torch. He staggered one step back, and then rocketed backward out the door like he’d been sucked out an airlock. He hit the far wall, then went careening down the hallway like a burning torch. The stink of scorched hair and flesh filled the room.

Dolly stood frozen, lighter and paint can pointed at the door and ready to fire at the next face to threaten her. Walking Bear stuck his head in the threshold.

“Hold up,” he said. “I thought you could use a hand, but that was before I knew you had a flamethrower in here.”

Dolly dropped her makeshift weapons to the floor and ran into Walking Bear’s arms. He enveloped her like a big warm blanket. She buried her head in his chest. His shirt smelled like pine needles.

“Am I glad to see you.”

She noticed that Denny and Chester lay in a crumpled pile at the end of the hall. She looked up at Walking Bear.

“Well?”

"They ran into each other in the dark. You ready to get out of here?"

"We can't," Dolly said. "The doors are locked."

"Lightning blew the generator. No power, no locks."

She looked up at his big broad face. "I'd face the storm before I stayed here."

"I have a car," Walking Bear said.

"You have a car?" Dolly said with surprise. "How come you never drove it?"

"Well, I didn't have anywhere I needed to go."

Dolly shook her head in wonder.

She knew the town's hurricane protocol. Andy would be at the DPW, ready to respond when the storm let up enough to get things back up and running. And her vision said she needed him.

"We have to stop this madness. At the source. I know just where to go for help," she said.

They walked out of the home and an armadillo stood at the edge of the sidewalk in the lee of a shrub. It looked up at Walking Bear and tracked him as he approached. Walking Bear nodded to the armadillo. Dolly gave Walking Bear a quizzical look.

"My spirit guide," he said.

The armadillo waddled up to Dolly. It stopped at her feet and sat up on its hind legs like a begging dog. It wagged its snout at Dolly.

Dolly never liked armadillos. They dug up her garden and looked like something God assembled out of spare parts. But she did not recoil, though this creature was just inches from her. It stared up at her with its tiny black eyes set in its pointy armored face.

The armadillo radiated some dynamic living power. She felt a strange, calm attraction, and an irresistible urge.

She bent over and reached out with two fingers. She touched the armadillo's forehead. Her fingertips went warm and energy soft as a summer breeze flowed into her hand. The armadillo dropped down on all fours and sauntered off into the woods. Dolly stared after it in stark amazement, as if the armadillo's touch had the same effect as Midas'. Walking Bear had to pull her back upright.

"Where's he going?" she managed to say.

"He will prepare our way."

"How?"

"I don't know," Walking Bear said. "But he does."

Chapter Fifty-Five

The mosquito swarm surged out of the Magic Shop doorway. It split into three and descended on Andy, Autumn and Felix. The insects coated Andy's arms like two throbbing black blankets. Bites like needle-pricks raced up his skin like machine gun fire. He dropped the rifle and swept a hand down his left arm. Mosquito bodies crunched against his skin and left a trail of bright red blood. Hundreds more dove in to take their place.

Mosquitoes swarmed his neck like their vampiric brethren. Twin groups surged up his pants and attacked his legs. Mosquitoes flew into his ears and up his nose. They alighted on his eyeballs. He shut his eyes tight and felt their bodies crush. The whine of the insects inspired visions of them inside his brain. He inhaled and insects coated his mouth.

He held his breath. He felt the weight of the creatures across his body. The insects pumped blood from his skin and he felt lightheaded. He flailed in panic. This was no way to die.

"Out here!" shouted Autumn.

Andy could barely hear her over the insects' screeching whine. He cracked his eyes to see where she was as he swatted at the black mass. She was outside in the downpour. Felix bolted through the doorway toward her. Andy spat out a mouthful of mosquitoes and followed.

The punishing rain swept the mosquitoes from his skin. Andy scrubbed his neck and head clear. He blew his nose into his hands and was rewarded with a ball of yellow snot, black bodies and bright red blood.

"They can't swarm in this," Autumn yelled over the wind and rain.

An inch of water surged over her feet and down the alley into the street. Behind her, a wave of mosquitoes swarmed out of the shop door and melted away under the rain's withering fire.

"We need to stop this before the town's washed away," Felix said.

Andy gave a rueful look at the rifle on the floor of the Magic Shop. Every inch of skin the mosquitoes had a run at was a mass of itching, bleeding welts. He didn't dare risk another trip into that maelstrom.

"This way," he said.

The three of them splashed though the rain back to the DPW parking lot. Autumn held them up short of crossing the street.

"As the wildlife biologist," she said, "I'm not the one who should be saying this but...what the hell are those?"

Across the street in the parking lot a half-dozen gray rabbits hopped around the white DPW pickup. The two rear tires were flat. One rabbit hung from the tread of a front tire, gleaming jagged teeth sunk into the thick rubber. As it swung its body back and forth, its teeth sawed through the radial. Air whooshed from the tire and the truck sagged closer to the ground.

"Side door," Andy said.

He led the group on a skittish, circular path to the DPW side door. Halfway there, the rabbits caught their scent. A hiss arose from the group and they bounded in pursuit. The three humans broke into a run.

Andy fumbled with a ring of keys as they approached the building. One rabbit raced yards ahead of the pack. Andy hit the door at full speed and used his shoulder as a brake. The key jiggled around the lock as he tried to insert it. It finally slid in and with a twist and yank, he opened the door. Emergency lights lit the hall in long shadows. The lead rabbit closed. Andy entered with Autumn and Felix right behind him. As Felix pulled the door shut, the lead rabbit launched itself into the air like a gray missile.

With perfect timing, the rabbit hurtled through the doorway's shrinking gap. The rabbit hit Felix's right leg. Felix spun and yanked the door shut behind him. He screamed in pain.

Andy and Autumn whirled around. The rabbit chomped a hunk of flesh and blue jean from Felix's leg and dropped to the floor. Blood sprayed the floor. Felix jammed the heel of his cowboy boot into its head. The rabbit's skull crunched flat and blood pooled beneath it.

Felix stood in shock for a moment, staring at the predatory creature. Then he leaned against the wall and slid to the ground. His eyes never left the wet carcass.

Andy ran to his office and returned with a first aid kit. Autumn knelt over the rabbit. She pulled a pen from her pocket and probed its mouth. Andy tore away Felix's pant leg and checked the bleeding wound.

He fought his initial instinct to recoil. Flashes of Afghanistan memories flipped though his mind. Amputated limbs. Screaming children. Puddles of blood on the streets. His hands shook as he unspooled a roll of cotton gauze. He fought back the urge to bolt down the hallway in panic and summoned his long-dormant military first aid training.

Felix's gouge wasn't deep. No arteries were cut. It could be worse. Andy focused on the wound and searched for some clinical detachment.

"This thing is bizarre," Autumn said in wonder at the rabbit, her clinical detachment apparently in full swing.

Andy sprayed some antiseptic on Felix's wound. Felix did not react. Andy made a compress bandage and bound the wound.

"This isn't bad, Felix, but you need a doctor. And you don't need to be walking around on it before that."

Lost in her analysis, Autumn lifted one rabbit paw with the tip of her pen. Scythe-like claws extended from the pads.

"Slashing feline claws," she observed. "Canid teeth. Fur coarse as ground flax seed. Rabbits are herbivores. This thing can't exist."

"There's a couch in my office," Andy said to Felix. "You should lie down there and keep your leg elevated."

Felix nodded and Andy helped him out of the hallway. Autumn followed them in.

"I don't need a DNA test to tell you that's some kind of chimera," Autumn said.

Andy gave her a blank look.

"A hybrid mix of multiple species," she said. "Nothing we could pull off scientifically."

"Just magically," Andy said.

Autumn shrugged and signaled the surrender of science. A door in the hallway slammed open and closed.

"Andy?" a timid voice called out.

Chapter Fifty-Six

"Mom?" Andy called down the hallway.

Dolly appeared in the doorway, Walking Bear behind her. Andy gave her a huge hug. Walking Bear spied the rabbit on the floor and knelt to investigate alongside Autumn. "What are you two doing out here? How did you get past the rabbits?"

Dolly relayed the story of Shane's rampage around the retirement home. She'd seen no rabbits around the building.

"The town has gone insane," Felix said.

"I think that Lyle Miller has some black magic going on down at–" Andy said.

"–the Apex plant," Dolly finished. "It's what I've been seeing for days."

"Your painting," Andy said. "We need to get down there and see what's going on. Mom, why don't you and Walking Bear go across the street to the shelter?"

Dolly snorted. "Not likely. I wouldn't have dreamed the place if I wasn't supposed to be there to stop something. And I need you and Walking Bear there."

"Mom..."

Dolly gave Andy an indignant stare until he sighed in resignation. He turned to Walking Bear. "I don't suppose you'll go to the shelter."

"I'm her bodyguard," the Anamassee answered.

Andy turned to Autumn.

"Don't even ask it," she said.

Andy balled his fists in frustration and looked down at Felix.

"You are sure as hell not going. Stay right here. If things get hairy, get over to the shelter. But this is one tough old building."

"No problem, boss," he said.

"Rabbits, snakes and gators," Andy said. "We're going to need some weapons."

He longed for the M-16 on the Magic Shop floor. Instead he opened the tool locker. He pulled out a machete he used to cut brush and offered it to Walking Bear. The Anamassee pointed to a knife on his belt.

"This has more stopping power," Andy said.

"I have help waiting," Walking Bear said.

Andy handed it to Autumn. She reached past him and grabbed a shovel.

"I've been pretty good with one of these lately," she said.

Andy sighed. He made a meek show of offering the machete to his mother.

"Andy, please," she said dismissively.

Andy raised his hands and gave up.

"My natural leadership is seriously going to waste here," he said.

The four went to the door to the DPW lot. There wasn't a rabbit in sight. The DPW pickup had four flats. There was an inch of water in the bed and it was still raining.

"We'll take my truck," Walking Bear said.

But Andy had another idea, a great plan he wanted nothing to do with. But it was the right plan. He pulled a key from the key box by the door.

"We need to also have something that will take more punishment," he said, "in case we meet up with more of those rabbits, some gators or worse." He gritted his teeth. "We should take the dump truck."

He couldn't believe he got the words out of his mouth. The last thing he'd planned to do was get behind the wheel of that thing.

"Does that run?" Autumn said.

"Yep. Only two forward gears and no reverse, but it runs."

Andy ducked into the rain first and ran to the truck. A pit opened in his stomach as soon as he stepped on the running board. He pushed on and climbed up into the cab. The familiar high view through the windshield brought back a surge of dark memories.

The passenger door opened. Dolly climbed in.

"Mom! Where's Autumn?"

"With Walking Bear. I told her I was riding with my son."

"Mom, you shouldn't be riding at all. Please, head over to the shelter."

"Andrew," she said.

Andy hadn't heard that chiding tone since he was a kid. Resolution had turned Dolly's face to stone.

"I've been at that home for years, fading in and out of the rest of the world. Don't think I don't know when it happens. It's embarrassing and terrifying. In an instant I am in an alien world, surrounded by strangers. But worse than not knowing who you, my own son, is, is not knowing who I am. Imagine experiencing your existence vaporize. And each event, it's just a signpost saying *Full Senility Ahead* and the miles to go get shorter every time.

"The last few days, I have been back. Back better than in years, perhaps better than ever. And through it all I've been haunted by Apex. The reason I'm well is to be able to confront whatever is there. Now I can walk there to confront it alone, or I can ride there with my son. Which way should I go?"

This was his mother, the one he remembered, who fought the powers that be, who led the crusade to save the Everglades, who managed their world after his father's death. Andy had missed her.

"Guess you'd better buckle up," he said.

He turned the key and the truck rumbled to life. The diesel sent vibrations up though his seat and he flashed back to assembling a convoy in Afghanistan. He shook it off and flipped on the lights and wipers. He remembered that the truck had no reverse gear. He thrust the gearshift into first.

"What kills me is I'm just going to have to fix this later," he said.

He let out the clutch and the truck crept forward. It flattened the chain link fence in front of it and rolled out onto Washington Street. Walking Bear and Autumn were already there in the pickup truck. They headed toward the Apex plant. Andy upshifted to second and followed.

A dead stoplight bounced on its cable in the stiff, shifting wind, three empty eyes watching the two trucks pass beneath it. Darkness reigned outside the headlights' narrow path. Each swipe of the wipers threw a sheet of water over the side of the truck. Andy took a deep breath to calm the dread that roiled in his stomach. He hoped he was ready to cope with whatever Lyle had in store for them at the plant. He prayed that whatever it was, he could keep his mother safe from it.

Chapter Fifty-Seven

Carlina drove way too fast. Rain fell like buckets of water against her windshield and all the wipers did was add a steady backbeat to the rain's rampage. She guessed and braked and prayed that no one else was foolish enough to be out in this weather. Her own safety never entered her mind. Her worries were about Ricky and Angela, home alone in the heart of this storm.

From the main road, she saw that the house was dark, just like the rest of town. The two great oaks on either side of the house swayed so low in the wind gusts she could not believe they were still standing. She barely had the car in park before she was out and through the house's front door.

As soon as she entered, Angela leapt from the living room's dim shadows and wrapped her quivering arms around her mother's waist.

"Mommy! Mommy!" she cried rapid fire. "You are home. You're okay. It's Ricky. Something's wrong. I wanted to run. Daddy said not to leave so I stayed. You have to fix Ricky!"

She pulled her mother down the hall and halted her in front of Ricky's open door. Carlina looked in and screamed her son's name.

Two candles burning at the ends of his desk lit the scene in an eerie flickering glow. Ricky sat at his desk, eyes glazed to a milky blue. He held both hands up before him and moved them like he was conducting some silent symphony. Above the desk floated a set of playing cards. With each flick of Ricky's wrist, the cards took on a new shape, flew a new formation. At his mother's cry, Ricky did not react, undisturbed in whatever world he now inhabited.

The wind gusted to a freight-train crescendo. Loose siding rattled against the walls. Two sharp warning cracks sounded outside. Carlina's maternal sense went to high alert, her subconscious cued to some unseen but half-processed danger. She reached for Angela.

The old oak outside exploded like a clap of thunder. Carlina jumped at the sound. Her hands missed Angela by inches.

The ceiling along the front of the house collapsed. Barrel-sized branches burst through the sheetrock like an invading organism. A blast of rain and leaves swept in like its humid breath. One branch brushed Carlina aside. Her head hit the wall and she saw stars.

The trunk plummeted straight into the hallway. Angela disappeared beneath it.

It was a strange delightful place Ricky floated within. The world was white. A swishing sound like small waves on a beach soothed him. All he could see were the cards as they floated before him and assumed new shapes at his command. Magic flowed through his fingertips with every flick and twist. It cruised through his body and left him without a care in the world. Had he been here minutes? Hours? Days? No matter.

Something large and scary stirred outside his blissful bubble. But it barely registered, like a wild bear scratching outside a foot-thick wall. Only the world in the bubble mattered.

Then Angela's screams pierced his dream place like a bolt of lightning. A high-pitched, terrified wail that sent a spike of fear up his spine. He'd heard her scared. He'd heard her hurt. He'd never heard her like that.

He had to save her.

He held his palm up and the cards retreated there into a neat stack. He gripped it and his room reappeared. The deafening sounds of Hurricane Rita blasted his ears. Wind whipped his hair around and rain splattered the ...hallway? Half the house was gone. Angela screamed again.

He saw her through his doorway. The old oak had snapped in half and crushed most of their house. Angela lay under the gnarled trunk, almost invisible amid a tangle of sheared branches and swirling leaves.

"Ricky!" she screamed. She reached out for him with a bloody hand.

Ricky responded instantly.

"*Bakshokah serat!*"

The coin in his pocket blazed. The cards flew from his hand, one after the other. They formed two flights, the cards overlapping with one corner pointing straight down. They dove at the branches that pinned Angela to the ground. Like two chain saws, they chewed through the tree on either side of Ricky's sister. White chunks of wood sprayed into the driving rain. The cards finished their pass and left the tree trunk in three pieces. They boomeranged back to Ricky's hand.

He ran out into the ruined half of the house and kicked away the chunk of trunk that still pinned his sister. He pulled her off the ground and she buried her sobbing face into his neck. He wrapped his arms around her tiny, trembling body.

If anything had happened to her...

He shielded his eyes from the rain and searched for his mother. She leaned against the wall, head in both hands. Ricky picked up Angela, though she was years too old to be carried. She wrapped her arms around his neck, her legs around his waist. He picked his way to his mother's side through the wreckage of the once great tree.

"Ricky! Angela!" She embraced them in a wet group hug. "Get to the car!"

They leaned into the wind and navigated through the wreckage that had been their home. At the car, Ricky slid Angela into the back seat. He had to pry her arms from around his neck. She grabbed a teddy bear from the floor and curled up into a fetal position across the seat. He got into the front with his mother.

"The shelter is open downtown," Carlina said. "We'll go there. Your father will find us there."

She started the car but did not put it in gear.

"Ricky, those cards...?"

Ricky shifted in his seat.

"They are from the Magic Shop," he said. "They were just supposed to be a game."

"The Reverend was right," Carlina said. "They are the Devil's work. Give them to me."

"They are out there in the storm," he lied. "Miles away by now."

"Thank God," she said. She backed the car down the driveway.

Ricky felt the lump of the deck of cards in his back pocket.

I should have left them in the storm. The cards took control of me and did who knows what while I was zoned out.

The coin in his front pocket was still warm.

But when I took control of them, I saved my sister.

He had a feeling he would need that power again before the day was over.

Chapter Fifty-Eight

The shelter was worse than Carlina expected.

When she opened the shelter's interior door, she was certain she would see the apparatus of local government hard at work with people tracking the storm and providing hot coffee and doughnuts to the poor homeless unfortunates like herself. The town backup generator would have the lights and air conditioning going and a big screen TV would be tuned to WAMM's Storm Tracker Update.

Instead she felt like she was entering a cave. The emergency lights barely kept the darkness at bay. Tired, wet, scared people sat on the floor or on old, threadbare canvas cots. The air smelled of mildew and the sweat of fear. When Carlina opened the door, expectant faces turned to inspect her and then looked back at the floor in disappointment. The shelter wasn't a ray of hope in the storm. It was a subterranean void of despair.

Mayor Diaz approached. Carlina sighed. Flora was a sweet person and an energetic town booster, but she would be way out of her depth in this emergency. Wasn't there someone from the state or county here to actually get things done?

Flora looked genuinely concerned. She was, for the first time in Carlina's recollection, washed free of any makeup. She gave Carlina a hug.

"Carlina! Come in. Are you alright?"

"I'm okay," she said. "But a tree crushed the house." She'd keep her son's magic act to herself, thank you.

"Oh God," Flora said. She knelt down before Angela, who had her face buried in her soggy teddy bear. Flora examined the girl's battered arms. "Are you hurt, Angela?"

Angela peeked up from between the teddy bear's ears and shook her head. "Just bumped."

"I've heard cookies help with bumps," Flora said. "Mrs. Wilson has some there in the corner if you'd like."

Angela gave her mother an expectant glance for approval.

"Just two," Carlina said.

Angela ran to Mrs. Wilson. Flora turned to Ricky. "They're good for all ages."

Ricky shook his head. He backed up to the shelter wall and sat down.

"He's not himself," Carlina said.

"None of us are," Flora said. "The storm took us by surprise. But all of you are safe. Anything lost can be replaced. Any building damaged can be rebuilt. Where's Felix?"

Carlina realized that the mayor knew everyone in town by name and, more impressively, remembered them all in the midst of this chaos.

"He isn't here? Oh God, that means he's out there. He was looking for Reverend Wright. He wasn't at the church this morning."

Flora gave Carlina a hug across her shoulders. "Don't worry. The town is full of safe places to be. If he knew you were taking care of Ricky and Angela, he probably found a dry spot to ride this out. He's got a good head on his shoulders. He'll be fine."

Carlina felt better for the first time in hours. Of course Felix would be okay. No one was tougher than her Felix.

"Now we are better off here than we look," Flora said. "In addition to Mrs. Wilson's cookies we have canned food. There's a bathroom on the right and we have water from the well on a battery pump. This place was designed to survive a Soviet nuclear attack. A hurricane is nothing."

Carlina decided she had been wrong. This place *was* a ray of hope, and Flora was the surprising bulb lighting it. The people around her weren't sitting in abject desolation. They were reading, or playing board games with one another.

"This storm will pass," Flora said. "And we are going to walk out into the daylight and make Citrus Glade better than it has ever been."

The mayor was right. The worst had passed now that she and the kids were safe in the shelter.

Except that the shelter was one Arroyo short.

Chapter Fifty-Nine

Ricky hadn't said two words on the harrowing ride to the shelter. His mother hadn't mentioned the cards or magic again, as if avoiding it made it go away.

He could not sort through all the negative emotions that bubbled up inside him. Embarrassment at having the magic take him over, shame that he longed for it to do so again, fear at what kind of living zombie he might have become if Angela hadn't snapped him back to reality.

But the main thing he felt was guilt. He knew, he could *feel*, when he was in the magic stream, that he was part of all this; the storm, the missing Reverend, even the renewed oranges on his family's trees. The world had been normal until he had started messing with Lyle and his so-called stage illusions. There was no way this magic wasn't one hundred percent black.

If he was part of the cause, he wasn't alone. The other three Outsiders were making their own contributions to this hell on earth. The others would be home doing magic, sprawled out in some catatonic state. Someone had to wake them up and break that connection.

Angela had stopped him. It was up to him to stop the others.

He watched the mayor lead his mother across the shelter. He swiped a penlight from atop a case of bottled water. He rose and cracked open the inner shelter door. He slipped through the opening and shut the door behind him. At the top of the steps to the exterior door, he paused and planned. Barry's house was closest. He'd go there first. He mapped the route in his head.

Rain pummeled the heavy metal door. The wind howled by and

stray branches scraped across the outside of the door. Ricky took a deep breath, braced his back against the door and pushed.

Rain lashed his face as he stepped outside. He steadied the door against the gusts and laid it back down. The latch clicked shut. He bowed his head against the deluge and ran for Barry's house.

He decided to approach from the back, to check Barry's bedroom from the window. If he had the magic hat going, it wasn't likely that he'd be pulling animals from it in the living room.

He splashed through one backyard and hopped the fence into Barry's. He shielded his eyes from the rain and didn't like what he saw. Barry's back window was broken. He ran to the back of the dark house.

The eave offered partial shelter from the rain. The room was pitch black. He pointed his penlight in and snapped it on. His fingers locked around the tube. Barry lay on the floor. The flashlight's beam made his eyeglasses' shattered left lens look like frosted glass. His head lay on one side, a jagged chunk ripped from his throat. His nose was a bloody stump. The hat lay sideways on his desk. Ricky aimed the flashlight beam inside it. Empty.

"Oh no, oh no," Ricky moaned. *Damn it, Barry. What the hell did you conjure up out of that hat?*

A watery trail sliced from Barry's window and across his backyard.

And where the hell did it go?

If Barry couldn't handle the power of the top hat, there was no way Paco could control the demolition derby his magic wand could conjure. Paco might already be dead. Or he might be near impossible to stop. But Ricky had to try.

He paused before he set out. There was something of Barry's he could use. He climbed in through his dead friend's window.

Glass crunched under his feet with each tentative step he took. He played his flashlight beam around the edges of Barry's body, unwilling to again see the damage done to his friend. Tufts of coarse gray fur clung to Barry's clothes. Ricky stepped in a puddle of congealing blood and it squished under his shoe. He knelt and took a guess. Fifty-fifty odds. He opened Barry's right pocket with his fingertips and slipped his other hand inside. He felt a handful of change at the bottom and pulled it out.

He flicked his flashlight on to the coins in his hand. One gold coin, the one given to Barry by Lyle, stood out in the collection of silver and copper. Ricky plucked it out. His own coin sat in his left pocket. He put Barry's in his right. He'd felt the heat one coin created during the magic. No point in doubling that in one location.

He returned the rest of the coins to Barry's pocket.

All Barry had wanted was somewhere, anywhere, to fit in.

"I'll fix this, dude," he said.

Ricky climbed out the window and paused under the shelter of the eave. The wind now blew the rain nearly horizontal. He ducked his head and made his way toward Paco's.

Chapter Sixty

Something slithered around Juliana's knees. She jerked awake and slammed her head on the roof of the truck cab.

"Goddamn it!" she cursed at the pain. She realized she was waist-deep in black, rushing water. Rain spanked the truck's windows. She put her last sentient moments back together. Driving the truck north in the storm, crossing the bridge, falling.

A catfish brushed against her foot again and she pulled her feet up as high as she could. The truck was buried nose first in the canal and she lay across the steering wheel. She did a quick check and flexed her hands and feet. Everything worked. Damn, after a crash like that you'd think...

But there was something, something inside her wasn't right. She ran a hand along her side and felt her rib cocked off at an odd angle. Something wheezed within her when she breathed. A punctured lung. Damn it.

Wait, she thought. *This ought to hurt like hell.*

But it didn't. In fact, not only did she not hurt, she felt great. Powerful. She could not know that with the stupefying cocaine flushed from her system, the door had opened up for something more potent to hit her. She caught sight of her face in the mirror over the twisted passenger sun visor. Her eyes had a hint of blue behind them.

Emotions boiled up within her. Jealousy. Rage. Vengeance. She could have been killed driving this damn truck in a hurricane. Goddamn Vicente, that unappreciative ass.

She wanted the two of them out of this crappy town and living on the beach somewhere. But no, all he ever said was how perfect this town was. Well she knew what it really was. He had another woman. He had to. Some skank who thought she could slip by and make a fool out of Juliana.

Juliana didn't have time to find the bitch, but she knew where she'd be tonight. Huddled in the shelter to ride out the storm. Juliana was ready to settle this. The hard way.

She pushed open the driver's door. Its weight and the wind sent it crashing against the nose of the cab. Rain blew in and spattered her face so hard it felt like pebbles. She pulled herself through the door, climbed up into the bed, and leapt to the edge of the canal. Her bare feet dug into the soft ground and she landed standing. There was something sharp under her foot, but the pain seemed miles away, well obscured by the fury she felt against Citrus Glade.

The wind gusted hard and she leaned into it for balance. The trailer of cars was sideways in the canal, a total loss for the Colombians. Yeah, well. She sucked in a slow, raspy breath and turned back to the road. Low clouds raced across the sky. Through the rain she caught glimpses of the town a few miles away. She walked out to the yellow line in the middle of the road and headed back to town.

The two hairs Lyle collected from Vicente were not both his. One had been Juliana's. Lyle's spell had touched her without delivering a mission. She had already created her own. A vision had welled up within her, a lovely picture that came from who knows where. The other woman's head on the tip of a spear.

Chapter Sixty-One

Ragged pavement on bare feet. Chilling rain against soaked cotton clothes. Lung tissue that tore with each inhalation.

Juliana didn't feel it. She sensed it, but pain was a thing of the past in her new state of mind. She walked the double yellow on CR 12 with one directive, an amplification of the thought she last had before the blue power had touched her and led her out of the wreck. The Other Woman's time had come.

Headlights flashed down the road. A car approached, a bland silver four-door. The plate on the front read *Ask Me About My Grandchildren.* The high beams kicked on and Juliana squinted. The car rolled to a stop at her side and the driver's window slid down.

The rain plastered Juliana's long black hair down across her face and her view into the car was like looking through prison cell bars. A little old man's face peeked out at her. Raindrops speckled his glasses.

"There's a hurricane going on," he said in a thin little voice. "Do you need a ride?"

"Great idea," Juliana said.

Before the old man's smile could leave his lips, Juliana reached in and yanked his head against the door pillar. His glasses flew out the window. His eyes rolled around and bounced. She slammed him twice more until his head went limp. She pulled him out of the car and tossed him in the road. She took her amazing strength in stride.

She sat in the driver's seat, gave the wheel four turns and slammed the gas pedal to the floor. The back end of the car swung around and she was pointed back to Citrus Glade. The car lurched as the wheels crushed the former driver.

In town, cars filled the lot at City Hall. Excellent. The shelter was full, as she expected. She would throw open those doors and...

The doors gave her an idea, a priceless and painless way to end this one-sided competition. Painless for Juliana at least.

She pulled the car up on the grass by city hall, aimed it at the backup generator, and punched it.

Below in the shelter, a muffled version of a car crash sounded from above one of the shelter's thick walls. The lights snapped off and the noisy air conditioning fan went silent. A collective gasp rose from the half of the occupants who were not sound asleep. Weak emergency lighting at one end of the shelter flipped on.

Flora snapped on her flashlight and waved it against the ceiling.

"No problem," she said. "No problem. We just need to restart the generator. We have gas if it needs it. Stay calm. I'll go check it out."

She pulled on her rain coat and opened the inner door. There was a thud at the outside doors and the metal creaked like a submarine's hull under pressure. She flipped the handle and pushed. The door didn't budge. She leaned a shoulder into it and tried again. Nothing. Something must have fallen on it, like a tree. Or more ironically, maybe the wind ripped the generator off its pad and it rolled on top of the doors.

The generator! No lights meant no power. No power meant...

She rushed back into the shelter and put her hand against the air vent. Dead still. The air conditioning was also the ventilation system. This little underground box was designed to survive a nuclear attack, all plutonium-tinged air kept on the outside. The lack of any insect life down here said the seals still worked.

There were dozens of people down here. She couldn't do the math, but they would have to use up the air in here pretty quickly. Someone was going to have to come in from the outside, and well before the storm subsided, or the basement of City Hall would be Citrus Glade's first wholesale morgue.

Back above ground, Juliana backed her carjacked four-door away from City Hall and left the blue compact car she had pushed atop the shelter doors. *Go ahead Ms. Slut-of-the-Year. Try to open those against a few thousand pounds of Detroit steel.*

Her first problem was solved, or would be when the air gave out. Now she was off to find Vicente. She knew where he'd be, guarding that investment he had in the NSA tower. She drove south to the mill.

Chapter Sixty-Two

Even in the barely navigable darkness of the unlit subdivision, Ricky knew something was wrong as soon as he turned down Paco's street. Dim, dancing candlelight flickered in windows of most of the houses, but nothing from Paco's. Just like Barry's.

He ran halfway across the Diaz yard and stopped short. The house wasn't dark. It was gone. All that was left in its place was a gaping crater. A few inches of rain had already collected in the bottom. Even in the storm, the ground smelled of sulphur.

No wreckage edged the pit. The house hadn't exploded outward. It had just collapsed inward, disappeared like the things Paco touched with the wand. Damn, had he disappeared the whole thing? With everything inside?

Ricky remembered the strange state he was in when the magic had possessed him. He had no idea what he was doing or what impact it was having in the real world. Paco could have done anything at that point. Vanished the whole house. Even vanished himself.

If that was what happened, there was one thing that wouldn't vanish, one talisman that had already stood the tests of time. He slid down the rain-soaked sides of the crater and pawed through the muddy water at the bottom. He retrieved something cold and hard. Paco's coin. He put it in his back pocket. His cards were in the other.

There was no body, but Ricky didn't need to see one. Paco was dead. The loss barely registered. Barry's death had already numbed him.

Hurricane Rita delivered a violent burst of wind. Shingles from the roof next door flew into the air like a flock of startled birds and disappeared into the clouds.

Zach's house was a few residences over. Ricky didn't run this time. Soaked to the skin, the weather was not a factor. He had to stop Zach. Lyle might have opened the door to all this black magic, but Zach pushed them all through the threshold. This disaster was his fault. Their friends' deaths were his fault. Zach was going to stop adding to this madness and he was going to pay.

Chapter Sixty-Three

Running in terror as his face burned away, Shane could barely make out the Elysian Fields hallway through the orange glow. He rounded a corner and glimpsed salvation. A bright yellow mop bucket sat next to the wall, mop handle sticking out of it like a giraffe's neck.

Shane plunged his head into the grimy water. His skin sizzled like oil on a hot skillet. Water rushed into his nose and he could taste piss and puke and the soles of a thousand shoes. He gagged and got a mouthful of the disgusting muck. He yanked his head from the bucket, rolled right and vomited.

He wiped his face with the sleeve of his shirt. It tugged at him and he looked down to see charred flesh stuck to the sleeve. He had to be fucked up. He didn't feel fucked up. There was no pain, but the fire... He thought back and even when he was burning, he screamed in panic, but not pain. He spit the taste of puke from his mouth and rose off the floor.

He walked down the hallway. Something, someone, had yanked him out of Dolly the Eco-bitch's room. He looked in her doorway. The room was mostly shadows but he knew she was gone. She and Injun Joe were both missing. Probably missing together. The power loss would kill the door locks. They could be anywhere.

He scooped his cane from the floor and strode down the hall to his two crumpled cronies. Worthless as they were at Apex. He gave each one a kick to the chest. They both stirred their heads in lazy circles. Denny looked up at Shane and cringed. He backed away across the floor.

"Shane," he said. "What the hell happened?"

Chester came to life and let out a yelp of fear. Shane walked over to the nurses' station and looked into a wall mirror that said *Always Look Your Best* along the bottom.

He was a monster. The tip of his nose had burned away and he had a clear shot of his charred sinuses within. His silver mane was scorched to stubble from his ears to up above his forehead. His skin looked like the ragged shrunken surface of a flambéed marshmallow. His eyelids were gone and tears ran down his cheeks in twin wet trails. With no lids he looked bug-eyed.

"Goddamn it!" He smashed the mirror with the head of his cane.

The bitch was truly going to pay for this now.

He turned back to Denny and Chester. They were on their feet and looked scared as whores in church.

"What's wrong with you two?" he snapped. "I'm fucking fine. Don't I sound fucking fine?"

"Yeah, boss," Chester said. "No problem."

"Then let's get out of here," Shane said. He had to follow the calling now. "We're going to the plant."

Chapter Sixty-Four

Zach's house glowed like a nuclear pile in the night. Amidst the black, unpowered homes of the subdivision, a strange blue-white light spilled out from a window at the rear of the house, Zach's bedroom window. The light pulsed and throbbed. Static electricity danced in the backyard as if kicked up by the falling rain. Zach was obviously hard at work.

Ricky wasn't going to hit the rear window like he did at Barry's. If whatever had killed Barry hadn't already escaped, it would have probably killed him too. He'd find another way in.

The choice was not difficult. The wide-open front door invited him.

He paused at the threshold under the porch. In the movies this was the moment where the undercover detective always pulled a big gun from the small of his back and carried it in that cool two-handed-half-pointed-at-the-ground way movie cops had mastered. There was something in this house worse than any cop ever faced and Ricky had nothing in his waistband but his scrawny waist.

What he did have though, was more powerful than anything a cop ever carried. He pulled the magic cards from his back pocket. Ricky would fight fire with fire, fight magic with magic.

If he could master the magic. When he'd dealt from this deck in his room, the magic used him, almost used him up. If he said the incantation and gave the deck life, could he keep it from consuming his own? What was to keep that power, amplified by Barry and Paco's coins, from devouring him first, re-wrapping him in that web of ecstasy and putting him into the stupor of the living dead?

Just his willpower could stop it. And that had better be enough.

He held the deck between both hands.

"Bakshokah serat."

The three coins blazed hot in his pockets. Magic ran up both legs, through his spine and down his arms. It hit the deck and the cards fluttered between his fingers like wild animals trying to escape. That heady, hazy, seductive feeling came over him. All he had to do was let the cards go. He could float away, free of the hurricane and any worries.

Instead he clamped down on the cards. He shook off the siren's song the magic sang. He focused on his family; his mother, his sister, his father who wanted his children to end up better than he had. He was going to save them, the town, the state. And these damn cards were going to help him do it.

"Bakshokah serat!" he commanded again. This time he did not let the magic run wild through him. He directed it, throttled it, and sent only as much as he needed, in the way he needed it, to the deck in his hands. The fluttering died down to a thrumming. The cards were his to command.

He edged into Zach's house. He passed the couch where he'd spent countless hours hunting aliens and bad guys in video games. It seemed like a thousand years ago.

Zach's room was at the end of the hall. The door was open and the blue-white light illuminated a rectangle in the hallway. Inside the light lay Zach's parents, mother sprawled face up on top of Zach's father. Both had bullet holes in their foreheads and ragged exit wounds from the back of their skulls. Looked like Zach had borrowed his father's pistol.

Ricky crept down the hall. With each step he took, the magic within him ticked up a notch as he tapped into the current Zach's conjuring had aroused. The hairs on his arms stood straight up. The air smelled like melted wiring. He held his breath as he peered into Zach's room.

Zach sat on the floor, legs crossed like some Eastern mystic. His head twisted back in an unnatural angle so that his cobalt eyes stared at the wall behind him. Both his arms stretched upward, fingers splayed wide apart. His hands were bone white, the blood drained from them long ago when he locked into this position. His mouth was an open smile.

The rings danced over his head like a trio of halos in a figure-eight race. Blue-white light pulsed from each one. On the floor at Zach's feet lay the pistol that had felled his parents.

Zach was gone around whatever bend the magic took him. He looked beyond coming back. But Ricky didn't know how bad he'd looked himself when the cards had a hold of him. He might have looked as bad as Zach. He might have looked worse. Angela brought him out of it. Zach's parents obviously failed to snap him out of it, but his parents were jerks. Maybe he could bring Zach around and not have to…

"Hey, Zach dude," Ricky said.

Zach's head pivoted toward Ricky in an independent motion no vertebrae would ever allow. His eyes were solid, burning blue. His face didn't show a hint of recognition. He lowered his hands to his lap. Then his right hand reached out for the pistol.

Zach brought the gun to bear on Ricky. The black barrel looked like the mouth of hell.

Ricky snapped into action. He let the magic charge the cards and they turned hard as steel. Like a Vegas dealer, Ricky spun two cards in Zach's direction.

The pistol barked, but the bullet barely cleared the barrel when one card intercepted it with a resounding ping. A second card flew by and severed Zach's right hand at the wrist. His hand seemed to hang suspended in the air for a second and then hit the floor, pistol still firmly in its grip, severed wrist cauterized clean.

Zach had no reaction, no cringe on his face, no scream of pain. He just raised his left hand and waved the rings toward Ricky. They flew to the doorway.

Ricky flicked cards forward like machine gun fire. They sliced through the rings but the rings did not stop. The rings dove for Ricky's head.

At the last millisecond, Ricky ducked beneath the whizzing steel and rolled headfirst into Zach's room. Two rings flew by, but one dropped lower. It passed through his left arm like a circular saw. Pain screamed up through his shoulder. His arm locked in place.

He came up on his knees and whipped a card at Zach's exposed neck. It went through it like a guillotine. The blue fire left his eyes. His body hit the floor.

Behind Ricky in the hallway the three rings buried themselves in the drywall and went still. The blue-white light winked out.

Zach's supercharged magic retreated from the room. Ricky let his magic seep back into the earth. He fell back against Zach's dresser. From across the room, the cards flew back to the deck in his hand. Some were coated in blood. The cards turned back into laminated paper and slept.

His left arm was on fire. He couldn't move it. He crawled across the floor to Zach's body and pulled the final coin from his dead friend's pocket.

He gave his locked arm a tug with his right hand. Nothing. He crawled to the wall and lay down.

At least I stopped the magic, he thought. *I saved the town.*

But the storm didn't stop. Outside, an outbuilding toppled over. Wind filled it and exploded it from the inside out. Something else was keeping this hell on earth going. No, *someone.*

Ricky hauled himself to his feet. He had a good idea where that one person would be. He left Zach's house to cut the magic off at the source.

Chapter Sixty-Five

Like spying an old girlfriend he hadn't seen in years, the first sight of the Apex Sugar plant brought back a rush of good memories. Shane drove the car down the potholed drive to the main parking lot, just as he had most days for decades. The shadow of the radio tower in the lot was new, but the plant was still there, just like old times.

"Damn, Shane," Denny said. "How long has it been?"

"Too long."

Just short of the parking lot, the wind and rain cut off to near nothing, like some big screen filtered almost all of it out save a hazy mist and swirls of ground fog. Shane hit the brakes. Above them bands of blue pulsed from the tower outward like electrical shockwaves across the bruised sky.

"What the hell...?" Chester said.

"Shane," Denny said, "this doesn't look good."

"Shut up you two," Shane said. He knew it looked good. Perfect, in fact, just like the vision he had.

Inside the plant, Lyle's eyes snapped wide open. He cut off the incantation he'd been chanting while standing at the center of the circle on the plant floor. The abrupt end to the inflow of magic felt like someone had cut off the water in the middle of a shower.

In the plan for the Grand Adventure, it made no difference. The energy stored within the cavern below was more than enough to sustain his new girlfriend Rita. But the end of the flow was unexpected.

The magic stream should have engulfed his four apprentices as they played with their little toys, used them as a conduit for the trip to the Apex plant. In a perfect world the four useful idiots would starve to death after days in the throes of ecstasy. Yet, one by one, the four stopped producing.

He could rationalize that the storm had cut them off, perhaps destroyed their homes. Or perhaps in a strange twist, their parents actually took an interest in what their outcast children were doing and got in the way. Neither explanation held water. The storm was least intense at Citrus Glade, though a true eye had yet to form, and the magic had enough control over the boys that parental intervention would be suicidal. No, something had gone wrong outside of the Apex plant, and it was inevitable that the same something would make its way here.

But two thousand years of experience counted for something. His next line of defense was just outside the production floor and on the way in.

"Shane and Company," Lyle called out. "Come in from the rain."

Shane stepped out onto the production floor, cane at a jaunty angle across his shoulder. "If it isn't the magician."

Lyle flashed his most disingenuous smile. "Sorcerer, if you please. And ready to make what you have now permanent."

"So I have you to thank for my renewed mobility?"

"And your benevolent attitude toward your fellow man," Lyle said. He nodded toward the shadows. "You brought some friends?"

Lyle gave his cane a forward flick. Denny and Chester advanced into the wavering circle of light. Lyle waved them to come closer.

"Step on up, gentlemen. The more the merrier. Stand by a candle."

The three men took positions behind a candle at the circle's edge. Denny and Chester exchanged confused, excited grins. Shane stared straight at Lyle.

"You know this place used to be our turf," Shane said.

"Then you'll be motivated to defend it," Lyle answered.

Lyle extended his hand before his face. Three shimmering black raven's feathers lay in his upturned palm.

"*Katsumi kimionis,*" he said.

He blew across his palm and a feather flew to each of the three candles before the Elysian Fields escapees. The feather hit the candle's flame and burst into a sparkling transparent blue mass. The little fogs enveloped each man's head and then split into wisps that penetrated through ears, nose and mouth. Each man shuddered and his eyes turned bright blue.

"Now, defend the room."

The three men moved to be equidistant around the circle, turned outward and waited.

Lyle closed his eyes and searched the land outside the plant. He found Vicente approaching the tower. Excellent. Lyle's last line of defense surrounded him in the plant. Now to work on his first. His next spell would strengthen the one outside the plant whose *whapna* he had awakened, just as he had bolstered his three new minions inside the plant. But while the three in here would not share Lyle's authority, the sorcerer would see fit to share a bit of that with the one outside. After all, a first line of defense that consisted of one person wasn't much of a line of defense at all.

"*Katsumi kimionis,*" he said and began the last steps to ensure the completion of his Grand Adventure.

Chapter Sixty-Six

Vicente spent a good deal of the slow drive to the tower cursing the missing Squirrelly Jones. Well, he'd seen Squirrelly install the skimmer. He'd have to just figure out how to uninstall it.

As he approached the Apex property, the storm disappeared. At the parking lot's edge, it was like he drove through a curtain. The rain shrank to a fine foggy mist. Black roiling clouds still filled the sky, but the wind dropped down to near nothing. The shock was the sight of the NSA tower.

Bands of thin blue energy emanated from the tower's tip. The widening circles rolled across the sky like ripples in a pond. Squirrelly's skimmer wasn't making that happen. He parked his truck by the tower gate.

Suddenly, he was filled with an upwelling of power, as if he'd absorbed energy from the air around him. He felt wide awake, his senses turned up to full. The realization dawned on him that he came here for the wrong reason. He wasn't here about the skimmer at all. He was here for the tower itself. It had to be protected, not from the storm, but from people. Others would want to destroy it and it must be preserved, so that it could deliver the blue energy pulses to the world. He didn't know how this important mission had escaped him earlier. In fact, all the concerns he had when he arrived: the Colombians, the storm, the coke, all passed into irrelevance. All there was in the world was this tower. This tower was the world.

This mission was too important to undertake alone. But, he would not have to. In the swamps around the plant he could sense hundreds of specks of life, like pinpricks of blue light through a black sheet, and they awaited his command.

"Come," he called out.

All around the plant rose a noise that could even be heard above the roar of the wind and rain, a simultaneous splashing and rustling and bursting of earth. Pairs of tiny cerulean dots winked into existence all around him in the fog. They moved closer and Vicente could feel vibrations through his feet. Yards away, they paused and he could make out what they were. Alligators. Snakes. All with blue glowing eyes.

Low scrub at the parking lot's edge shook and two massive feral hogs burst onto the cracked pavement. Mud matted their long coarse hair to their sides. They stood waist high and each easily weighed more than two hundred pounds. Foot-long tusks curved from their upper and lower lips. They grunted and the blue in their eyes pulsed deeper.

"Defend," Vicente said.

The two pigs snorted and charged off into the mist toward CR 12 The reptiles faced outward and waited.

Whatever's out there, Vicente thought, *hasn't got a chance.*

Chapter Sixty-Seven

The view from the cab gave Andy chills.

The two-vehicle convoy rolled down CR 12 as fast as the poor visibility would allow. He had a perfect view of the pickup truck ahead, with Walking Bear in the driver's seat and Autumn in the passenger side. The pickup had the high beams on, but all that did was light the sheets of rain into a bright reflective wall. Everything more than a few feet from the side of the road was just a gray mass.

The whole thing was way too familiar. A lead escort vehicle. A hostile environment. The unseen enemy close by. Being surrounded by steel but feeling helplessly vulnerable. He had to put the steering wheel in a death grip to keep his shaking hands under control.

"Are you alright?" Dolly asked.

"Yeah, Mom. I'm fine."

"I don't think any of us are 'fine' right about now."

"No, I guess not."

The selfishness of his reactions hit him. He was reliving the past while everyone around him was struggling with the present and needed his full attention right here, right now.

"Are you up for this, Mom?"

Dolly patted his arm, the same reassuring gesture she gave him when he was a child. "Absolutely. In my dream I crossed a hawk's feather and pruning shears, and the NSA tower went down. It said I needed to bring you and Walking Bear here."

"You need to stay safe," Andy said.

"That's always been the plan."

The pickup's brake lights painted the front of the dump truck red. Andy made a hurried downshift and hit his brakes. The old Apex Sugar sign peeked out from behind a screen of young cabbage palms on the left. The pickup swung down the cracked two-lane driveway.

Suddenly, two massive hogs charged in from the edge of the road. Heads down, they slammed into the driver's side of the truck like a pile driver. Their tusks impaled the door. Metal bent with a hollow groan and the truck rocked up on one side. The hogs held it up and a tire on the low side blew out like an explosion. The hogs backed off and the truck careened into the drainage ditch on the side of the driveway and stopped.

"Holy shit!" A hundred images flashed through Andy's mind. RPGs, IEDs, Taliban ambushes. Trucks blown thirty feet into the air. Bodies in pools of blood.

Andy spun the wheel and jammed on the brakes. He missed the pickup's bumper by inches. The dump truck lurched to a halt. Andy held his breath and fought back the panic that threatened to consume him.

In the glare of the dump truck's headlights, the hogs took position in the center of the driveway, as if daring the humans to make the next move.

Andy's stomach did cartwheels. More casualties, more death. Everything he feared seeing from the cab of a truck was back with a vengeance. He wanted to run screaming back to the main road.

But something more important than self-preservation kicked in. He looked across the cab. His mother stared out the windshield. She was all he had for family and he wasn't about to let her die out in this magic-stained no man's land. And this wasn't some spot on the other side of the world. This was his home. If he ran, that would be one less person in the battle to keep Citrus Glade from being wiped off the map. He relaxed his grip on the wheel.

"You okay, Mom?"

Dolly nodded and shook off the shock from the attack. She threw open her door and stood in the opening. "Walking Bear!"

The pickup's driver's door swung open and Walking Bear pulled himself out. He gave Dolly a chopped reassuring wave. Walking Bear reached in and pulled Autumn out after him, her face a mask of anguish. Walking Bear pushed her toward the dump truck.

Autumn climbed up into the cab and Dolly gave her the passenger seat while she remained standing.

"Damn pigs speared us right through the side of the truck." She pulled her wet hair away from her face. "Non-native bastards."

Walking Bear climbed up the driver's side of the dump truck and cracked open the door.

"For now, we're safe up here," Andy said. "The pigs can pound the side of this truck until their skulls cave in."

"Unless they run those tusks through one of these rotten tires," Walking Bear said. "Those tusks are sharp as hell."

"I'd never get this heavy truck to go anywhere on flat tires," Andy said. "We'll be stuck here with who knows what between us and the plant."

"Something gave those hogs the brains to go for the driver in the pickup," Walking Bear said. "It would also give them the brains to go for your tires."

A dozen yards down the road, the two hogs snorted and waved their snouts in the air. Their eyes pulsed blue with a heartbeat rhythm.

In the near area of the headlight's beam, an armadillo waddled out onto the road. It paused and looked up at Walking Bear.

"I've got this," the old Anamassee said. He leapt from the cab and pulled his hunting knife from his belt. The armadillo headed toward the plant.

All three occupants shouted in protest, but Walking Bear ignored them. He walked the driveway's double yellow line, eyes locked on the snarling hogs. One of them scraped its tusk against the rough pavement like a barber strap-sharpening a straight razor. The other pawed the ground.

With Walking Bear halfway there, the hogs charged, a quarter-ton of furious beasts ready to kill.

A yellow blur of panther fur flew from the underbrush and hit one of the hogs. The hog rolled right like a ship hit by a broadside. The attacking panther bit into the hogs' neck and tore out a thick chunk of meat. Blood sprayed the big cat and the hog flopped over dead.

But the assault gave the second hog a lead. The panther leapt in pursuit, but the hog had Walking Bear in its sights. The gap closed to feet. The hog snorted. Walking Bear stared him down like a Western gunfighter.

The armadillo raced into the hog's path at an impossible speed. The hog sidestepped to miss the armadillo and swung its massive head for a slashing attack. A tusk caught the armadillo and threw it skyward.

"No!" Walking Bear screamed.

The hog lost just a step, but it was a step too much. The panther caught it from behind and the two animals skidded across the slick pavement past Walking Bear. The panther grabbed the hog's chin with one powerful paw and pulled. It drove its canines into the boar's exposed neck. The hog gurgled and died.

Walking Bear ran to the armadillo and knelt at its side. He cradled the animal's head in his hand. The armadillo cast its black eyes to Walking Bear's face. Its mouth opened slightly and a wisp of white mist snaked out and vanished. The armadillo went limp. Walking Bear bowed his head. His lips moved in silent prayer.

Dolly had run from the truck as soon as the panther dropped the second hog. She knelt behind Walking Bear and hugged his broad shoulders.

"Your spirit guide?' she asked.

He nodded, eyes still closed.

"I'm sorry," Dolly said. "He was courageous. You both were."

Walking Bear looked down the road toward the Apex plant's hulking outline. A flash of lightning backlit the structure. The panther stood with its forepaws on the body of the dead hog and spit out a scratchy roar. Walking Bear's eyes narrowed.

"Let's go finish this."

Chapter Sixty-Eight

At the edge of the parking lot, the rain stopped like it hit a pane of glass. One second the truck's wipers were slinging a torrent of water off the vertical windshield, the next they parted mist. Andy stopped the truck. Walking Bear hopped down from his place on the running board and slicked his long hair back from his eyes. The panther trotted up to his side.

Autumn looked at the panther with longing.

"Researchers spend years and don't see a Florida panther. I'm hunting with one."

Hurricane Rita had formed her eye. Overhead, the sky was completely clear. Stars twinkled like angels in heaven. The full moon cast down its light and gave the crumbling plant a gray, ghostly glow. From the top of the tower, the bands of blue energy had transformed into a continuous counterclockwise swirl that stretched out across the sky to the whirling clouds at the storm's inner edge.

"That's where it's going," Andy said. "The energy travels through the pipes and then up through the tower."

"Hurricanes need energy to form," Autumn said. "It's usually from warm water, but all this would supercharge the whole process. No wonder the storm rose up so fast."

"And if we cut off that power?"

"The storm runs out of steam fast. Enough of it isn't over the ocean to recharge."

"Sounds like a plan. The winch on the front bumper has enough power to yank one leg of the tower free. That will be enough to topple it.

"Say you plug this fire hose feeding the storm," Dolly said, "what about all that energy? The hose will burst somewhere."

"Mom, there are millions getting pounded on both coasts. The Keys are going to be washed away. I'll chance it. You two had better get out."

Dolly climbed out of the cab.

"No way," Autumn said. "Lose all that chivalrous crap. You need me. You're going to drive up, I jump out and hook the tow cable, and you reel it in."

"That's the plan?" Andy said.

"It is now," Autumn said. "Get driving."

Dolly watched the dump truck lurch away toward the tower Walking Bear joined her, panther at his side.

"We have our own task," Dolly said. "We have to go into the plant The man in there is making everything go on out here."

"We can wait until Andy takes out the tower."

"Once the tower is down, Lyle will make good his escape."

"Ah, the element of surprise," Walking Bear said. "You have some mystical immunity?"

"I have a strong spirit," she said, "a wise friend, and a panther. I'm covered."

The moonlight cast shadows around the lumps in the buckled decaying asphalt. The panther trotted ahead of them in a beeline to the Apex plant. Walking Bear and Dolly followed its path.

The dump truck's headlights lit the chain-link fence at the base of the tower. Vicente Flores stood outside the perimeter. He stared down the truck with his solid blue eyes.

"Who's that?" Autumn said.

"Vicente Flores. General lowlife with a good façade. At least that' him on the outside. Looks like something else happening on the inside. He's got the same look in his eyes those mosquitoes had."

"I'm starting to hate that look."

Vicente raised his hands in the air like a priest at Mass. Pairs of blue eyes winked open on the ground all around him and Andy could see he faced an army of alligators and snakes. A machete wasn't going to be much help now.

"A few days ago I would have been happy to see this many alligators," Autumn said.

Two gators sprinted to the nose of the truck. They clamped onto the front bumper. In unison, they rolled right. The bumper tore free with a wrenching sound that sent a shiver up Andy's spine. The bumper clanked to the ground. The wiring for the winch yanked free in a shower of sparks.

"Holy shit," Andy said.

Gators attacked from both sides. Great jaws snapped shut on tires. The truck rocked back and forth as the tires burst one by one.

Before Andy could react, the air around the truck lit up with a million points of blue light. They swarmed the cab. Insects popped and splattered against the windshield like they'd been thrown against it by the bucketful. Andy and Autumn reflexively gave the door window cranks a tightening tug. The cab darkened as the windows grew thick with insect bodies. Blue eyes appeared in the recesses of the dashboard vents.

"Andy!" Autumn yelled. She slammed the vents shut on her side.

Andy closed his vents but the slats had gaps. A mosquito squirmed through the crack. Andy slammed it into the dashboard with his palm. He grabbed a rag from the seat and shoved it into the vent. Autumn grabbed yellowed papers and followed his lead. Andy bent over and stuffed some dirty paper towels into the floor vents. He turned the vent controls to off.

A snake slithered across the base of the windshield. Its brown and tan scales scraped a temporary clearing through the muck. It spiraled around a windshield wiper and ripped it free. Another brushed the outside of Andy's door. The door handle jiggled and Andy pounded the door lock down.

Blind, immobile and surrounded, Andy thought. *Could we be more screwed?*

Autumn reached over and grabbed his hand.

At that moment across the parking lot, what Dolly thought were lumps of buckled asphalt came to life. Luminous eyes flicked open and dozens of alligators rose from the ground.

The panther snarled and with one great bound leapt to Walking Bear's feet. It turned to face the new threat. Its head and tail swung in opposite defensive arcs as it growled a warning at the advancing horde. A python slithered out in advance of the gators.

Walking Bear drew his big knife from his belt and took a half step in front of Dolly.

"We'll try to clear you a path," he said. "Stay away from their jaws."

The python coiled itself for a strike. The panther pounced. Its jaws caught the snake and snapped it in half. The cat threw the rest of the snake away with a toss of its head.

The gators came on at a run.

Chapter Sixty-Nine

Vicente's high dwarfed anything drugs had ever done. Beasts at his command. Human lives in his hands. The million-watt thrum of magic that passed under his feet and into the tower behind him. He could even sense the energy in the bubbling clouds that swirled around the calm center over Citrus Glade. In seconds, his creatures of the night would destroy the two interlopers at the entrance of the Apex plant.

The dump truck idled on four shredded tires. Pythons had strewn exterior parts like bumpers and mirrors all over the parking lot. The thick remains of thousands of suicidal insects blackened the windows. Three pythons encircled the cab, ready to pop it open like Popeye crushing a can of spinach.

Instead of collapsing the cab, the snakes paused. Their heads twisted outward and their forked tongues licked the air. The gators across the parking lot paused mid-stride.

Something was wrong. The power Vicente felt, *his* power, was weaker, drained away to somewhere else...

"Cente," called a voice behind him.

He whirled to see Juliana step out of the scrub. Her feet were torn and bloody, her long legs scratched. Her hair hung down in wet strands across her face but could not obscure her bright blue eyes.

Pale memories fluttered by of a girl and a truck the girl should have delivered to Georgia by now. At one point all these things had been important. Now all that mattered was Juliana might be a threat to the tower. If she could divert power from him, could she pull it from the tower as well? Were the rest of these people just a diversion for her attack?

"Get out of here," he said. "Before I kill you."

He focused his waning power on the three pythons around the dump truck cab. They uncurled and slid down to his feet.

"The skank you are doing is dead by now," Juliana said. Her voice had an eerie, childlike quality to it. She walked straight to Vicente, eyes locked on his, face devoid of expression. "Now it can be the two of us. Together. Forever."

With every step Juliana came closer, the power within him weakened. Vicente sent the pythons forward. They didn't move. Juliana took a last step and wrapped her arms around his neck.

"Forever," she whispered in his ear.

Before he could push her away, the pythons rose and spiraled up around their bodies like three stripes on a barber's pole. Cold, slick scales slipped across Vicente's damp neck as one wrapped around the couple like a collar. Vicente squirmed and the snakes constricted. His lungs whooshed flat. He choked out a gasp.

"We are so in love," Juliana said.

The snakes squeezed. Ribcages cracked. Vicente groaned and the blue fire left his eyes. Juliana rolled her head back, stared at the stars in the sky, and followed her lover to whatever came next. The two corpses toppled to the ground.

All across the parking lot, the eyes of the sentry animals returned to normal.

Chapter Seventy

A tree crashed outside the DPW and woke Felix with a start. He tried to sit up and pain lit up his leg like a solar flare. He eased himself back down. The bandage on his leg had only dried blood. Thank heaven.

His watch said four-fifteen. He'd been out for hours. Rain blasted against the office window and outside random bits of the town scraped across the street. He hadn't slept through the hurricane.

His first thoughts were about his family. The old wooden farmhouse wasn't built to take this kind of pounding. The wind outside conjured up visions of the metal roof peeling off or uprooted trees crashing through walls. Carlina would use her head and protect the kids if the storm threatened the house. No, Carlina would get them to safety *before* things got dicey. She would take no chances.

He rolled himself off the couch, careful to keep all his weight on one leg and drag the other. He hobbled over to the window.

The pounding rain nearly grayed out the view of the City Hall parking lot. He wiped away condensation on the glass. A wind shift parted the curtain and he caught sight of Carlina's car in the third row.

Gracias, Padre en el cielo.

They made it to the shelter. If the place could withstand Russian nukes, it could withstand Rita.

But something had gone wrong. A car was parked on the shelter doors. The crumpled remains of the generator were bashed into the wall of City Hall. That meant everyone down there was trapped with no light and no air. Rita or no Rita, that door needed to come open. He was about to venture out into the storm when something around the car moved. The sight made his leg throb.

Rabbits. The same gray scruffy bastards with the ragged ears and the teeth like a mangled bread knife. Their eyes glowed blue.

His family was down there. It was up to him to get that door open.

He limped out the back door, into the storm and to his truck parked in the street. He shielded his eyes and shuffled through the items in the bed of the truck. He pulled his machete out from under an empty orange sack and slipped it into his belt. Then he pulled out the long-handled pole saw. He was reminded of a movie where he saw knights selecting weapons as they prepared for combat. Where's some chain mail when you need it?

He turned into the wind and headed for City Hall.

"Just relax," Flora said softly. "We'll all be fine."

Her flashlight beam lit each face one at a time as she moved from person to person in the shelter. They might have looked relieved when she welcomed them in earlier, but now they all looked scared. Few others in the pitch-black shelter had flashlights with them. The atmosphere had turned thick and humid. Between that and Flora's order to blow out any candles, everyone knew without asking that the air inside wasn't being scrubbed. They all lay on the cool concrete floor. Soft sobs and hushed prayers echoed off the walls. A few of the older occupants wheezed out labored breaths in the dying air.

Flora paused at Carlina, who lay with her arm wrapped around Angela. The day had caught up with the girl and she was asleep. Carlina's eyes were red from crying. Flora knelt down beside her.

"Ricky will be okay," Flora said. "The town is full of safe places to ride out the storm. He is a smart boy."

"I'm not crying for him alone," Carlina said. She hugged Angela tighter.

"We'll get out of here," Flora said. "Andy is out there. He'll be pulling open that door any minute now."

"Do you really think so?"

Flora could not dash the hope in Carlina's eyes. "Absolutely."

Flora moved on before her true assessment betrayed her. Andy would assume that the shelter was safe. This would be the last place he checked.

Someone else would have to get that door open, and soon, before the town shelter became the town tomb.

Felix turned the corner of the DPW building and faced the shelter entrance at the base of City Hall. He yanked the pull cord on the pole saw and it ripped to life. Four rabbits turned their shining eyes toward him.

"Come and get it, Thumper," he said.

He lurched toward the shelter doors. The rabbits perked up and bounded to intercept.

The lead rabbit came on at a surprising speed, jagged teeth bared for the kill. At a dozen feet out, it leapt for Felix's throat. Felix swung the pole saw like a broadsword and caught the rabbit mid-flight. The whirling chain sliced the rabbit clean in two. The haunches dropped to the ground. The lifeless head kept flying forward and hit Felix in the chest.

Two more charged from the right. Felix caught the first with a glancing backswing of the pole saw. It disappeared in an explosion of fur and blood. The second leapt through the mid-air remains of the first, aimed at Felix's face. Felix swung the heavy motor end of the pole saw up just in time to swat the rabbit away. Its teeth crunched against the metal casing.

The pivoting swing on his one good leg set Felix off balance. His left went unguarded. A last rabbit jumped in and chomped down on his injured leg. The bolt of pain made him shudder and scream. He dropped the saw and grabbed the rabbit by the ears. The skin below its mangy fur crawled like an army of maggots squirmed within. Felix fought his revulsion and yanked the rabbit away. The bandage and a chunk of his flesh came with it. He slammed the rabbit against the concrete curb. It spit out the bloody muscle in its mouth and hissed. Felix bashed it twice more until the blue light in its eyes died.

Raindrops pummeled the gash in his leg and he felt like he was hit with a flight of arrows. He clamped the wound with his hand and fresh blood oozed through his fingers. This wound was deeper than the first. He was sure he'd seen bone. His head swam. He staggered over to the car on the shelter doors. He opened the car door and yanked the shifter from first to neutral.

He was about to pass out. He dragged himself along the side of the car to the rear, leaned his back against the trunk and pushed. Wind ripped a shredded palm frond against his face. His feet slipped out from under him and he slammed the back of his head against the car. It didn't move.

He raised himself back into position. The world spun like he was on a carnival ride. He dug his feet in against a ridge on the shelter door and took a deep breath. He thought of his wife and children trapped just inches below him. He pushed.

The car rocked up on its springs and stayed there. Felix strained against it.

The car nudged forward.

Felix exhaled and gave another push. The car kept going. In two steps it rolled off the shelter doors.

Felix dropped to his knees and crawled onto the doors. He let loose his bleeding wound and pulled at the door handle. It didn't move. His strength was gone. He collapsed against the door.

Inside the shelter, all was still. Flora sat with her back against the open interior exit doors. Each labored breath drew in only thick, stale air. She knew it would wind down like this. The people at her feet were either passed out from oxygen deprivation or dead. She did not want to know which. She had tried to save them all, and instead suffocated them all to death. Her mind wandered off to a day she'd spent at

Sanibel Island as a child. Bright sun, warm water, wet sand between her toes...

A thud sounded behind her and she snapped back into the shelter.

My imagination...

It sounded twice again. Weak, but there.

Rescue? Was she dreaming?

She crawled up to the exterior doors, put her shoulder against one and pushed. It opened a few inches, then the wind outside caught it and threw it wide open. Fresh air blasted through the opening and rejuvenating rain splashed Flora's face. She sucked in deep draughts of air and her mind came back to life. She saw Felix crumpled on the other door and pulled him down into the shelter.

The noise, the air and the ambient light brought the people in the shelter back to life. Sighs of joy and laughter rose from the floor.

Flora propped Felix up on the steps. She examined his bleeding leg with her flashlight.

"That's one nasty bite," she said.

He nodded to her. She grabbed a roll of paper towels from the supplies at the base of the step and started to wind them around his leg.

"Felix!" Carlina rushed to his side.

"Daddy!" Angela ran up and wrapped her arms around his neck.

Felix managed a weak smile and scanned the room through drooping eyelids. "Where's Ricky?"

Carlina looked out through the shelter door into the heart of the storm.

"I wish I knew."

Chapter Seventy-One

Outside the Apex plant, Walking Bear crouched in defense, knife drawn, with Dolly at his back. The panther was poised to spring at the lead alligator.

Then the sea of blue eyes faded away. The advancing animals paused as if they had just awakened from a strange collective dream. The panther snarled in confusion. The reptilian mass turned from the exposed parking lot and lumbered off to the safety of the surrounding scrub.

Dolly and Walking Bear watched in grateful bewilderment. The big cat trotted off to assist the gators in their retreat.

"Your son must have done something right," Walking Bear said.

"Let's get in there before something else goes wrong," Dolly said.

The entrance door to the plant was off its hinges with the *No* in the *No Trespassing* sign spray painted over with a black X. They entered the plant straight to the former production floor.

Magician Lyle Miller stood within some kind of inscribed circle. He chanted in a strange language, arms outstretched. A blue aura, the same soft hue as the pulses from the tower outside, coated his body. Candles burned on stands around the circle, but something worse outside the circle caught Dolly's breath. Denny and Chester stood guard, stony-faced and eyes aglow. Shane stood front and center, cane at the ready, face a charred misshapen mess from their last meeting. The evil power she'd felt within them at Elysian Fields was now off the charts. Lyle paused and gave the two an annoyed look.

"Well, the Addled Artist and the Chief," he said. "Charging in to save the day. Too little and way too late."

Lyle's inner line of defense advanced on Dolly and Walking Bear. Shane pointed at Walking Bear.

"You two take the Indian," Shane said. "I owe this bitch a new face."

Denny and Chester rolled in on Walking Bear like a rogue wave. The Anamassee would normally be able to hold his own against the two smaller men, but Denny and Chester were no longer normal.

Shane grabbed Dolly by the front of her shirt and threw her into the wall. The hit knocked the wind out of her and she saw stars. Shane stalked after her and grabbed her again. He stuck his burned face right next to hers. His eyes watered and bulged in their lidless sockets. His breath reeked of charred, spoiled meat. He raised his cane to strike her.

"Take a last look at this face," he said. "Your whole body is about to feel this way."

The added life force within Shane practically crackled off his skin. The spirit guide had felt the same way. The armadillo's message to her...to show her how...

She reached out and touched two fingers over Shane's heart. The power within him flowed through her fingertips, a hundredfold stronger than when she touched the armadillo.

What little of Shane's face still moved registered profound shock.

"You biiii–"

His grip on her loosened. As the energy drained from him, his legs went weak. He wobbled and collapsed on the floor.

Dolly felt the power of a goddess within her. She scooped Shane's cane up from the floor and ran to Walking Bear. She pulled Denny off her friend and tossed Walking Bear the cane. She put her fingers to Denny's heart. Energy drained from him, though not nearly the voltage Shane had on tap. Denny's eyes went from blue to white to normal. Then he passed out.

Walking Bear hauled off with the cane and walloped Chester on the side of the head. Chester's eyes drooped shut and he dropped like a sack of rocks.

Dolly turned to face Lyle. The life force that swelled within her made her feel invincible. She marched toward the circle.

Through the fight, Lyle had continued his incantation, eyes closed and seemingly unaware. But when Dolly stepped into the candlelight, his eyes snapped open and he turned to face her.

"What the hell?" He waved a hand in her direction. "*Bakshokah gerza lop!*"

The candle flames expanded into a defensive wall of fire around the circle. Dolly recoiled from the heat.

"I can't finish this if I'm wasting time with you," he said. "I always have to do everything myself."

He chanted a lengthy spell. The fire around the circle billowed and swayed until it rose up in a pillar. The pillar tip formed the head of a dragon with great pointed ears and a crocodilian snout. It spread its jaws and lunged. Dolly covered her face.

The fire dragon's teeth snapped closed around Dolly's shoulders and pulled her off the ground.

Chapter Seventy-Two

Outside the plant, the truck cab was eerily quiet. Andy dared hope that something good had finally happened. He rolled down the window an inch.

Near the fence, two enormous pythons held Vicente and a young woman in an intertwined death grip on the ground. One had already swallowed Vicente's head. The other was up to Juliana's calves. The alligators moved off into the scrub. There wasn't a fleck of blue to be seen anywhere on the ground.

"I don't know how," Andy said. "But I think we won one."

Autumn opened her door to the same scene of retreating reptiles. Above, the tower still sent out its swirling blue power bands. She stepped out of the cab and checked the twisted front bumper on the ground.

"Gators got the winch," she said. "I am *so* doing a research paper on that. Plan B?"

Andy rolled down his window and looked up at the tower.

"Three tons of truck."

"You can't drive into that! Whatever that blue juice is will probably fry you!"

"I'll jump out long before that. Climb out. I'll need a running start on these rims."

Autumn stifled a final protest and climbed down from the cab.

Andy wiped a section of the windshield clear. Back inside, he threw the truck into first and started a wide circle in the parking lot. Shredded rubber flapped around the rims as they sent up sparks from the pavement. As the truck headed back at the tower it was doing twenty. Fast enough for this much mass to crush the fence and cream the tower, but not too fast to do a Hollywood exit from a moving vehicle. He hoped. He popped the door open.

He straightened the wheel and gave the gas pedal one last stomp. He slipped the truck into neutral, held the wheel straight, and balanced in the open door. The truck sped toward the fence. He waited until his self-preservation instincts hit max and jumped.

His ankle collapsed when he hit the ground and he rolled away onto his shoulders. The truck flattened the fence like it wasn't there. It smashed through the tower legs. The vehicle lit up bright neon blue. The tower legs sheared away. The blue swirl in the sky disappeared. The air sizzled as escaping energy vaporized the mist around the tower. The truck burst into a ball of flames and a red and black mushroom cloud rose up and engulfed the tower. The tower toppled over like a felled tree. It hit the ground in an explosion of cobalt sparks.

Andy lay on his back and watched in stunned amazement. As elation took its place, the ground rumbled so hard that he bounced off the asphalt. Cracks spread from the tower base across the parking lot. A sinkhole formed and sucked down the concrete platform and the burning truck. Blacktop crumbled in an expanding circle.

Andy's heart thudded in his ears. He scrambled backward in a crab crawl as the earth beneath him tilted downward. The flaming truck disappeared into the infinite void. The tower followed, sliding into the pit like the tail of some great retreating leviathan. Andy's palms slipped against the rain-slicked asphalt and he slid down the angled slab toward the darkness.

Chapter Seventy-Three

Walking Bear dashed after Dolly as the fire dragon yanked her into the air. He grabbed her around the waist, lifting off the ground after her. He squinted against the brilliant flames.

Something popped and sizzled. The blue glow in the center of the circle disappeared. The fire dragon and the flames around the inscribed circle vanished. Walking Bear dropped back to the ground, Dolly hugged in his protective arms. She looked dazed, but incredibly, unburned.

Lyle gave his hands, no longer cloaked in the cerulean magic aura, an incredulous stare.

"No, no, no, NO!" he roared. "This cannot be happening!"

The earth rumbled and the entire plant shook back and forth. Sections of the ceiling fell in a series of overlapping crashes. Overstressed metal beams moaned a chorus of warnings. The concrete floor shattered into a sea of expanding cracks.

Lyle pointed at Dolly and Walking Bear.

"You'll all pay for this. This is not over! *Patenda excovchel.*"

As the floor of the plant within the circle crumbled and fell into darkness, Lyle vanished. The candle holders tumbled into the void.

Walking Bear wrapped a big arm around Dolly's shoulder and hurried her to the exit door. The expanding sinkhole followed them at each step. As they reached the doorway, the unconscious bodies of Chester and Denny rolled into the blackness.

"Wait!" cried Shane. He lay on the floor, his arms dragging his body toward the door. A stain of urine trailed back between his useless legs. The eyes that stared out from his face of charred flesh no longer glowed. "Don't leave me here."

Walking Bear looked down with contempt, Dolly with compassion. She knelt, grabbed the doorway with one hand and reached out with the other. She leaned forward and Shane grabbed her wrist.

The ground collapsed out from under him. Shane hung over the void, fingers locked on Dolly's wrist, his nails drawing blood. She teetered in the doorway and leaned toward the abyss.

Shane managed a toothy, evil grin from his mangled face and laughed. "Bitch."

Walking Bear drew his knife and with one great stroke severed the tendons in Shane's arm. Shane's hand flew open and he plummeted into the dark, screaming.

Walking Bear grabbed Dolly around the waist and pulled her to her feet. They ran through the parking lot as the ground caved in behind them.

Rough asphalt scraped Andy's palms as he fell into the sinkhole. He jerked to a stop and his collar choked him. Autumn had caught him by the back of his shirt. She pulled him back to the edge. They turned and scrambled for the exit road.

Behind them the sinkhole grew. The Apex plant creaked and groaned and then collapsed into the growing hole, as if the earth decided to ingest all that was evil. Andy and Autumn were halfway up the access road before they felt safe enough to stop. By then the hole had devoured even the edges of the parking lot. On the far side, the hole had taken the tip of the Everglades, and water poured in over the edge in a waterfall. The rain had stopped. The wind was gone.

Andy scanned what was left of the parking lot.

"My mother? Walking Bear?"

"I saw them walk into the plant," Autumn said, voice filled with sadness. "Just before the tower came down."

Andy was about to call out when Walking Bear loomed out of the scrub. He had his arm around Dolly's shoulder.

"Mom!" Andy rushed to her side. Walking Bear released her but she did not move. Andy hugged her. She did not respond. "You're all right?"

"Where am I?" Dolly said.

Andy's relief at her survival waned, replaced by the familiar dread of her incoherence. He looked up from her shoulder to Walking Bear.

"In the plant," Walking Bear said. "There was a...she went through a lot. Give her a few moments."

"Lyle?" Autumn asked.

"Escaped before the collapse," Walking Bear said. "Sometimes justice is not fully served."

The water rushing into the sinkhole had a soothing, cleansing sound to it. The eastern horizon fired up a promising pink ribbon.

"Let's see if we can roll your truck onto its tires and get back into town," Andy said. "Otherwise it's a long walk."

Chapter Seventy-Four

That was as close as Lyle wanted to cut it. He could actually feel the ground collapse under him as his teleportation spell extricated him from the sinking Apex plant. How could so much have gone wrong, so many lines of defense breached? He'd be leaving this fly-speck town a few presents before he departed. They had earned it.

He rematerialized in the rear of the Magic Shop in the center of the runic circle. He had to collect his talismans and get out of here. He rushed for the back door and bounced off the edge of the circle.

"What the hell?"

Gold coins glowed at the compass points of the circle. The coins he'd given those stupid kids. The amplifiers. All in one place? Oh shit...

Ricky stood at the wrought-iron lectern, the thick yellowed spell book opened before him. A single red candle burned at his side. His right arm hung in a makeshift sling.

"I knew you would come back," Ricky said. "Too many toys to leave behind."

"Impudent mortal bastard," Lyle raged. "You don't have the power.

"I do," Ricky said. He pointed at the book. "A binding enchantment. It keeps you in there with the rest of us out here. For the length of your immortality."

"You can't do this," Lyle said. "You are just a useful tool. You are bound to me!"

"Some ties are stronger."

"I'll get out of this," Lyle said. "And the first thing I'll do is hun you, your family and your friends down. You will die so slowly."

"Someone will need to know the reversing spell," Ricky said. "And it will be gone."

Ricky picked the open book up by the edge of its cover with his good hand. He suspended the dry, brittle pages over the red candle's flame. Fire leapt across the small gap and the book went ablaze.

"You stupid child! Centuries of incantations are in there. Do you know what you are doing?"

Lyle flashed back to a thousand years ago, to the night his master died at his hands. The last words his master said were, "Do you know what you are doing?"

"One break in this circle," Lyle said with panicked desperation, "one movement of a coin, and I'll work my way free. You can't keep this undisturbed forever."

"I can't," Ricky said. "But we can."

Chapter Seventy-Five

One year later.

The crowd at the new marina exceeded all expectations. Anglers from both coasts were ready for the opening of the Lake Anamassee Recreation Area. The deluge of rain from Hurricane Rita had been more than enough to fill the sinkhole that consumed the closed Apex plant. Now on the anniversary of the freak storm, Citrus Glade was ready to reap one of the benefits. Tourism tasted sweeter than anything Apex ever churned out.

Mayor Flora Diaz looked sharp in a coral linen dress and high heels. She carried an enormous pair of scissors she had borrowed from the mayor of Miami-Dade. A foot-wide red ribbon stretched across the spanking-new boat ramp. A flotilla of boats sat on trailers waiting for that ribbon to part and so begin the day's catch-and-release contest. Word had spread that Lake Anamassee was going to be south Florida's prime fishing destination. A dozen dignitaries sat on folding chairs in the shade of a white canopy. A few local heroes were there as well.

The mayor stopped first at Felix Arroyo. He'd taken up an end chair to give him room to extend his right leg. The "Shelter Savior" walked with a cane now, but he walked, which was more than the doctors hoped for a year ago. Flora smiled and bent to shake his hand.

"Where's the family?" she said.

Felix pointed to the edge of the lot.

"Fleecing the tourists," Felix said.

Carlina, Angela and Ricky were working a table that sported an *Arroyo Groves* banner along the edge. They were doing a brisk business in citrus and preserves. Ricky looked over and waved.

"Ricky looks completely recovered," Flora said.

"You should see him working the trees," Felix said, beaming. "And remember, he's *Ricardo* now. And touchy about it."

Autumn came up behind Flora and hugged her shoulder. "Big day, Madam Mayor."

"You are sure we have some fish in there, right? We don't need a bunch of fishermen returning empty handed."

"It's brimming with fish," Autumn said. "Spring was a riot as nature filled this new niche. We're lucky they aren't climbing up the ramp to escape the overcrowding."

"Are you sure you'll be happy managing the lake?" Flora said. "It won't be as thrilling as it matures and stabilizes."

"I've found that I have a little swamp cypress in me." Autumn said. "Time to put down some roots."

"Speaking of which, where is your fiancé? Andy oversaw the construction here. He told me he'd be here for the opening."

"He was planning on bringing Dolly. But I'm not sure..."

Flora looked solemn. Autumn didn't have to say more.

Andy sat next to Dolly in her room. Dust coated a half-finished painting on the easel. Walking Bear stood at the window, alternating his view between inside and outside the room.

"I'll have this painting done soon," Dolly said. "In time for the grand opening of the marina."

Andy gave his head a sad shake. "Maybe not. The marina opens today."

"Really," Dolly said, a bit confused. "Well, sometimes time gets away from me these days. I'll finish it soon anyway. My son oversaw the marina's construction. He heads the DPW. You should meet him. You'd like him."

Andy blinked back a tear and went to Walking Bear as Dolly inspected her painting.

"She doesn't get much better than this anymore," Walking Bear said. "Since the hurricane–"

"The hurricane" was the standard euphemism. No one, even the inner circle who knew the whole truth, ever mentioned Lyle or sorcery by name.

"–she really hasn't recovered. She went through a lot during those days."

Andy was certain that the magic she had tapped into, the good energy as opposed to the bad that had fueled Shane and Vicente, had burned through what continuous coherence Dolly had left within her, run the rest through on fast forward. Before each visit, he held out hope for just a few moments with the mother he knew, with the woman who saved the state.

"You know," Andy said. "The week after the hurricane, she once had a few good hours. She knew that she was slipping in and out, now more out than in. We talked some about that night. She said the sacrifice was worth it."

"You should have seen how brave she was," Walking Bear said.

"She still is," Andy said.

Most of the town was out at the marina opening, far from the other reminder of the events one year ago today.

On the town square, where once stood the building that housed Cooper's Tack and Harness, Everyday Shoes and finally the Magic Shop, the new mini-park now bloomed. Brilliant flowers and lush bushes lined a short path to the monument at the center, a thick box clad in polished marble and inscribed with the names of those lost during Hurricane Rita. A select few, under the personal direction of the mayor, had built the monument within the walls of the building, so that when the condemned structure came down, just the memorial was left standing.

The team had taken great care in the clandestine construction. Beneath the marble veneer, the two walls of steel-reinforced bricks had an outer sheathing of lead. It was designed to last forever and was dense enough that even on the quietest night, with an ear pressed to the cold, slick surface, one could not hear the howling screams within.

Acknowledgements

Eternal gratitude goes to my wife, Christy, who demands I take the time to create and endures strange looks from all her friends who read my works.

To my faithful beta readers, K. P. Hornsby and Janet Guy, whose frank honesty keeps me humble and saves my dear readers many painful reading experiences.

To CSM Larry May, USAR, for sharing his experiences during combat operations in Afghanistan, and for his decades of service keeping our nation free.

To Don D'Auria and the folks at Samhain for the white magic they do turning my collections of words into something greater than their sum.

About the Author

Russell James lives in hurricane-prone Florida and weathered three direct hits in one year. As far as he knows, no magic was involved in attracting any of those storms.

Black Magic is Russell James' third horror novel following *Dark Inspiration* and *Sacrifice.* He has also published the paranormal alternate history short story *Touch and Go.* Visit his website at www.russellrjames.com, follow on Twitter @RRJames14, or drop a line to complain about his writing at rrj@russellrjames.com.

Who can save the children from the Woodsman?

Sacrifice

© 2012 Russell James

Thirty years ago, six high school friends banded together to confront the Woodsman, a murderous specter whose prey was children. None of the friends will ever forget the horror of those weeks...or blood chilling image of the Woodsman.

Now the six have returned to town for a long overdue reunion. Except the Woodsman hasn't finished with them yet. As a new nightmare unfolds, ripping open old scars and inflicting fresh terror, what will each of them have to sacrifice this time to keep the children safe and the Woodsman at bay?

Enjoy the following excerpt from Sacrifice...

Lightning arced across the night sky. In its flash, the Sagebrook water tower stood like a gleaming white beacon above the trees on the hill. Ten seconds later, thunder rolled in behind it, the way every event has an echo that follows.

Five figures scurried along the catwalk around the tower, one of the old-fashioned kinds, where a squat cylinder with a conical hat sat on six spindly steel legs a few hundred feet in the air. A newer tower served the people's water needs, but the old girl was an icon for the Long Island town, so the trustees kept it painted white and emblazoned with the "Sagebrook-Founded on 1741" logo to remind themselves of their heritage. Once per year, the logo changed to celebrate the graduation of the Whitman High senior class.

The boys on the catwalk were going to see that this year it changed twice. These seniors had committed more than their fair share of pranks; stolen street signs, a tap into the high school PA system, swapping the state flag in front of school with the Jolly Roger. But this stunt would top them all

They had all met in the sixth grade, where their teacher had dubbed them "The Dirty Half Dozen" due to their inseparability and penchant for trouble. (The title had stuck.) They hadn't done anything as dangerous as tonight's foray, but anything worth a good laugh was worth doing.

"Who's got the red?" Bob whispered, though no one but the boys could be within earshot. He crouched at the base of the new banner that read "Congratulations Class of 1980" with "Go Minutemen" painted underneath in red letters. Bob was rail thin with an unruly head of brown hair that consented to a part on the right and little else. An unlit cigarette dangled from the corner of his mouth.

"Right here," Paul said. He handed Bob a can of red spray paint. Paul stood several inches taller than the rest of the boys and his broad shoulders made the narrow catwalk a tight fit. He wore his Minutemen football team jacket, though Dave had told him the white leather sleeves would look like two glow worms crawling across the tower at night. His hair was cropped close and he sported the shadow of what he euphemistically called a moustache.

A blast of cold wind hit the tower. The snaps on Paul's jacket hit the metal railing with a reverberating ping.

A third boy, Jeff, hung over the catwalk railing. He had a long face with ears that had stuck out just enough for a good round of elementary school ribbing. He held his New York Mets ball cap tight as he looked down at the perimeter fence. A ten-year-old Olds Vista Cruiser station wagon idled near the hole in the fence. There was a slight lope to the modified V8's rumbling exhaust through the turbo mufflers. The headlights were off, but the parking lights lit the edges of the car. Jeff spoke into a cheap Japanese walkie talkie.

"Dave," he said. "What the hell are you doing with the lights on?"

"Damn," Dave answered from the Vista. "Sorry man." The marker lights in the car went dark. "It's clear down here."

"At two a.m. it had better be," said Ken, a red headed kid with a rash of freckles across his cheekbones. He slipped behind Jeff to join Bob and Paul. He brushed against Jeff's butt as he squeezed by.

"Watch it, homo," Jeff said.

"It's your ass," Ken said. "It's so enticing. We're here in the dark..."

"Hey," Bob snapped. "You girls want to shut the hell up and start spraying?"

Twin lightning flashes lit a big cloud like a floating anvil-shaped lantern. Thunder crackled across the sky five seconds later.

Marc, the last boy on the tower sat at the opening where the access ladder met the catwalk. His feet dangled through the opening. Both hands gripped the catwalk rail. He was the slightest of the group and he had to brace himself against a renewed gust of wind that rocked his thick curly black hair back and forth. There were only four cans of paint, so he could have stayed in the car on watch with Dave. But there was something to prove by climbing the tower, though he wasn't sure of it was to the others or to himself. The journey did enlighten him about one thing. He was definitely acrophobic.

"We better hurry," Marc said. "We don't want to be up here in the rain."

"You said we'd have clear weather," Paul said to Ken as Ken handed him a can of white spray paint.

"No," Ken said. "I said there was a twenty percent chance of a shower. When I have a few free hours, I'll explain probability to you, Jockstrap."

"There's a one hundred percent probability I'm going to throw you all off this damn tower if you don't shut up," Bob said. The spray can in his hand started to hiss. "If we don't do this tonight, they'll have time to paint over it before graduation. Let's go."

"All for none..." Paul said.

"And none for all," the group finished. The teen's unofficial motto, in its sarcastic denial of camaraderie, completely represented theirs.

Paul, Jeff and Ken joined in and the side of the tower sounded like a den of spitting cobras. The "G" in "Go" lost a few of its edges. A "B" took shape on the tower's side.

Another bolt of lightning arced from the anvil cloud to the ground. This time the thunder reported only a second after. The smell of rain wafted in on the breeze. A spray of fat drops splattered against the tank like machine gun fire.

"Hey, guys," Dave's voice said from the walkie-talkie in Jeff's belt. "It's starting to rain down here. Is it raining up there?"

"No," Ken answered to himself with a roll of his eyes. "It always rains from the ground up."

Jeff gave a quick look at the peak of the tower, then at the approaching cloud. "This thing is one hell of a conductor. We should..."

Lightning split the sky above their heads. The thunder was simultaneous and sharp, so loud that the boys could feel it rumble.

"Hang on, wussies," Bob said. He gave the tower one last blast from his can. He stood up and leaned back against the railing. "Go Minutemen" had been transformed into "Blow Minutemen."

Paul gave his "L" one final shot of red. He appraised his work with an admiring stare. "How did Ms. Kravitz ever give me a D in Art?"

Marc stood at the ladder, one foot on the first rung. "Let's go!"

The air around them seemed to come alive, as if the molecules had decided to dance in circles around each other. The hair on the boys' arms stood on end. Jeff's walkie talkie buzzed like a cicada. A freezing downdraft swept the catwalk. Five heartbeats went into overdrive.

"Lay flat!' Jeff shouted.

The boys dove for the decking. Marc, already on the ladder, just hung on.

A white light blinding as the power of God enveloped the tower. Deafening thunder blanketed the boys and the air turned hot and dry. Uncountable volts pumped through the tower as the lightning bolt ripped from the spire on the peak to the ground below. Jeff's radio exploded in a shower of sparks and melted plastic. The boys' bodies jittered against the catwalk decking, belt buckles clanging against the steel. Clothing smoked and there was the disgusting smell of burnt hair. The split second seemed to last forever.

Available now in ebook and print from Samhain Publishing.